D0713222

OTHER BOOKS BY JACK OLSEN

Alphabet Jackson
Massy's Game
The Bridge at Chappaquiddick
Night of the Grizzlies
The Man with the Candy
The Girls in the Office
Silence on Monte Sole

# THE SECRET OF FIRE 5

# JACK OLSEN

# THE SECRET OF FIRE 5

Random House • New York

Copyright © 1977 by Susan Yvonne Olsen. All rights reserved under
International and Pan-American Copyright Conventions. Published in the United
States by Random House, Inc., New York, and simultaneously in Canada by
Random House of Canada Limited, Toronto.

Library of Congress Cataloging in Publication Data

Olsen, Jack.
The secret of fire 5

I. Title.
PZ4.04985Se    [PS3565.L77]    813'.5'4    76–48306
ISBN 0–394–41174–9

Manufactured in the United States of America
9 8 7 6 5 4 3 2
First Edition

This book is for
all the brave men
who run into buildings that others run out of

# THE SECRET OF
# FIRE 5

Crazy guys, they use more energy sleeping than they do fighting fires. Squirm, sneeze, snore, snort, huff, puff all night long. Sounds like a factory instead of a bunk room. Why can't they twist and turn nice and quiet, like me?

Two racks down, that heavy breathing—Vincent "Plummer" Brown must be on another date with Raquel. Or is it Sophia's night? Chewed me out when I woke him for a light. "Goddamn, Charly, I was getting into Brigitte, and Ann-Margret was waiting."

"Sure, sure. What's with you and Charo?"

"She went back to Coogie."

"Coogie who?" I says, but he don't answer.

Plummer's the only guy in the house that's looking forward to female firemen, which we're expecting the first ones any day now, courtesy of the equal rights law. "It'll be beautiful," Plum says the other day, showing those Moon Drop teeth that drive the little girls wild. "We'll be banging 'em right on the rig."

"Who'd want a broad that could pass our physical?" Ax Bedrosian asks.

"Me?" Plummer hints.

"Yeh? Well, fuck off, why don'tcha?" Ax says, that's his favorite expression. If you say, "I can't stand ketchup on spaghetti," Ax'll probably explain, "Oh, yeh? Well, fuck off, why don'tcha?"

Me, I can't imagine a fire station with women. I don't think the brass hats can, either. They can't even agree on what to call them. Somebody suggested firefems, somebody else said firegirls. What's that make us, fireboys? Plummer suggested firebroads. Has a nice ring.

"I know how to handle 'em," he says, dancing his sailor's hornpike around the pool table. "Just leave it to me. First one comes in, she'll say, 'Probationary firefighter reporting for duty.' I'll say, 'Listen, Probie, hold on to this for a minute, will ya?' "

Cap Nordquist says he heard there's one or two at training school that're really strong. Bulldaggers, no doubt. They can hump a line, sure, but will they back me up? Say my mask gives out in a cockloft and the air's superheated and I drop. Does she pull me out, the way I'd save Ax or Plum or any of the other guys? Or does she get quirky and run? That's what worries us.

Mustacci begins his patented snore. First he's a stock car throttling down and then he's a sea elephant with the asthma. I shake him by the shoulder, the way he asked me to. "Mike!"

"Timezit?"

"Three something. You're snoring again."

"Okay, Charly."

A few minutes later it starts again. *Mike?* I whisper.

"Hey, man," a gravelly voice speaks up. "Fuck off, why don'tcha?"

"He's snoring, Ax."

"Let'm snore. You make more noise'n he does."

"Check, Ax." Mustn't upset our star roofman and workhorse. "Go back to sleep, pal."

"Fat chance, with your motor mouth."

"Up yours, Ax."

4

"You too, Charly." I hear him stifle a yawn.

"Yeh, well, g'night, Ax."

"Night, Charly."

Don't know how he fits his rack, him being six five and maybe 260 pounds, depending on how many beers he sucked up. Him and his Feinblatz lager. The night we had the fire at the Polack's rathskeller, Ax and I worked clean-up for two straight hours in the furnace room and we finally come upstairs so dry and parched we could barely talk. Our throats were the Sahara desert, and the Polack draws two overflowing steins of beer and slides them across to us, and Ax takes one sip and spits it out. "Ain't Feinblatz," he says.

Wish we'd taken a couple Feinblatz to Flatley's basement with us yesterday. Grown men, shopping for bloomers. Me, I think Ax should always start out by explaining the situation to the saleslady, how he caught the allergy and can't wear anything but nylon next to his private regions and men's nylon shorts cost about six bucks the pair, so he keeps his eyes open for special sales on the women's bloomers extra extra large.

But instead he walks up in his Class B fire uniform and says, "Lemme see whatchew got in a plain white bloomer."

"Certainly," the saleslady says. "What size?"

Ax reaches down and feels his hips and says, "About a fifty-two."

"Fifty-two?"

"Yeh." I look at him. The old donkey, he's playing it nonchalant. "Give or take a coupla inches. Ain't this the special sale for stouts?"

"Ye-e-e-es," the lady says. She rubs her fingers along the back of her thinning hair and glances around the store. A few minutes later she comes back with a box of pink drawers, and Ax says, "I wanted white is what I requested."

"The whites aren't on special, sir."

5

Ax holds a pair up in the light. They look like marine flags. I kind of edge away. "Hey, Charly," he calls out, "whattaya think?" He's been buying these things for two years now, all of a sudden he wants my advice.

"You're the customer," I says.

"Some place I can try these on?" Ax says.

He comes out a few minutes later, tells the woman they fit fine except for a slight bind in the crotch, and we walk out with a dozen pairs of ladies' nylon bloomers. He would of bought more, but there's a store limit.

"Know how much we saved at that sale?" he says as we climb into my station wagon. "About fifty bucks is all. Was it worth the trouble?"

"Ax," I says, this question's always been on my mind, "whyn't you just wait and pick up men's nylon shorts on sale?"

"J'ever see men's nylon shorts on sale?"

I got to admit I haven't.

"Mens're a luxury item," Ax explains. "But broads wear nylon all the time."

I'm not gonna argue, because the last thing I want is for Ax to think I'm razzing him. Nobody makes fun of Ax's bloomers any more. Not since he threw Mike Mustache through the crapper wall.


Funny I don't fall asleep the way I use to. Some of the guys, they sleep on command, wake up on command. Not me, pal. Let's see, should I do the Presidents or the capitals? The capital of New York is Albany. The capital of New Jersey is Trenton. The capital . . .

That's one problem I never had when I was married. Sleeping. Let's see, how long did it last? The honeymoon plus two, three days, then it started to slide. I don't know why. God bless you, Marilyn, it wasn't your fault. Plummer says keep a steady string going, don't stick to one, that's the solution. Calls me the gray divorcé.

Easier for him to connect, he don't even have a bald spot. Talk about a steady string, I can't even start a string of one. Imagine Maybelle Morgan the thirty-eight-year-old meter maid insisting we jog three miles around the park first. Says it heightens her feelings. That's the only thing it heightens, I guarantee you. Maybe she'll give me another crack.

There goes Lester Dawson grinding his molars again. Chills your blood. Why does an independently wealthy fireman grind his teeth all night long? Dreaming about fire, that's it. Hates fire, goes googly, can't control himself. What was it he said in the watch office the other day? "Charly, fire makes me see red."

A regular Jackal and Hyde. He hurts himself and don't remember how it happened. At a hotel fire, we're building a sand dam to drain off the roof-water, and he steps in an airshaft and falls two floors. In the hospital five weeks, still limps a little. Then he tries to get at a fire in a hotel ceiling and pulls a chandelier down and it drives him right into the ballroom floor, he's still got glass baguettes three inches up his ass.

And yet he's a very calm guy most of the time. Does macramé, knitting with knots and rope. He's a magician with the stuff, a pro. Give Les the right string, he'll knit you a fox. In my mind's eye I can hear him correcting me, "Knot, not knit!" It sure looks like knitting to me.

By God, I'll get to sleep if it takes all night. Let's see. Nevada. Reno? Las Vegas? No, Reno. The capital of California is Sacramento . . .

Tyree just belched in his sleep, you could hear it all the way across the bunk room. An iron man with a tin stomach. Me, I think it's the soul food he eats at home before he comes down here and gets in every clutch we got: breakfast, lunch, dinner and late snack. He don't miss a clutch, I'll tell you, man. Tonight it was casserole of venison, cooked to perfection by one of the world's great firehouse chefs, which modesty forbids me to mention him by name, but if you was to say "Charly Sprockett" you wouldn't be far off. Amerston "Tyree" D'Arcy had himself three full and complete servings, plus dumplings each and every time, and if I'm lying, then he's white and I'm black and Truman Capote's a weight lifter.

Jeez, didn't the house captain get on Tyree's case today? "D'Arcy, you gotta get ridda that lard." The two of them, they went at it hot and heavy—Tyree didn't get on Fire 5 by being a shirking violet.

"Them weight rules," he said, "does they apply to everybody in the station, Cap?" He stared at the shiny buckle that sits on old Nordquist's potbelly like the Lincoln Monument.

"What I said goes," the house captain stormed back. You could see his porky old face heating up under that snowfall of hair. "You gotta take off some of that black—I mean fat."

"You mean black," Tyree said, and stomped off toward the firemen's "hot line," fifty cents per man per month, and the phone don't go through the department switchboard, so we can enjoy a little privacy. Tyree's always on the hot line, calling the Equal Rights Commission, calling the NAACP, calling the U.N. Keeps the officers scared to death, that's how he stays on Fire 5. It also don't hurt that he holds the battalion record for hooking up to a hydrant: eleven seconds from wrench to water. Now if he'd only take off some of that black . . .

"Hey, Charly, you awake?" Sonelius "Sonny" Wicker can't sleep either. Poor Sonny of a bitch. Used to sleep like a rock before his wife ran off with the milkman.

"Yeh, Sonny." I try to keep my voice in a whisper. The other five guys in the bunk room are all drawing $7.56 an hour while

8

they sleep, but that don't mean they want to wake up and earn it.

Sonny slips over and sits on my rack. "W-w-wonder who set the Atlas fire?" he says. He don't fool me. He's not laying awake wondering who torched the Atlas. It's something else that's burning up Sonny Wicker, but I got better sense than to mention it.

"Search me. Gasoline Gomez, that's all I know." Gasoline Gomez is our word for arsonist, he's a make-believe character like Smokey the Bear or Blackie Carbon. Some shifts he drives us apeshit, some shifts we're ready to thank him for breaking the boredom.

"No sense to it," Sonny says, starting a cigaret. His pale white skin and his lemon-colored hair light up and then go dark again as he hands me the pack. Our elderly beachboy. "C-c-crazy," he says.

He's right. At headquarters, they're off the wall. No pattern, no clues. It use to be we could figure out a motive, start from there. Ghetto kids, they go into abandoned buildings and steal the radiators, the toilets, anything they can pry loose. Then they torch the building and wait for us to break open the walls with our tools. The next day they grab the exposed plumbing. It practically goes on a timetable. The day after the radiators disappear, there's a fire. You can set your watch.

Well, our marshals have it tough. The way the law reads they practically got to catch the perpetrator striking the match. I know arsonists that stand on the fire ground laughing at the top of their lungs and they can't be arrested, let alone convicted. We had one a few years ago torched his house to kill his wife, and when they brought her out in a body bag, he run up and spit on it. He's walking the streets today. Some of the torches, they'll stretch wire across hallways to trip us up, or they'll hang

9

cundrums full of gasoline from the ceiling, so they'll go off in our face. Funny little tricks. We just die laughing.

"Couldn't sleep, huh, Sonny?" I says after he relapses into silence.

Jeez, it's terrible how a guy can change in front of your eyes. Before Alice left, Sonny was the most contentedest guy in the whole station. A simple soul, raised in a little town that he always claimed it was named Pavement Ends. Wouldn't hurt a flea, wouldn't hurt a rabbit, either. He bought a mating pair of New Zealand whites to make a few bucks on the side, and now he's got over four hundred of them, can't bear to butcher them, says he knows every one personally. It's good Sonny likes rabbits. It's bad he married one.

All's he ever use to do was sit around the bullpen reading his favorite magazines, *Organic Gardening* and *Countryside & Small Stock Journal.* One day he says to me, "I'm reading a g-good article. It's called 'Rabbits Love Squash.'"

"They do, they do!" Plummer Brown called out from the doorway. "I never could get my rabbit off the court."

Sonny just laughed in that good-natured way of his. About the only thing that upset him was somebody talking against the good old U. S. of A. Sonny's the one put the red, white and blue cockomania on the side of our rig, God forbid anybody should think we're the Bulgarian fire department when we roll up. He's proud to be an American and proud to be a firefighter. "Other guys go home at night," he'd say, "and they ask themselves, 'What's it all about?' But a fireman, he never wonders what it's all about, he knows he's d-d-doing something useful."

Now look at him. Can't sleep, can't eat. No more hooray for the red white and blue. He use to be the first one on the roof when the afternoon orders came over the squawkbox: "Lower the United States flag." Now he's laying on his rack half the time, brooding, gargling Maalox.

10

Well, one day you're happy and dumb and the next day you're wiser and miserable. But what a way to get the news, in his wife's note to the milkman: "4 half-gallons, 1 pint ½ and ½, all my love, Alice." Sonny showed her the note, the next day she was gone.

Use to be a saying when I come on the department, "Fireman, take care of your own," which we never failed, even if it was off-shift. Now we got cradle-to-grave medical and a bunch of fringy benefits, and it's a job now, not a profession. Where's the pride, where's the concern for a fellow worker? In the old days Sonny's milkman better watch his ass. Nowadays who knows?

"Well, g-g-g'night, Charly."

"Night, Sonny. Try and get some rest."

After he leaves I slip out to the scullery for a glass of ice water. I like it around here at night. The brass keep threatening to tear down the station and transfer us and I figure that's when I'll put in my papers. Not that anybody cares when Charly Sprockett retires, but the idea of working another house aggravates me. Change is the pits, you get tired of rattling around when you're my age. I know every brick in this dump. I know where the apparatus floor's wore, I know where the old water tower use to park. I know every groove in the banister, every scratch in the sink. What do we need a new firehouse for? This one works. A thing works, they ought to leave it alone.

It's not bad enough we got firefems on their way, we got to break in a new chief, too. Well, Grant couldn't run the battalion forever. Can't blame him. Fancy new title: Deputy Fire Chief Allan M. Grant. Some mouthful, huh? Hate to see him go, but he deserves the promotion.

They say our new battalion chief's a dooze. H. Walker Slater, the H is for Hitler. Just promoted from captain, had a headquarters job the last few years. Nobody knows him, not

11

even his closest friends. He don't joke or jack around, don't drink or smoke, don't fraternize with anybody below his rank. The exact opposite of Al Grant.

Damned near my best friend, Grant, and him a chief and me a plain old firefighter all these years. We come on the department together, went through training school together, and friends're friends, that's the way he looks at it. Rank don't matter. Except to guys like H. Walker Slater. The word's out the new man's headed up: battalion chief, deputy chief, assistant chief, and then into the superchief's job as soon as the superchief retires. That's all we need around here, one of them upward mobility types.

I tippy-toe past the other bunk room where Ladder 10 sleeps. The nighttime concert's going full blast. Not so bad when you get used to it. Ax says he don't sleep as good at home, it's too quiet. Francine might have something to do with that, the frustration she gives him. Forget it. Plummer says I worry too much about the others. "What're you, a mother hen?" he says. "These men are adults." I wish he was right.

Must be around four, four-thirty by now. The capital of Oregon is Salem. Feeling a little drowsy finally. The capital of Maine is . . . Salem? The capital of Madrid is Salem. The capital of Salem is . . .

The houselights?

Okay, okay, I'm awake. Count the seconds: one two three. Now the bells. *There!* Look at Plummer, practically does a back flip when the bells hit.

One round of three. That means only one company goes. Fire 5 or Ladder 10, which?

I draw the heavy bunking pants over my underwear and slip the suspenders on my shoulders in one smooth motion, like a ballerina at the Met. Forty-one years old and I'm ready for action in seconds, not even breathing hard. That's why I like the lights going on first, three seconds before the bells. The lights wake me up, so I'm never shook by the noise.

I stand at the edge of the pole hole and peek down at the apparatus floor while the rest of the astronauts slide by. You're not suppose to dawdle, but I'm not gonna slide the pole at four in the morning and then have to walk all the way back upstairs for nothing. I always look down and see which officer runs toward the watch office. If it's Lieutenant Steicher from Ladder 10, I just go back to my rack. If it's our own Lieutenant Kirkpatrick, well, he's still got to listen to a second round of alarms, that's the rule, so I slide the pole, grab my coat and helmet off the back of the rig and get to my seat as quick as him. Whole thing takes thirty, forty seconds, all the time in the world.

Oops, it's Kirkpatrick, hustling toward the watch office. Slide, fool, slide!

Plummer's already got the engine sputtering and the radio turned up, and we hear the dispatcher saying, *"Fire Five, Fire Five, Fifteen forty-five Wilkes, Fifteen forty-five Wilkes. Service call. Code Yellow."*

The most boresome kind of fire! "Service call" usually means a defective alarm went off in a building, or maybe a citizen put out a fire in his sofa, something like that. Code Yellow means drive at lawful speed and obey all traffic signs. What a thrill, to be woken up at four in the A.M. on a service call. And it's raining on top of everything else.

Turns out a Dempsey Dumpster's smoking behind a warehouse. "Big whoopee!" Plummer says, hitting the air brakes so the rig skids to about six feet away from the metal box of trash and street-sweepings and old newspapers.

"I know how to put this one out," Ax Bedrosian mutters, but before he can open his fly Sonny Wicker and Lester Dawson douse the fire with the pre-connect to the booster tank. We roll back on Code Yellow, the bell jangling gently but no siren, and everybody's griping about the world's biggest ashtrays, Dempsey Dumpsters. Halfway home we hear the alerter tones on the radio—*beep beep beep*—and the dispatcher drones, *"Fire Five, Fire Five. Six and Sable, Six and Sable . . ."*

"Go, Plummer," Lieutenant Kirkpatrick says in his soft voice. It's the first words he said since we left the station, he never says much anyway. If we get to a fire before the chief, Loo'll set up the early lay, but then you won't hear a squeak out of him till the fire's tapped. He'll be inside on a line, or working with a Halligan tool, or up on the roof helping the laddermen. He has an instinct for knowing how to put out fires,

14

where to attack with maximum effect, not like certain other loots that like to stand outside and pour tons of water and then go running into the house like the Indians riding up San Juan Hill.

Plummer floors the hammer on our modified Kenworth pumper and Loo touches his boot to the siren switch, and we're boring through the dark streets, waking up Skid Row.

Inside my heavy turn-out coat, I can feel the thumping. Almost twenty years in this business, and my heart bangs every time our big diesel starts pounding and the siren growls in my ear and I look through the windshield and see the storefronts turning pink from our lights. We're businessmen off to business! It's not the 8:02 commuter special, but it's the only business we know. Among ourselves we talk about "good" fires the way cops talk about "good" murders. A good fire's something that tests your medal, wrings you out, makes you feel satisfied with yourself when you crowd into the shower later. Jeez, I'm beginning to sound like Sonny Wicker.

What's that address again? *Sixth and Sable?*

"That's the fucking station!" Plummer yelps.

When we drive up, there's not even a wisp of smoke, just a scorched spot covered with foam in the middle of the apparatus floor where we park our rig. Five or six sleepy truckmen from Ladder 10 are standing around rubbing their eyes. Off to one side the house captain's writing on a clipboard. You can see by his face how he feels about the whole thrilling event.

Poor old Captain Nordquist, he's scared to go on sick call for fear they'll give him an EKG and find out how bad his heart is. He should be upstairs getting his sleep, let us young studs handle deals like this. But I guess even a sick old captain has to turn out when the fire's in his own station house. I notice he's wearing his old-fashion high-top slippers.

"Gasoline Gomez?" Lieutenant Kirkpatrick says.

15

"What?" Nordquist says, cupping his ear. Jeez, forgot his hearing aid again.

"Arson?" the loot says louder.

"Nope," Cap says. "It was intentional. A red flare."

Lately these misunderstandings have been getting worse. At an apartment fire last week, a civilian ran up to Captain Nordquist and said thanks for saving his cat.

"Trapped?" Cap said, trying to listen to the citizen and his mobile radio at the same time. He pointed to the fire room on the second floor. "Up there?" he asked the guy.

"In a bedroom," the civilian said. "One of your men went in—"

Cap pushed his transmitting button. *"Portable One, a man here says his wife's trapped in a bedroom."*

*"Trapped in a what?"* Loo's voice come back.

*"Inside the fire room."*

Lieutenant Kirkpatrick came out of the building and explained that the fire was completely knocked, nobody could be trapped inside. "I'll be damned," Cap said, looking around for the citizen. "That guy gimme a false report. I'll be damned. Get his name, Kirkpatrick." Luckily the man was gone.

Well, Nordquist isn't that much different from a lot of the older officers. They're all half deaf from listening to that 120-decibel siren year after year and half blind from the fumes and the gas. You automatically talk louder when you see a chief's white hat. At the Rialto Theatre fire, the superchief himself walked up to a full-length mirror that he couldn't see through the smoke, all he can make out is the reflection of his own white hat, so he says, "Oh, hello, Chief, made a full search?"

Then the smoke parted and he seen the mirror and three firemen working a few feet away, and he just said, "Keep moving, boys!" and skipped back down the stairs like it never happened.

Nordquist gets down and sniffs the wet patch on the apparatus floor. "I'll write it up in the morning," he says. A wisp of foam is stuck on the end of his long pointy nose. "Goddamn firebugs, won't even let a man sleep." He turns to Kirkpatrick and says, "Where you been, Lieutenant?"

"Dumpster smoldering. Code Yellow."

"Code Yellow? With a kid smoldering?"

*"Dumpster, Cap,"* Mike Mustache yells.

"I hope he makes it," Cap says, and limps up the stairs toward his third-floor room. His sprained ankles still aren't completely healed from last month. Poor guy, he slid the pole half asleep and miscounted the floors and let go at the mezzanine. It was an eight-foot drop to the watch office.

"Okay, fellas," Loo says after Cap's out of sight, "let's get started." We're less than halfway through our twenty-four-hour shift, but we'll have two full days to relax. A nice work schedule, once you get used to it. Twenty-four hours on, forty-eight hours off. You develop a rhythm, like a bear.

Pretty soon everybody's doing his job, hosing the floor, wiping the rig for rain spots, washing street stains off the bottom-plates, topping the booster tank, recharging fire-foam jugs. At least we won't have to hang any wet hose in the tower. Always makes me feel like a washerwoman, running hoses through the wringer and hanging them up to dry.

We work quiet. Daylight's beginning to slip through the cracks between the apparatus doors. An old bus rattles by.

For a second I wonder why a Gasoline Gomez would throw a red flare into a fire station. What's gonna burn on a concrete floor? And how'd he get in? I mean, those big doors close automatically as soon as we leave, a cockroach couldn't crawl under. There's a little window that opens for ventilation, but it's only a foot across, and it's safetied, with chicken wire for

17

a middle layer. I look up. The window's about half open, but it isn't broken.

A dumb stunt, anyway.

Maybe the flare's a warning. But from who? Ten years ago it'd been a calling card from the urban Mau-Maus, telling the F.D. to get off our ass and hire more blacks. In those days we use to come under sniper fire in the ghettos. But now we got six black loots, two black captains, even a black battalion chief. And don't forget Amerston "Tyree" D'Arcy of Fire 5, a fine figure of a man with his forty-one-inch waist, and still the fastest sprinter in the department. A credit to his race, which is the twenty-yard dash to the dinner table.

It's five-thirty in the morning, I been up practically all night, and the alarm hits again. Three rounds of three this time. Working on the apparatus floor, we can hear the first call over the squawkbox in the watch office. *"Fire Five, Ladder Ten, Battalion Four, Ninth and Coulbourn . . ."*

Skid Row again. Plenty action there lately.

By the time we're rolling about thirty seconds later, the alarm office is calling out two companies in the big headquarters house, Station 10, a mile uptown. We hear it over the radio in the cab: *"Engine Twelve, Eighteen, Ladder Six. Ninth and Coulbourn. Engine Twelve, Eighteen . . ."*

"That must be the Harbor Light Mission," Plummer says as he careens our pumper around a corner. "Big response." Them night dispatchers, they shoot first and ask questions afterwards. If a fire's in a high-density area, it's better to have six or eight companies standing around playing with theirselves than one company getting suffocated. Overkill saves lives.

A block from the location we can see a bright red glow. When you're first-in at a fire, a bright red glow almost always means arson. I don't know exactly why, but I seen it a thousand

18

times, your arson fires burn brighter and redder than your others. Maybe because they get a loving start.

It's the Harbor Light, all right. Must be fifty winos hang out here, and forty-nine are on a drunk or just got over one, milling around on the street and swatting away the bluebirds. The fire's confined to a corner of the dingy old building, at a loading entrance, and it's flaring up pretty good, but there don't seem to be human endangerment.

We hit a home run on the hydrant hook-up. It's maybe twenty feet from the fire, and Tyree D'Arcy's skin reflects the flames while he does one of his eleven-second specials with the hydrant wrench. Half our crew runs inside looking for extension, and the rest of us tap that fire in twenty minutes flat. You never know, some fires won't go black for two days and others are pussies. The size of the initial burn don't always mean much.

The new battalion chief, H. Walker Slater, tells the first-in companies to stay for the clean-up and sends the others back. Gee, thanks, Chief. Those candy asses from 12's and 18's probably been sacked out all night. If they hurry, they can catch another nap before morning roll call.

Well, he'll never hear us complain. The chief could tell us to work till next Tuesday and we'd work till next Tuesday with Loo right alongside, whistling to himself and doing twice as much as anybody else. There he is now, stacking hose with Ax Bedrosian. Old Ax, he follows the loot around like a six-foot-five-inch puppy dog, says he figures Kirkpatrick saved his life at least twice and kept him from being canned a dozen times. If you see Loo, look for Ax no more than a few feet away.

As best we can figure, this fire started in a small service entrance and then walked up a wooden porch into the kitchen. The porch fell in and it's a big lump of smelly waste now. There's no fire extension to the second floor or the office, but

19

this corner of the building is a total loss. Too bad the whole place didn't go. There'll be another fire here before long, there always is, these places. Some old wino drops his cigaret on the floor and craps out. The city's been trying to rehabilitate this neighborhood, but there's not enough money for everything.

"Hey, how about a blow?" Plummer calls out, and Loo nods. We don't go anyplace special, Alcapulco's closed for the summer, we just lean on our shovels and light up. Full daylight now. The fire marshal's white car comes wheeling around the corner.

Two deputies climb out with their hydrocarbon indicator, "sniffer" we call it, and right away one of them says, "Holy balls!"

The other one comes over to check the reading, and I sneak a peek. The needle's into the red zone. The fire debris isn't far from the curb, so I says, "Maybe you're picking up gasoline residue from parked cars."

"Not this big a reading," the deputy says. "Hey, push down in there with your shovel, will ya? Open up the ashes a little?"

I dig into the smoking mound of charcoal and splinters and plaster. My shovel hits something and makes a sucking noise, like it's in mud, except there's no mud within a mile. I reach down in the hole with my glove, but then I catch the smell. Like roast lamb.

I draw my hand back and the hair on my neck goes up like it's charged. I still get the whim-whams when I find a body. Especially if it catches me by surprise.

Must of been six, eight firemen walked right over this one, tromping and tromping on him, the poor dead man was getting his face flattened under the rubble.

A couple guys hoist him out of the ashes by the armpits. One leg's burned off, the abdomen's split down the middle, I'm staring at a set of poached organs. Too dumb to turn away in time.

20

One of the deputy marshals gets in their car and calls the coroner's office, and Fire 5 starts to take up. I hope the coroner enjoys his work.

The other marshal talks to Loo. "Me, I'd say suicide. Soaked himself in gasoline, set himself on fire. Musta got the idea off the TV."

What a way to go. With all the different choices a man can take—pills, suck a pistol, turn on the gas . . .

That's the thing about your basic wino, he don't think straight to begin with. They're not like you and me. It takes terrific pressure to turn a man into a stew-bum, and then the alcohol gets to be one more pressure. Sick. Sad. Can't even kill theirselves right.

"Men," the new battalion chief says, smiling through his thin lips, "we didn't get properly introduced at the fire the other day. Some of you I've met from time to time, but for the record, I'm Chief H. Walker Slater."

The "B" platoon of Fire 5 is lined up at attention, double chins tucked into our Adam's apples, run-down heels together, stomachs in, those that can still manage it. Why don't he give us parade rest?

The smile flicks off. "I'm in charge here," he snaps. *"Fully* in charge. Make a note of it." How're we suppose to make a note when we're at attention?

"Men," he says, "we're a proud outfit." He's short and wispy, with a built like a C.P.A., but his bass voice rattles the apparatus. I imagine Ladder 10's taking it in from the mezzanine, waiting their turn for the fun and games. "I'm glad to have you in my battalion."

The fourth battalion's been here ninety-seven years and H. Walker Slater's just been promoted from his desk job at headquarters, and already we're *his* battalion. Tyree D'Arcy lets a rose, but lucky the new chief don't hear it.

"A few points," he says, folding his arms across the front of his Class A jacket with the polished gold buttons. "From now on, we do things one way. *My way!* There's no right way and wrong way any more, there's only the H. Walker Slater way."

He's got a short whip, I think they call it a crop, the first one I ever seen, since us firemen very seldom ride to the hounds, and I'm halfway thinking he's gonna crack somebody with it. "If I tell you men to suck eggs," he says, rapping his own leg with the crop, "I'm gonna expect you to suck eggs. Don't even bother to think if it's right or wrong, just do it! It's not your job to think, it's mine. If I make a mistake, I'll take the blame, I'll back you up. Fair enough?"

A couple of the guys say, "Um-hmmm."

*"Fair enough?"* the chief says louder.

"Yeh, right, Chief." "Fair enough." "Yes, sir, Chief!" We're falling all over ourself to agree with him.

"I'm here to make this the best damn battalion in town." Stupid me, I thought we already were. "I expect Fire Five to lead the way. You're the best, you're hand-picked." Now he's talking, but why won't he give us parade rest? "If I'm a little tougher on you men, it's because I expect you to set the standards, carry the guide-on." I hope that horny Plummer gets it straight. That's *guide*-on.

My back's cracking. Next to me I can hear Tyree breathing hard, his overweight's killing him. Chief Grant never held us at attention unless the superchief was in quarters, and then only long enough to show respect. But then, Al Grant thinks we're firefighters, not Annapolis cadets.

At last. Inspection begins. Slater walks along the row peering up at everybody, he's only about five seven in his elevator boots. He sticks his bulldog nose right up under our chins, and I know why. H. Walker Slater won't tolerate booze and boozers.

He stops short at Mustacci. Mike is cue-bald but he has a thick mustache that's his personal trademark and muttonchop side whiskers big enough to hide a family of mice. "Barber up!" Slater snaps. "Get that fungus off your face! How d'you expect your mask to seal?"

"Seals fine, Chief," Mike says. I wish he'd of just kept quiet.

Slater leans up to read Mike's name off his nameplate. "You have one shift to meet regulations."

Regulations? Nobody pays any attention to our hair regulations, those rules belong to the dark ages. "Side whiskers may not extend past the bottom of the ear hole . . . Mustaches may not extend past the outer limit of the lips . . ." Poor Mike. I don't even think he has a barber.

The chief passes Les Dawson and stops at Ax. With that big beefy face and a nose like uncooked dough, there's no way Ax can look dignified, plus you can always read our latest menu off his tie.

"Get that uniform to the cleaner!" Slater barks.

"It just come back, Chief," Ax says.

"Send it again!" He stands on tippy-toes to read the nameplate. "Oh, yeh, you're Bedrosian," he says. A smirk comes over his face, he looks like a bleached bulldog. If you can imagine a blond-haired J. Edgar Hoover, you got the picture.

"Right, Chief, I'm Bedrosian, yes, sir."

"The one that won't wear regulation."

"Whattaya mean, Chief?"

"You know what I mean," Slater says, tilting his head back and peering at Ax like he's looking at a tall turd. "Your underwear, if I have to say it."

"Chief," Ax says, "I didn't know there was a regulation about underwear."

"This battalion's a team," Slater booms out. He jots something on his clipboard. "That means we conform. Your shoes need attention, too." He can't complain about Ax's crew-cut,

24

the last one in the station. We always like to kid Ax that his hair and his face look like they were carved out with a Halligan tool.

I sneak a peek at his shoes. Ax has terrible feet, bunions, calluses and corns, everything but hemorrhoids. His size 15s always look like they got about a dozen golf balls inside.

"What're *you* looking at, Fireman?" Hitler snaps at me.

"Nothing, Chief," I says, snapping back to attention.

For ten minutes the new man struts up and down the row, making complaints and scribbling on his clipboard. Sonny's sideburns are an eighth of an inch too long, Tyree better lose thirty pounds, Plummer cocks his hat too far, my tie's crooked, etc. etc. and so forth.

Then he comes back to Ax. "You don't even look like a firefighter," he says in a lowered voice.

Loo jumps in and says, "Chief, this here's the man that ventilated the retarded school. Went on the roof by himself and opened the fire room?"

Ax starts to roll up his sleeves to show the scars where the fire back-drafted and laid him up for three months of skin transplants, but the chief says to the lieutenant, "That was last year, wasn't it?"

"Yes, sir."

"When's he gonna wash up?"

Before Loo can answer, Slater snaps, "Dismiss the platoon! I can't stand around here jabbering." I guess he can't. The Fourth Battalion's got four houses with six engine companies, four truck companies and a fireboat. If he's gonna give this same treatment to everybody, he'll have a long day.

Upstairs in the scullery, I pour coffee, and my hand's shaking. "How old's that midget scumsucker?" Mike Mustache says, and Sonny Wicker says he thinks thirty-nine.

25

"He'll never see forty," Mike says.

"Hey, I got a flash for ya," Plummer says. "That's our next superchief."

"Who's his rabbi?" Tyree D'Arcy wants to know.

"Only the mayor," Plum says. "Remember when he worked as the mayor's assistant on arson problems?"

"Two years," Les says.

"That did it for him," Plummer says. "Sucked in real good. Now he can't miss."

Ax sits at the long table and rests his cheeks in his hands. "Hey, you guys," he says, "tell me the truth. Don't I look like a firefighter?"

"Only at fires," I says. I'd tell him more, but by this time he ought to know what we think of him. Best I ever seen with an ax or a chain saw. There's intelligence in that, though not everybody would recognize it.

"How'd you like those razor creases in H. Walker's uniform?" Mike Mustacci says. "Punctilious. They say his wife irons his shorts."

"What's punc—punctilious?" Ax asks.

"Keeping razor creases in your pants," Mike explains. "Or sending back memo pads."

"Memo pads?"

"When he was at headquarters, he requisitioned a couple dozen personalized memo pads, and they came back with a line across the top, 'From the Desk of Captain Walker Slater.' "

"Why'd he send 'em back?" I says.

"The printer forgot the H."

I stare out the window. The sun may never shine again.

We're in the scullery, which is our dining room and kitchen, but you'd never mistake it for the Howard Johnson's. The whole room's about thirty feet long by fifteen across, with two ovens along one wall, a cracked sink, a sagging cupboard, two old refrigerators and a chest-type deep-freeze. We use to have two electric light bulbs hanging from the ceiling, but they put in a long fluorescent tube that shows up the cracks and stains. There's usually a stack of newspapers on the long table, plus a couple decks of cards and a cribbage board and sometimes a checkerboard that some of the guys on Ladder 10 make do as a chessboard. We share the whole place with Ladder 10, but you very seldom see the two companies socializing together. Different types, that's all.

Down at the far end of the table Mike Mustacci's working on an exercise for his correspondence writing course, he got started after he sent in a sample of his penmanship and won a free scholarship to a correspondence school for authors, seventy-five dollars off on the regular two-hundred-dollar course. He's a tiger on words, learns a new one every day from his *Reader's Digest* check list. He does his school assignments in felt-tip pen on the cardboard stiffeners you find in laundered shirts.

"How's this grab ya?" Mike asks, and begins reading from one of his laundry boards while everybody lets out a groan.

"It is arbitrary to explain the connection between firefighters and arsonists, as they are very definitely related in what the social scientists call the sympathetic sense, for one could not do without the other. It has been observed that arsonists are the source of scorn and alacrity by we firefighters, as they cause us to turn out at all hours of the day and night, but it has been equally observed by thousands of firefighters, 'I'm indeed happy there are such perpetrators around, as they keep our job from being too boring.'"

"Hey, baby, don't write that down!" Tyree D'Arcy says. "Speak for yourself. I don't dig no torches, man."

"Hey, Mike," Les says, winking at me, "what's that word alacrity mean?"

"Wouldn't you like to know?" our author says, turning huffily back to his felt-tip pen. He dreams of publishing his life story and making six million dollars and driving a Mercedes. Fat chance anything like that ever happening to a fireman.

"You guys seen the bulletin board?" It's Neal "The Eel" Steicher, the lieutenant on Ladder 10.

We tromp out in the hall and read an order signed H. Walker Slater:

Effective 0800 hours tomorrow, roll calls and inspections will be conducted in Class A uniforms.

"Fucking asshole," Ax says.

"Understatement," says Mike Mustache.

Class A's are white shirt, black tie, double-breasted peacoat, black pants, black shoes and sox and service cap. The Class A jacket alone goes for a hundred bucks, and we pay for the whole uniform out of our own pockets. Up to now, we been standing roll call in Class B's, which is just your simple on-duty outfit.

"Fucking pogue," Ax says. He's had the rag on all morning. Plummer put a sticker on his bumper, SUPPORT GAY LIB, and Ax just found it after three weeks.

"Got a flash for ya," Plum says. "That new chief, he's whacked out, he's psycho."

"The walls have ears," I says.

"Oh, yeh?" Mustacci says. "Well, they better keep the hair trimmed off 'em."

We slouch back to the scullery, and I start to beat up eggs for the onion omelets that everybody in the clutch is panting for. I brought in a basket full of wild scallions, picked them on the off-shift. Lester Dawson comes over to drool. "Man," he says, "it's great to have you back."

By that he means it's great to have me off booze and cooking again, because when I was lushing it up after the divorce, I didn't cook, I didn't do my share of the housework, I didn't do anything except lap up vodka. Maybe I could of gotten by till the d.t.'s wiped me out, because firemen take care of their own, and it use to be a tradition for half the guys to be alcoholics. The old-timers, they'd have a snort when they got up, another at lunchtime, an eye-opener in the afternoon, and in between they'd run out to their cars for a shot.

For a while I was never completely sober. Never! People ask me didn't you have terrible hangovers? Nope. To have hangovers you got to quit drinking now and then. I started and finished every day with a half pint and I thought nothing of having another one in the middle of the night the way normal people get up to take a leak. I was like the drunken old chief Daniel Patrick Morrison, whom they used to say, "Let him do anything he wants at a fire, but *don't let him blow on it!*" He retired two years ago and died within a week, and he was cremated one piece at a time, may they all rest in peace.

What saved me was Lieutenant Kirkpatrick, when we were

both working at 17's. I knew I was beginning to look bad. I was using a bottle of Visine a day, I was shaking and trembling and having a hard time at fires. I looked at myself in the crapper mirror one morning and I was *old*. Kirkpatrick slipped in and saw me peeling my eyelids back and he said in that soft voice of his, "Charly, friend to friend, what're we gonna do about this problem?"

What're *we* gonna do about this problem?

"Loo," I said, "I gotta hurry," and I brushed past him. Embarrassed, I guess. Both of us.

A few weeks later the first big budget cuts come down, and ten percent of the department got terminated. Kirkpatrick was asked to form a commando company, Fire 5, that would rove all over town, plus fill in gaps. They'd have a modified Kenworth pumper with 1,000 feet of inch-and-a-half and 1,000 feet of two-and-a-half, a 325-gallon booster tank full of the new fast water, a 1,500-pound ball of Purple-K for chemical fires, and a set of six ladders ranging from babies to a 35-footer. The idea was that a fire company in trouble could get help from Fire 5 —ladder help, pumper help, search and rescue, even medical.

I almost fell over when Kirkpatrick asked if I'd volunteer.

"Loo," I said, "I'm thirty-nine years old. Get some of them young guys."

"Charly, I need somebody that's done it all."

Man, I had to look away. I'd been a truckman, nozzleman, hydrantman, chauffeur, tillerman, an instructor at the training school, I'd been a deputy marshal with the stimulated rank of sergeant, I'd even been a probationary lieutenant once, before they wised up to my boozing. I worked in three-man houses, where the days are twenty-six hours long, I worked out of headquarters where you're a guppy in a bowl, I even crewed on one the fireboats.

But my wife left me and I drank, that's all that mattered any more.

The day Fire 5 lined up for its first roll call in the old Station 12 on Sable Street, I was there, shoes shined and buttons polished. I recognized a second chance when I seen one, and I been straight ever since. Oh, I drink beer with the guys, ale if I'm feeling fancy. A fireman that don't inhale suds is a misfit right away. But two things I don't do, I don't drink hard liquor and I don't think about Marilyn. She left, she left, that's all. And she's not coming back. Who needs married life? I got a couple airy rooms over a bakery two blocks from the station, I got the use of a nice backyard with a grapevine, I got six good dudes working with me and a great lieutenant to boot. I got the world by the nuts, sittin' on a rainbow, however that song goes.

Lester Dawson leans over my shoulder and sniffs while I slice the scallions into pieces. I lift the edges for the last time, letting the butter slide under the eggs. I'm ready to fold the omelets over and serve them up to the sound of thunderous applause, and the goddamn bell rings.

Three rounds of three.

That means both companies go, the house empties.

I snap off the heat and slide the pole. By the time we get back those omelets'll look like something fell out of a baby giraffe.

That's why we keep a locker full of Cap'n Crunch.

It's a big run-down house with a sign in the front window, ROOMS TO LET. A plume of smoke curls from a roof turret. Must be a bed fire, or an overstuffed.

We're first in, and Kirkpatrick gives the orders. "Lay your pre-connect, Sonny. Les, take the can." His usual flat voice. The can's an extinguisher with fifty pounds of dry chemical, usually it's enough for a job like this.

The new battalion chief rolls up in his lime-yellow command car, and I notice he's riding in the back seat. That's a first. Even the superchief sits in front with his chauffeur. Closer to the action, gives a better view as you approach.

"Whatta we got here?" Slater wants to know, jumping out.

"Nothing much, Chief," Loo says.

H. Walker Slater peers at the thin ribbon of smoke above the roofline, then grabs the mike from the dashboard. *"Battalion Four at the location,"* he says. *"We got an inch-and-a-half fire in a three-story house. No problem."*

*"Okay Battalion Four,"* the dispatcher answers. *"Do you want some backup?"* Usually on fires this close to downtown they send four or five companies anyway.

*"I said no problem,"* Slater snaps. *"We can handle it with what we got."*

He's barely hung up the mike when there's a whoosh and a

big cloud of yellowish smoke comes out a second-story window.

"What—" the chief says.

Les Dawson staggers through the front door with his face flushed. "Something blew," he says. He wipes his chin with a smoking glove. The whole upstairs is burning.

Loo glances at the chief, but Slater's glassy-eyed. He never seen a body of fire like this when he was president of that desk down at headquarters. The red of the flames reflects in his brownish-yellow eyes, and I wait for him to start giving orders.

Then Loo makes a few hand signals, and pretty soon Fire 5's got itself in gear. We needed a good fire, the guys were getting antsy. Sonny Wicker grins as he humps a hundred-foot bundle across the lawn. That's eighty pounds dead weight, and he handles it like a package of Chinese noodles. Ax carries the chain saw on his arm like a charm bracelet and disappears inside. Plummer Brown's already gunned the Kenworth a half block to the hydrant, while the supply line spills off behind him in a perfect reverse lay, and before the rig stops rolling, Tyree D'Arcy whacks at the hydrant with his wrench and the pressure charges the lines like a stud horse's wang.

"Take an inch-and-a-half and get inside," Lieutenant Kirkpatrick says under his breath. The chief's suppose to be running the show, but this fire don't know that.

Sonny grabs the pipe and I move in behind him as we run through the front door. Nothing's burning downstairs, so we head up and walk smack into a hall full of flames on the second floor. Son spins the Elkhart nozzle to full fog, and we push ahead knowing we can always follow our line back out if we get in trouble. We're doing the job that Fire 5's famous for. Penetration. Our middle name.

"Beautiful, beautiful," I says in Sonny's ear, and by the look on his face he's forgotten about his missing wife, at least for a while. He opens the nozzle and works the heavy stream around the hall counterclockwise, floor, ceiling, floor, ceiling. Steam stings back into our faces, our noses are dripping— having wonderful time, wish you were here.

Then the smoke thickens and banks back on us, it's like breathing raw sewage gas. Probably a sofa split in the heat. Ax should be on the roof by now, slicing holes, ventilating, giving the flame and the smoke an outlet so we can advance our line.

Sonny turns his head as though to ask what next. He coughs a few times and spits up, and I nudge his shoulder to tell him to get down, inhale some of the cleaner air on the floor. We take a couple of deep sucks and keep on trucking.

Around us we can hear crackling, popping, glass breaking as windows blow out from the heat, ceilings creaking as they buckle, and the whistling sound you get in all good fires, from superheated air forcing its way through cracks at high pressure. Once in a while there's a loud hiss, sometimes a dull thud or a low explosion. A bottle blows up, a framed picture falls off the wall and shatters, a kid's ball splits from the heat. Then it's quiet.

The fire's gathering itself.

The smoke thickens again. Where the hell's Ax with the saw?

Thuds from above us. Hip, hip, the axman's on the job!

Hey, Sonny's moving too slow. "Wow, Son, terrific!" I yell, but the poor guy's slumped over the nob, and I halfway drag him out the way we come in.

I can't believe what I see on the street. No relief companies. By now, there ought to be at least another couple of pumpers and a truck.

"What's going on?" I says to the chief's driver. He's a fireman first, a chauffeur second, he knows what's eating me.

He spreads the palms of his hands. "He won't call for help, that's all."

I remember his words: *"No problem. We can handle it with what we got."* Now our new chief can't admit he was wrong.

"Come on, you men, get inside!" It's Slater, shoving at me and Sonny with his white gloves.

"We just come out," I says. "Chief, we—"

"Get in, get in, *get in!* Goddamnit, *move!*" He's almost screaming now. I guess he'll beat us to death before he'll call for reinforcements.

I look up at the old wooden house, and all I can see is smoke from the second floor up. This is ridiculous. The chief pushes me from behind, and I grab Sonny. "Come on, kid," I says, helping him along. "I'll take the pipe this time." We follow our line inside and crawl back up the stairs.

Tyree and Les are crouched in the second-floor hallway, and when they spot us, Tyree says, "It's in the walls, man. Need us somebody to take down these walls."

A bulky form comes inching along on his hands and knees, and I make out the red helmet. "Loo," I says. "You okay?"

He shakes his head and stands up, inhaling like a pearl diver. Ax is right behind, and I see he still has the chain saw.

"Quick!" I says, and I wrench the saw out of his hands. He slumps to the floor, his swampwater eyes are rolling wildly.

"Cover me," I says to Tyree and Les, and they hit me with a spray. The saw turns over at the first yank, and the blade tears into that wall *brrrp brrrp brrrp.* Pretty soon it looks like I'm ripping the husk off a hornet's nest, except there's no hornets underneath, there's fire. It's licking up and down the lath and extending in every direction.

"Hit it," Loo says, and Les opens the hose all the way and blacks that lath down like a man blowing a match. It's simple, once you got the wall exposed. The rest of us cut out, the hallway seems to be knocked.

I slip outside again, and Lieutenant Kirkpatrick stumbles by me, he looks like a marathon runner at the finish line, but I never seen the fire that could keep him down. "Something about a baby," he blurts, and runs around the side.

A blue-haired woman's pacing the lawn near Chief Slater. "Baby!" she's screaming. "Oh, my baby!"

"What is it, Chief?" I says.

He don't seem to notice me. He's mumbling to himself. I pull back my helmet to hear better, and he's stomping his boot and saying, "Out, goddamnit. *Go out!*" He's ordering the fire to black! A new technique they're teaching in India.

"Where's your baby?" I ask the woman.

"In his little room on the second floor," she says between gulps. "Where that man's going."

I turn and see Loo disappearing inside a window.

A few minutes pass, and he comes back down the ladder, his face streaked, his turn-out coat charred. "Can't find it," he says between heaves. "An old bed, that's all."

"My baby!" the woman screams again. "Please, please, somebody save my baby!"

I yank a Survivair off the rig and pull it over my shoulders with the bottle pointing down my back. Kirkpatrick reaches out and flips the switch to On, which gives me fifteen to thirty minutes of pure air, depending on how hard I work. I hate anything covering my face, especially this bowl of cold hard plastic. "Pretend it's a pussy," Plummer told me once. We try to help each other's problems.

The fire's darkening, but there's still plenty of smoke. I can hardly see as I step through the window and into the room, taking care not to catch my air hose on the broken glass.

I work my way around the wall in a half-crouch, feeling and touching. There's a small bed, a wardrobe. Then I almost break a leg tripping over something. It's a rocking chair.

I keep touching and feeling till I get all the way back to the rocker again.

No baby in this room.

A narrow door leads into a stand-up utility closet and a faint red flicker. Must be where the loot got burned.

I shove into the tiny room and see a crooked line of flame running up the wall. I drop to the floor to get below the heat, but too late. It's like I walked into a furnace. The tips of my ears tingle under my helmet, then go cold, like somebody's stroking them with dry ice. I been through this before. Those ears are scorched.

I crawl around in the smoke and grab whatever I can grab. *There!* Is it a crib? A small bed?

A flaming panel of wood flakes off the ceiling and flutters to the floor, just missing me, and a blast of hot air slides down my back and puffs out my coat like a balloon. I shove my gloved hand through the slats and poke around.

My mother didn't raise me for this kind of work. The fun's gone out of this fire. After you carry out a dead baby, there's not enough capitals in the whole world to put you to sleep.

I slide my glove across the mattress. Can't feel anything. I can still hear that poor woman: "Baby! My baby!"

I take off a glove and watch the hairs on the back of my hand curl up and disappear, *pfffft!* If I wasn't breathing compressed air, I'd be smelling myself burning. I start at one end of the bed and work my bare hand up and down.

No baby.

I grope around the floor. Maybe the kid fell out.

Floor's bare. Charred and hot. I crawl backward out of the utility room toward the window I come in at.

Kirkpatrick's waiting at the bottom of the ladder, and I yank my mask off. "Nothing, Loo," I says, breathing hard. He slaps at a couple of sparks on my coat.

"Check it all?"

"Bedroom and utility room. If there's a baby, it's not in either one."

A pumper pulls up. "We getting help?" I says.

Loo nods.

"He finally broke down and called 'em in?"

"I called 'em in," the loot says. "Take a blow."

I can hear four or five more rigs coming, and I know it won't be long till the fire's out. I reach back and feel my ears. It's like I stayed home and sent my ears to the beach all day, plus the back of my right hand is as bare and red as a baby's ass.

*A baby's ass.* Somewhere inside, there's a baby. Helpless.

Where's the mother? There, surrounded by neighbors. Kind of old to have a baby. Makes it all the more precious, I guess. Jeez, they're all bawling. What that poor woman needs is the fire doc to hit her with a couple cc's of oblivion. She's lost a kid, no way out of it . . .

The brown smoke turns to black and the black thins down and Kirkpatrick hustles out the front door and over to Battalion Chief H. Walker Slater. "Chief," he says, looking at the ground, "there's nobody in there."

The chief grabs Loo by the front of his coat. "Goddamnit, Kirkpatrick, there's a dead kid in there!" Underneath that foghorn voice, he sounds practically hysterical. Who can blame him? It don't look too good in your file, losing a kid in your first week as a combat chief.

Loo disappears inside, and the mother wobbles over in her bathrobe and starts moaning. "Stand back, lady," the chief orders. "We're doing all we can."

"My baby, my poor baby!"

Out of the corner of my eye I see an off-white French poodle about the size of a large rat. He's peeking around the side of the house next door and baring yellowish teeth and he's got a dirty red ribbon tied in the fur behind the head.

*"Baby!"* the woman yells.

The mutt skips across a tangle of hose lines and spurts into her arms like a tiddlywink. "Oh, my baby!" she says, and squeezes the little beast till his eyes start to pop.

I reach back and feel my Krispy-Kritter ears.

I look down at my toasted hand.

Someday I'll come back and strangle that goddamn dog. And the woman too.

Chief H. Walker Slater looks down at his watch and speaks into his portable unit. *"This fire is tapped,"* he says. *"Two thirty-four P.M."* I guess he's proud of his afternoon's work.

Today we got the natural highs, there's no problem in a station house that a good fire can't solve. My ears are responding to gallons of goose grease, and a new crop of turf is sprouting on the back of my right hand, fertilized by ale.

"Our hero!" Mike Mustache says in a falsetto voice and grabs me by the jewels.

Plummer Brown waltzes onto the apparatus floor singing the firefighter's blues, "My asshole's tore, my tits are sore, I don't give a shit if I don't work no more." Lyrics by Burt Bacharach.

"Fuck off, why don'tcha?" Ax calls out.

Lester Dawson shows up with an eleven-layer chocolate mocha rum cake that must of set him back eighteen or twenty bucks and kept the bakery up all night making it. There's a little candy poodle screwed into the top of the cake like a bride and groom. "A work of art," I says as I grab the dog and crunch it under my shoe.

While we're waiting for Loo, I tell a story that happened to my pal Allan Grant long before he made chief. He hauled a Doberman pincher out of a fire, stuck his thumbs in its skinny ribs and give it artificial respiration, and when that didn't work, he did mouth-to-mouth.

Nobody believes me.

"Mouth to mouth on a d-d-dog?" Sonny says.

"Yeh, well, the poor dog," Plummer says, "he didn't have no choice." Wise guy.

"I hope they're at least engaged," Mike Mustache says.

Up theirs, I won't give them the punch line. On the first anniversary of the Doberman's rescue, Grant was invited back to the house, and the dog bit him.

We're suppose to drill one hour a shift, but Loo's a soft touch after a good fire. If we screwed up, that's another story, he'll drill us till he's satisfied, which may be a month.

"Memo from the battalion chief this morning," he says at the line-up. Great. The new chief's human after all. Every man in the platoon knows we done a good job at the dog fire, but it's nice to have it in writing.

"I'll read," Loo says. " 'Members of Fire Five "B" shift have been dozing during daylight hours and this is strictly forbidden by regulation. Elbows may be on desks and tables, but heads may not be on arms.' "

"Anklebone connected to da wristbone," Tyree mutters.

"Quiet down and listen," Loo says, which we all quiet down and listen. " 'Feet must be on floor or apparatus at all times, and racks may not be broken down for sleeping till ten P.M. Repeat ten P.M.' "

"Shit, Loo," Ax says, "we—"

"End of memo," Kirkpatrick says. "The marshal's office called. That body we found in the flophouse fire? A one-legged wino, been around Skid Row a couple years."

"I remember him!" Plummer says. "Gimp Eddie they call him. Saw him panhandling in Joe's a couple times. Smelly old dude."

"Lab test showed definite xylene and toluene," Loo goes on. "Murder One."

Nobody talks for a second.

"He was t-t-t-torched?" Sonny Wicker finally says.

"Soaked in gasoline first," Loo says. "Then torched."

For a few seconds it's quiet again. Then Tyree says, "Hey, Loo, c'mon, man, this ain't Boston, man. How they know it's murder?"

Loo says, "All I know is what they tell me."

"Spooky," Ax says, his clown-face bleached white-on-white. "What a way to go."

"Sadistic," Mike says. "Eclectic."

"Okay," Kirkpatrick says abruptly. "Drill time."

Nobody moves.

"Drill time," Loo repeats. "The book says an hour a day."

"Hey, Loo," Plummer calls out, "make it short, will ya?"

"How about a Q&A drill?" Kirkpatrick says, and everybody relaxes. "Charly, list the training manuals."

I recite the list, feeling stupid at being asked such a dumb question. "And 'Fire Suppression,' " I finish up.

"Any other manuals?"

Ax pipes up, "There's Manual Perez at training school."

Loo throws up his hands. That's it for the morning. Life's easy after a good fire. Discipline's relaxed. Like if the loot needs a volunteer for a detail, he'll get on the intercom and say, "Two minutes, you got two minutes." We run and hide, and whoever he catches, that's the volunteer. I'm not kidding! Grown men.

Some of the guys burrow under the equipment, and some wrap theirselves up in hose, but Loo's no idiot, he knows what a standard set of line looks like, and if it's got a bulge in the middle, he knows that's not an ardvark in there.

Sonny Wicker had a good hiding place for almost a year, he'd hang from the top of the hose tower and wrap a tarp around himself. Me, I use to hide in a big cupboard in the compressor room till some of the others found out about it.

They'd crowd in and giggle and play goosy-ass and make so much noise Loo'd catch the whole pack of us.

Lately I got the perfect hideout, in the fifth wheel housing on Ladder 10's truck, just above the springs where the steering box comes down. Cramped, but when you stand five foot ten and 150 pounds, you can snake inside there, and the only way the loot can find you is if he snakes inside himself, and how can a six-footer with oak-tree shoulders do that? So I never get the dirty details any more. And why should I anyway, doing almost all the cooking?

I can hear Plummer now, "You cook because you like it, Charly."

I can hear my answer, too, "I cook in self-defense."

We use to rotate, and then Plummer got a wild hair that he was some kind of gourmet chef, and damn near poisoned us. Plummer's specialty is ginch, not food. "One of the department's finest hosemen," his F.D. biography says.

During the month that Plum cooked, we had treats like chop suey with chili sauce and spare ribs almondine, and that's nothing compared to what he was serving us for lunch and supper. "I'm taking your basic chink menu and blending some international touches," he explained one night as he served us egg rolls with sour cream.

At first the rest of the guys were in hog heaven. They got no taste anyway, and they hate to cook. Me, I learned about food from Marilyn—a real Cordon Blue cook—and I knew Plummer and me'd have a shoot-out.

"Hey, pal," I said after he served the mint omelets for breakfast, "how about something simple tonight? Hate to see you going to so much trouble."

"Trouble?" he says. "Since when is rice noodles with bearnaise sauce trouble?"

"That's on for tonight?"

"Jellied asparagus spears on the side."

I thought I was the only fireman living off Alka Seltzer II till I overheard Ax get on Plummer's case late one night. "Hey, kid, where'd you learn to cook?"

"I use to be a first-grade cook in the army."

"Yeh? Well, this ain't the first grade. How'd Ho Chi Minh like your cooking?"

A few days later the guys had a meeting and voted me cook. First thing I put up a sign:

THIS IS NOT YOUR HOME. YOU HAVE TO SHARE THIS SCULLERY WITH OTHERS. DO NOT BE A CHAUVINIST PIG OR PIGETTE OR PIGPERSON. WASH YOUR OWN GODDAMN DISHES AND SILVERWARE. THANK YOU.

I signed it "The Management," but somebody crossed that out and put in "Geheime Staats Polizei." A Nazi general.

I keep the menu simple. Soups, stews, ham and cabbage, fried chicken, corned beef, potato salad, dumplings, your basic good old U.S. of A. cuisine. Our hunters keep us stocked with venison, elk and birds, and our fishermen bring in trout and bass. We started out the new clutch with a buck a man for spices, and it's been running good ever since, three months now, with your average six-course dinner costing ninety cents, maybe a buck, and breakfast figuring around forty cents or less.

I have no trouble with the guys on Fire 5, they're too scared I'll quit cooking, but those pogues on Ladder 10 are aggravating. One night they got into our storage locker and liberated a half a jar of fresh mushrooms, and I went out to the bullpen and announced with a long face that the whole Fire 5 platoon come down with mushroom poisoning and several weren't expected to pull through and could any of the other crews give blood? Ladder 10, they all crowded into the crapper, eating their fingers.

The only trouble I have now is rarely. When Tyree first come on, I told him to serve from the left and take the dishes away from the right. "Hey, man," he grumbled. "You superstitious?"

The bells ring and we take a slide. Les and I make a detour through the watch office to see what Plum's scribbling down: "398 Worthington, service call."

"Heaven's sake, Plum," Les says. "How come we get all the service calls lately?" *Heaven's sake.* That's as profane as Les gets. "What's the matter with Ladder Ten?"

"Them pussies?" Plum says, snapping his suspenders and grabbing his bunking coat.

Lieutenant Kirkpatrick comes running in. "Stay cool, Loo," Plummer says. "Service call. Three ninety-eight Worthington, marked down from four dollars."

"One nice thing," Plum says as we ease out of the station, "we won't have the chief on our ass." Battalion chiefs don't roll on singles, they don't roll on service calls, they usually only roll when a whole house turns out.

"Stow it," Kirkpatrick says.

The address turns out to be an apartment building, and a man meets us at the door. "It's . . . it's . . . Four A," he says. "A lady's in trouble."

We grab the elevator to the fourth floor. No answer at 4A. Loo looks at Ax and Ax grabs my Halligan tool. One stroke and the lock's shattered. That's why his nickname isn't Horse.

Inside, we hear a screechy voice, sounds like a scared kid: "This way! *Help!*"

We tromp through a room with a rumpled canopy bed and just off it we find a door where the squeaks are coming from.

"May we come in?" Lester says in his cultured voice, and the squeaker says, "Fuh Gawd's sake, come in!" It's an advanced case of hysteria, we can see that already.

A woman's in the bathtub. She weighs four-hundred pounds if she's a day, and she's got herself squeegeed in by suction. She sees us and says, "Oh, I'm so embarrassed."

Plummer reaches down and tries to lift her, but she don't budge. She's about twenty-eight years of age with a Kewpie doll face, not bad at all underneath the calories, and out front she has two giant Crenshaw melons, I'd guess about a 46D. There's enough there for the whole battalion, but who thinks of things like that at a time like this? Plummer maybe. But don't go by him, he'd screw a stove.

"God love ya if ya get me out," the woman squeals.

"We gotcha," Ax says. He reaches around her waist and says, "May I?" He thinks he's playing Simon Says.

"Certainly," the woman says.

Ax heaves. The tub lifts a half inch, but the woman don't budge.

"Once more," Ax says. He grabs her by the crotch and the upper arms and lifts straight up, at the Olympics they'd call it the snatch-and-jerk. The woman screams. Ax lets go and bends over. *"Ooo-ooh,"* he says. *"Ooo-ooh.* I got the hernia."

"What now, Loo?" Tyree says.

"Oil," Kirkpatrick says.

"In the kitchen," the woman yelps. "Under the sink."

Tyree comes back with a bottle of safflower oil, good for dieters. "God love ya," the victim says.

47

"Relax," Loo orders her. "Who has the smallest hands?"

Everybody puts their hand behind their back. "Charly," Loo says, "try to push in and break the suction."

"Where, Loo?"

*"Ar uh,* wherever you think best."

There's nothing I like more than to make my own decisions. I shove my hand behind her, and Tyree pours in the safflower oil, and the woman tries to say something but nothing comes out. She's a little hoarse, and no kidding. She tries to talk again, and Plummer says, "We know, lady. God love us if we get you out." She nods her head and tries to smile.

Then Plum takes one arm and Tyree takes the other and Sonny and Les grab her feet and they all heave at once. There's a pop like somebody opened a giant champagne bottle and out she comes like a baby whale. She slips and falls back in, drenching everybody, but this time she don't stick.

"My firemen!" she says, and reaches for the first one, which happens to be Ax. She gives him a watery squeeze, and then she sighs and looks for somebody else, but by that time we're all elbowing our way through the bathroom door.

"Nice place you got here," Les says politely.

"You like it?" she says. Her voice isn't squeaky any more, it's dropped about an octave. By this time we're all in the living room, and she points to a cowboy picture on the wall, an original James Fenimore Cooper.

"Yes, ma'am, lovely place," Loo says.

"Crocheted the antimacassars myself," the woman says.

"Do tell," Ax says. It looks like he's fully recovered, the way he's high-stepping toward the exit. "Who knitted all them things on the furniture?"

"Those're antimacassars."

"Oh?" Ax says. "She has nice taste."

"Would you like to see the kitchen?" she says, and Loo says

48

no thanks, we got to be toddling off, and just then the lady puts her hands over her mouth and lets out a shriek and lifts one kneecup over her private areas and her arms over her big tickets.

"Whatsa matter, lady?" Plummer says. He jumped about three feet when she shrieked, the same as he does when the alarm goes off.

*"I'm naked!"*

She waddles into the bedroom and comes back wrapped either in a tent or an oversize shimmy-sham, I don't know which, and by that time we're all out in the hall except Loo. "Fireman Bedrosian," he orders, "get the information."

"Loo—"

"Get the information." That means Ax has to write down the time of accident, nature of accident, how it come to happen, name of victim, time in, time out, etc. and so forth.

We leave him to his work and head for the rig. *"Fire Five in service,"* Plum says into the radio, and the dispatcher acknowledges. A few minutes go by and Ax comes running out the front door like he's pursued by vampires, and we roll away on a Code Yellow.

"She gimme this before I left," Ax says, still breathing hard, and hands me a slip of damp paper. It says "457–4745, Miss de Boliver."

"Burn it and stir the ashes," Plummer says. "That way you'll never be tempted on a cold night."

"You should talk about being tempted," Ax says. "Fuck off, why don'tcha?"

And so we roll merrily back to the house, a bunch of harmless firemen returning from another hair-raising experience. If the public only knew our suffering.

49

Just before dark we get special-called to Avenue H and the Freeway, and we all try to guess what could possibly be burning on an overpass above the Interstate and nothing flammable within a hundred yards. Must be a traffic accident, probably some spilt gasoline to flush. "Another one of them elite jobs, eh, Loo?" Plum says.

There's a crowd on top of the overpass, it looks like somebody's crawled on one of the light standards that reach out over the Freeway. If the younger generation'd just go back to booze, we wouldn't have to make these stupid runs.

Down below on the Freeway, police cars are skidding into position to block off two lanes of rush-hour traffic. It's maybe sixty, seventy feet, straight down.

"Wonder what they need us for?" I says.

Loo shrugs. In cases like this, we use to get below with a life-net and make the catch like Willie Mays, but that's gone out of style. The last one of those capers I was on, a guy was standing naked on a seventh-floor ledge. Our crew sneaks around the corner and Loo says, "Okay, run!" *Splat!* He stepped off the second he seen us move. Hit on top of a parked car about twenty feet away, would of killed anybody he hit.

Most of the jumpers we get nowadays, they're high. "Don't fuck wid me, man. One more step I take you wid me, man."

Those type. We're experimenting with a thirty-foot-wide air bag that inflates in ninety seconds with two electric fans. The idea is put it underneath, back off and wish them luck.

Two cops are trying to handle this case, and they look disappointed when they see our rig. "Oh, you're an engine company," the older cop says. He sounds sleepy, probably this run interrupted his collections. "We need a good ladderman to go out there and talk sense to that bitch." The cops have everybody typed—if you're a truckman you can climb like a monkey, if you're an engineman you hump hose, if you're a woman you're a bitch.

"Don't worry," I says, "we're not a truck company or an engine company, we're an anything company."

"That's Fire Five," the younger cop says, turning around and staring at the number on my helmet with the lightning bolt through it. He's been standing at the railing of the overpass screaming orders at the jumper, a definite no-no, but I doubt if she can hear him in the traffic and siren noise.

"Can you get out there?" the older cop says.

Loo says, "That pole won't hold much weight."

"It'll hold," the cop says. "It's cemented in."

There's two reasons why I'm good at this particular line of work. One is I only weigh a hundred fifty, which is the lightest in our platoon, at least till we get our first firefem, and two is I'm forty-one years old and I look kind of fatherly. I already talked three jumpers down, assuming they were really gonna jump in the first place, which is usually doubtful.

It's quieter now, with the northbound traffic stopped and no more sirens, and I can hear the younger cop still hassling the subject. She's a hippie chick, maybe twenty-two, twenty-three years old, and she's shaking like she's got the palsy. "Listen," the cop hollers at her, "if you wanna go, this is a stupid goddamn way. It's only a short drop and there's no traffic to run

51

over ya. Come on, climb back, I'll lend ya my gun."

She's got long chestnut-colored hair that hangs down her back and a pretty face and a slender figure. She's crying and once in a while she lets go with one arm to wipe her eyes while she straddles the horizontal pole with her legs. A crowd's gathering, people are getting out of their cars down below, and any minute I expect to hear some moron holler, "Go ahead, jump!" There's always one.

I start to ask her name, but the young cop's hollering at her over my voice.

"Hey," I says softly, "quit breaking her chops."

By this time Plummer's unpacked the nylon rope and the harness and rigged me up with a belay to the railing, so I inch my way a few feet out on the light pole. "Whatsa matter, miss?" I call out.

She starts to shinny toward the end, but she's already at the light mount. One more inch, they'll be picking her up with eyedroppers.

"Excuse me," I says, trying to keep my voice calm. "I didn't make out what you said."

"Let me d-d-die," she says, shaking all over. She talks like Sonny Wicker.

I shinny out a few more feet till I can see her big blue eyes in the bright light. "Don't!" she says.

I stop cold. "Listen, honey," I says. Another siren's approaching, it's a ladder truck headed down the Freeway with its hundred-foot aerial halfway extended. "I'm not coming after you. What you do, it's your own business. I just wanna talk, okay?"

She looks at me, her eyes narrowing, and then she turns her trembly head and checks the whole scene, high and low.

"C'mon, hon, what's bothering you?" I says. "Tell me about it. I'll be glad to listen. No extra charge." I give her my Pepsodent smile. Just one capped incisor, and the rest my own.

She mumbles something, but the ladder truck comes careening up and she turns. One leg's got a good grip, the other's barely holding by the ankle. She looks like she's letting go.

I wave at the truckmen to stop. Loo's securing my belay at the railing. "Get on the radio," I call back. "Tell 'em to hold off."

I look at the girl. She's taken it all in. Whacked out or not, she knows what's happening. They're smart, these jumpers, they're like cornered animals. She sees the aerial pull away and she renews her leglock.

"Listen," I says, "you can trust firemen. We got a job to do is all."

She's watching me in the glow of the mercury-vapor light, and she's waiting for me to make one false move, so I kind of relax on the pole and I says, "Now why's a pretty girl like you doing something like this?"

She sniffs a couple times and begins babbling about her boyfriend went away and there's nothing left.

"Honey," I says, "c'mon, crawl back and we'll talk about it." She turns and takes a deep look at me, and I says, "Miss, you're way too pretty for this."

She lets go one arm and dangles it over the open air, as if to show me. It's withered, maybe half the normal length, with tiny fingers like an elf. That's her answer to me. Well, what I said is dumb anyway. What's looks got to do with suicide? Suppose she's ugly, what should I of said then? "You're way too ugly for this?" What I meant was she's a human being, she should lighten up on herself, give herself a break.

So I come right out and say it, in simple English.

We talk maybe twenty minutes, her mostly. The whole world's against her, her mom died, her boyfriend run off and got married, her Siamese kitten got squashed by the plumber, she's all alone. Then somebody heisted her stash. Uppers. That's why she's shaking.

"Honey," I says, "nobody's all alone. You're never all alone unless you want to be. Look at me," I says. "My wife left me, took our four kids." There weren't any kids, but what's a little bushwah if it'll help save a life? "Thought I'd *never* get over it. But I did, sweetheart. You just gotta take things one day at a time."

"My n-n-name's Cindy," she says, digging her knuckles into her eyes. "What's yours?" A good sign.

"I'm your friend Charly Sprockett."

She starts to bawl again, and then she says she's scared of the cops, and I says, "Listen, don't worry about 'em. You climb back, I'll take care of you. Get you to a doctor, get you some help. Okay?"

"Promise?" she says. She's beginning to sound weaker.

"Just pull yourself back," I says, holding out my hands.

"No c-c-cops?"

"Swear to God."

She starts to inch toward me, but I'm not sure she's gonna make it. Not after kicking cold turkey and hanging out there for maybe thirty, forty minutes.

"Wait!" I says. "Hold it, hon." I can see her grip's weak and if she keeps trying to pull herself along that narrow bar, she could slip off. "I'm coming out," I says.

I'm still three or four feet away when her one good arm lets go and she slips around and hangs upside down by her legs. Her long hair's dangling straight over the Freeway. Out of the corner of my eye I see the ladder truck lurch forward. If she can hold on for a few more seconds, they'll save her. Those guys drill every day, they can stuff that aerial up a bat's ass in a windstorm.

54

She's slipping.

I grab a handful of blue jeans. *There!*

I snap my harness to her belt. The crowd goes ooh and ahh, but there's no danger. I been belayed all the time, couldn't of fell if I wanted to. The nylon line I got around me, it'd support a bull elk.

"You want to go down the ladder?" I says.

"No," she says. She's panting now, completely wiped out.

Inch by inch I work her back toward the railing, and Loo and Plummer lift her over the side. A couple of idiots start to clap their hands as if this is a rock festival. "Take a bow, take a bow," somebody calls out, and I says under my breath, "Take a walk, take a walk." Ghouls.

I'm wriggling out of my harness when I see the young cop jerk the girl around by the good arm. He puts her in a tight half nelson and starts frog-walking her to the squad car. "Hey, wait!" I holler. "I promised no cops."

"Stand back," he says.

I turn to Kirkpatrick. "Loo, I give her my word out there."

The loot moves over in front of the open door on the black-and-white. "We'll get her to the hospital," he says to the cop. "Book her later if you want."

Perfect. This way the doctors can take care of her, ease her withdrawal.

But the cop don't go for it. He's still got her good arm mashed against her back, and she's bent almost to her knees, gasping for breath.

"Let go!" Loo snaps out.

The chain of command don't mean much from P.D. to F.D., but when somebody with a silver bar on his collar tells somebody with a bare coat sleeve to let go, they usually let go.

"You'll hear from our watch commander," the cop says, smoothing out his blouse.

"Great," I put in. "I'll acquaint him what fine officers he's got."

"Goddamnit, she's gotta be booked for disorderly," the cop insists.

Kirkpatrick takes a look at the spectators standing around. He lowers his voice. "You're the one oughta be booked," he says.

We walk the girl back to our rig. Inside the cab, she's gone boneless and her face is pitch-white, not a drop of color. I throw a coat over her. I can see she's younger than I thought, maybe eighteen or nineteen. Her eyes aren't blue, that must of been the reflection from the light. They're kind of hazel, wide and red and wet.

While Loo's signaling our aid car over, I put my arm around her shoulders. She's still shaking, and her head flops on my chest, and she lets go this big sigh. I reach for her hand. It turns out to be the withered one. It don't feel bad, kind of like a baby's. I give it a nice squeeze and she looks up at me and smiles.

Pretty soon the aid man comes and takes her away.

A psycho hippie chick, and yet kind of sweet in her own sick way.

Who would of dreamed?

Man, I think I'll retire from the social whirl, just buy me a book on whacking off. Lately I been the strike-out king of the whole shift. That specialty shopper the other night, she drags me into a flea market. "I don't even have a dog," I says, but we spend the whole evening looking at gewgaws and knickknacks of the type Marilyn and I use to drive nine miles to give to the Goodwill, glad to get rid of them. Glad to get rid of the specialty shopper, too. I drive her home, she says she don't go for a goodnight kiss on the first date. Forty-two years old, married twice, wears a teentsy-weentsy ribbon in her hair.

Then I go out with a red-haired type that candles eggs, not bad-looking if you don't mind a thin little curved nose that reminds me of a chicken. Rhode Island Red, I called her. Plummer says I'm overparticular, she's got too good a shape to waste, so I give him the phone number. "Take your shot," I says, "and bring me back a dozen of eggs." He takes her out and says she's terrific, a four-way chick. But he forgets the eggs.

Then I make a date with the senior secretary in arson records, but she won't take my dictation.

That's three for three—strike-outs, I mean. Never reach the majors this way.

Well, there's more important things in life. I can hear Plummer saying, *"What's more important than cooze? You crazy?"*

For one thing, Fire 5's going to hell under this eager new battalion chief. He keeps everybody on edge, likes to pop in and look around, tighten the screws. He's all over Cap Nordquist, he don't mind ragging the old man in front of everybody else. Cap's hard of hearing, he has bad eyesight and a heart condition, outside of that he's Mr. America. When he has to turn out in the middle of the night he gets confused sometimes, but usually he's all right by the time the fire's out.

The other day Cap puts his helmet on backward, with the bill in back, he looks like Smoky Stover. "Tell me," Chief Slater purrs in that deep voice of his, "didn't they ask you on the captain's test how to put your hat on?" Right in front of the men!

One night Cap's suppose to be inside a fire room, leading a crew, but usually we park him outside and go in alone. He's just an old guy waiting out his pension. It's a taciturn agreement. This time we got him stashed behind the rig, where nobody can see him. He keeps his mobile radio turned up, and in the meanwhile Loo and the rest of us fight the fire on the third floor.

*"Battalion Four to Portable Two,"* we hear Slater call over the radio.

Nordquist's voice answers, *"Portable Two."*

*"What's your location?"*

*"Ar eh, inside the fire room, Chief."* I look out a window. Cap's standing behind the rig, smoking a cigar.

*"How's it look in there?"*

Nordquist gives a complete description of how the fire's licking at the ceiling and we're gonna pull it in a minute and there might be some extension in the walls but we can't tell for sure yet.

Jeez, Slater's inching his way around the rig. He must suspect something. *"Hot in there?"* he says into his portable unit. He's looking right at Cap.

*"Not too,"* the old man says, puffing on his stogie.

Then he sees the chief and flinches like he's hit by a truck. It's a wonder he don't have his final heart attack on the spot. Slater just smiles and goes back in front. You can be sure it'll go in Cap's file.

All afternoon we been working clean-up at a liquor store, a weird assignment for a guy like me that almost become an alcoholic. The law says any booze that's been in a fire is contaminated, it has to be destroyed even if the seal's intact. We're snapping the necks off hundreds of bottles—Chivas Regal, twenty-year-old cognac, Beefeater gin, liqueurs and brandies in fancy bottles, whole cases of Jack Daniel's and Old Forester and Smirnoff vodka. Then we pour it down the drain —*glug glug.* Funny thing, it don't bother me. I guess I been off the hard stuff long enough. Wouldn't mind a cold ale, though.

The guys are taking a lot of breaks. Every time I turn around, they're out at the rig, resting. You'd think they'd be able to break ten or twelve bottle necks without getting the heat prostration.

Something's happening, I can smell it. Look at Ax, he always walks with that clumsy giant's stride, like his thighs are rubbing together, but now he looks like a six-foot-five toddler with a load in his pants. Plummer Brown almost steps right out of his boots. Mike Mustache walks by and I hear a squish. Down the aisle Tyree D'Arcy's holding up a fancy bottle. "Um-*ummmm*, Ameretto," he says. "Speak to me, baby." He pours the bottle down his boot and clomps outside.

I look around for Loo, to see if he's in on it. No, not him. *Never.* If he was in on it, they wouldn't be using their boots, they'd just carry the hooch out by the case and throw it up on the skidload.

When we're all finished, I sniff around the rig to see where they got it hid. There's plenty of fumes, but no booze. Maybe they put it in one of the side lockers, but I doubt it. Those spaces are already full of gear. "Where's it at?" I ask Plummer.

"Where's what at?"

"The booze."

"I thought you were cured of that, Charly."

We're rolling back toward the station on a Code Yellow when I hear the radio: *"Fire Five, Fire Five. Clay and Vine."*

We pull up to a trash fire—people're always using litter cans for ashtrays, just like Dumpsters. In a situation like this, whoever's closest to the pre-connect just grabs the pipe and squirts the booster tank on the fire.

Nobody makes a move.

"What's the matter back there?" Loo says, turning around in the cab.

*"Ar eh . . ."* Les Dawson says.

"Well *uh . . .*" Ax Bedrosian says.

The rest of the guys are studying cloud formations.

"C'mon, for Chrissakes," I says, and I jump up and grab the pipe and start to give it a twist. Then I catch the smell. It's like I'm in an aging room with the Benedictine friars.

*"Om ah,"* Mike Mustache blurts out, "don't waste the tank!" He grabs a chemical extinguisher and squirts the fire out.

"Easier that way," he says, climbing back on with the empty canister.

"Easier than water?" the loot says.

"Loo, this here ain't water," Ax says, patting the booster tank. He knows they're caught, might as well confess. "We stashed a few gallons."

60

"How many's a few?" Kirkpatrick says, his eyebrows climbing up his forehead.

"Fifty, sixty," Sonny Wicker says.

"Souvenir of the clean-up," Tyree says. *"Heh heh."*

"A nice remembrance," Plummer says. *"Heh heh."*

The loot shakes his head from side to side. "Firemen," he says under his breath. He clucks his tongue. "You guys," he says. Then he shakes his head some more and says, "Firemen." Very eloquent, for him.

On the way back our pre-connect dangles off the tailgate and we lay a trail of booze a mile long. You should see the expressions on the pedestrians.

The loot's smiling, up in the cab, but when I look at him he shuts it down fast.

We're off-shift at eight o'clock, and it's a balmy summer night, nice breeze stirring. I stop at Joe's for an ale and walk home figuring I'm gonna catch up on the sleep the F.D.'s been costing me lately. It's still a few minutes to ten—no sense turning in till the bakery closes downstairs. I thaw a herring for my cat Tom and glance through the paper and turn up the scanner so's not to miss any action.

That's something Marilyn could never understand, how practically every firefighter in town is happy to shell out a hundred bucks or a hundred fifty for a short-wave scanner so we can listen to calls, as though we don't get enough action on the job. "Married to your work, married to your work!"—I still hear you, Marilyn.

"A" shift is working the next twenty-four hours and then "C" comes in, and I got two full days to kill. Already I can tell what's gonna be bugging me the whole off-shift, rattling around in my brain day and night. The long-haired chick hanging over the Freeway. Something kind of appealing about her, hippie hophead or not. Bittersweet. I wonder how there could ever be a happy ending for her. No way. A doper with a withered arm. What a prospect.

Still, I seen sadder cases. The toughest on me is dead kids.

Loo told me a trick. "I just turn my brain off," he says to me one night when we're riding arson patrol.

"Don't sound like you," I says.

He don't answer, but I guess he figures he can't let it stand, so he says, "When I was a probationary, I near quit the department. My second fire, I had to carry out a dead boy, maybe three years old. There was a little sister, too. The mother, she'd been too drunk to tell us there was kids in back."

"Got to you, eh, Loo?" I says when it looks like he's not gonna open up any more. But then I realize he's composing himself.

"Up to then, it was all a lark. Go to the fire, put it out, go back to the station and play games. Went home that night and told the wife, and we talked about quitting two straight days."

I pull the Plymouth behind a dark warehouse and cut the lights. "What'd you finally do, Loo?" I says, realizing what a stupid question.

"Went to the chief to turn in my papers. Old Stieglitz? I says, 'I'm sorry, Chief, I'm not firefighter material. Something like those kids the other night, it bothers me too much.'

"Chief says, 'Ya like kids, do ya?' You know how gruff he talked. I says, 'Who don't, Chief?' He picks up my personnel jacket and leafs through it, and he says, 'Two little kids of your own, eh, Fireman?' I just nodded my head. He takes a long look at me. You remember those clear green eyes he had, Charly, like looking into a lens? And he says, 'Son, you're not gonna quit.'

"I says, 'Why not, Chief?'

"He says, 'Cause there might be two more kids at the next fire.' "

This is the longest speech I ever heard Loo make. "Go on, go on."

"Oh," he says, like I woke him from a dream. "Well, that's

63

all, I guess. I realized Chief was right. It never bothered me again."

"Dead kids don't bother you?"

Loo bites his lip. "I turn my brain off," he says real slow. "But I still can't . . . I still can't . . ." His voice trails off.

"Aw, that's okay, Loo," I says, getting embarrassed.

"I still can't think about those first two kids," he whispers.

I look over, but he's turned toward the window, and I put the car in gear and drive off.

Well, you make an adjustment or you quit the job, that's all. Me, I'm a lot like Loo. I don't exactly turn off my brain, but I try to concentrate on the fire problem, like a professional, pretend I'm dealing with units, not people. Sometimes it don't work, like the night I had to tell a young father that his four-year-old daughter was still alive, because the father's hysterical and in shock, and all the time I knew the kid was on the way to the morgue. I lied, and it upset me, still does. But the one that torments me the worst is the one I should of forgot an hour after it happened. I was on aid cars, and we had a call that a sixteen-year-old shoplifter hanged herself in her cell. The body didn't bother me, but it happened on Christmas Eve, which that stuck with me for a long long time. Why didn't she do it on the twenty-third or the twenty-sixth? Why pick Christmas Eve?

The door slams downstairs in the bakery. Slotnik's closing the shop, he'll be in the back baking beagles a couple hours, and he's pretty thoughtful and quiet about it. I'll listen to the scanner awhile and doze off. The only thing that bothers me is the EKG's and the EEG's when the aid men radio them to the hospital, all that high squealing and squawking, but it don't bother me half as much as it does Tom my cat, he's out his porthole on the second note.

*Medic One doctor, use telephone.*

It's like a Brahms waltz in my ear, better than doing the capitals.

*Battalion Three at Station Twenty-five.*

Crazy chiefs, they roam around all night long. You wonder when they sleep. Well, they didn't get to be chiefs by sleeping.

*Engine Eight returning. Over.*

You can always tell when it's a pumper or a ladder truck on the air, you can hear the bells and the siren behind the radio voice. If it's an aid car you hear the howler, and if it's a fire officer he's usually got that high-pitched siren going and sometimes the warbler. Jeez, how Marilyn use to hate those sounds, I guess all the fire wives do. It's not what a wife wants to hear.

*Aid Three a hundred milligrams of E.M. Twenty-six and notify me if the PVC's aren't relieved. Over . . .*

Those poor bastards, they never quit. Couldn't hack that aid-car assignment again, me. What's the rule? "If the face is red, raise the head. If the face is pale, raise the tail. If the face is blue . . . If the face is blue . . ." What to do? It rhymes.

*Battalion Four at Twelve's and going to Eighteen's . . .* Hey, Chief, go to sleep, will ya? Give the boys a break. They don't want brass dropping in all hours of the night.

*Medic One doctor, switch to channel three . . . Roger that, meet the aid car.*

If the face is blue . . . Goddamn, can't remember anything any more. Getting up in years. Forty-one. When's the social security begin? All the slogans and gimmicks to remember. "When in danger or in doubt, run in circles, yell and shout." Better yet, pretend you're a chief, stand around and look important and tell two-alarm fires they better black down or you'll put them on report.

*Duty doctor call Station Thirty-one we have a sick fireman.*

65

Thirty-one's. That's the famous Hofbrau station, home of the world's foremost consumers of beer and ale. Somebody's been boozing back in the utility room. Sniff of oxygen'll fix him up. Learned that when I was boozing myself.

*Fire Five Fire Five Broad and Pine . . .*

Still can't figure how I got in so deep. A quart a day there before Loo straightened me out . . .

*Fire Five Fire Five One-sixteen Pine One-sixteen . . .*

Stuff rots your liver *hey that's us!*

I sit up and spin the volume control, and I hear the dispatcher ordering Fire 5 to the heart of Skid Row again, a four-block run. I count the time on my sweep second.

Lieutenant Melvon Simmons comes on the air. *"Fire Five at the location. We got a small fire on the sidewalk, looks like trash from here."* The siren's dying in back of his voice. They must of just pulled up. Two minutes, thirteen seconds total elapsed. Not bad, considering it's "A" shift and not us.

I dampen the volume and roll over. Fire 5's on another one of its elite runs, the ones that take advance training and special technique. Trash burning on the sidewalk. Glad I'm off tonight.

*Fire Five to dispatcher we got a D.B.*

I must of fell asleep and this is another run. Where's my watch? Quarter to twelve. "A" platoon's been at a trash fire five or six minutes. How can there be a D.B.?

*"Fire Five okay,"* the dispatcher says. *"I'll notify the coroner."*

After a few more minutes I hear Mel Simmons say, *"Fire Five returning."* I let ten minutes go by and call the watch office.

"We just rolled on a trash fire," the housewatchman says.

"Yeh, I know. Who's the D.B.? Spectator? Heart attack?"

66

"Nope. It wasn't really a trash fire, Charly. It was an old man. Soaked with gas and burned to death."

"Suicide?" I says without thinking.

"No," the housewatchman says. "Torched."

We got problems.

We just finish lunch when a man in a gray-felt hat and a cashmere overcoat with a velvet collar walks into the watch office and introduces himself as Gary Heilman, attorney at law. He explains that the D.B. the other night was his father.

"We tried everything," he says after we pour him a cup of coffee, "but Dad wouldn't stay at home, he wouldn't allow himself to be hospitalized, he just walked the streets and drank. Ever since Mother died . . ."

He stops to compose himself. "Ever since Mother died, he's been a wino—an alcoholic. But never—a bad man."

I see that he's here to be comforted, so I says, "You don't have to be a bad man to be an alcoholic, Mr. Heilman." Everybody perks up around the table, the voice of experience is talking.

The lawyer looks up with puffy eyes. "What're the chances?" he says.

"Of what?" I says.

"Catching the son of a bitch."

How can I answer? How can I tell the man that maybe one percent of all arsons end in a prison sentence?

"We're just firemen, Mr. Heilman," Les Dawson puts in, looking up from his knitting—I mean knotting. "We put fires out, that's all. The way this perpetrator's operating, we'll always be too late."

"He gets 'em when they're passed out," Mike Mustache says. "He pours gasoline and lights a match. It's over in seconds."

I start to add that winos are half dead to begin with, they don't have the stamina to fight second- and third-degree burns, but I keep still. I hate the subject, winos are so pathetic, you see them sprawled in doorways with snow and ice and blood matted together in their hair. They're always cut up, bandaged, limping. They fall down, they get mugged, they fight amongst each other, even kill each other sometimes. Poor souls. Tear your heart out.

After the lawyer leaves, a delegation of kids arrive for a tour of the fire station, and Tyree and I show them around. Visitors are allowed between two and five P.M., but the neighborhood's deteriated so much we don't get near as many as we use to. Once in a half-moon some teacher brings her students, or one of the neighborhood regulars drop in for a handout, which we're usually dumb enough to give it to him, being firemen.

Today it's two social workers with a group, deprived or something, and tagging along is a black kid maybe nine years old.

"Hey, whatchew doin', li'l brother?" Tyree says.

The kid jumps backward. "Jes' lookin'," he says in a pip-squeaky voice, shielding his face with his hands. He's maybe four feet high and so thin he looks like a used pipe cleaner.

"Glad to see ya, son!" Tyree says, and he reaches down and grabs the kid and gives him an airplane spin, and when the kid finally gets down to earth he's giggling his head off. Tyree puts an arm around his shoulders and says, "Come along, hear? We inspecting the house, maybe you could he'p us out."

We walk on the apparatus floor, me up front and Tyree

bringing up the rear with his new soulmeet. We show off our big red Kenworth pumper and Cap's command car, and then we steer over to Ladder 10's truck. One of the ladies points to the aerial and says, "How do you ever get unconscious people down that thing?"

"Tie their hands together," Tyree says, "then pop your head inside their arms and sling 'em over your back."

"You does dat?" the black kid says, looking wide-eyed at Tyree.

"Three times a day," Tyree says, chuckling. He juts out his jelly belly and says, "That's how I keep my figure," and the little girls laugh.

As usual, our visitors are curious about the tillerman's cabin in the back of the ladder truck, and everybody has to climb up and sit in the seat and beep the button that signals the driver. "How on earth do you steer back here?" the lady asks.

I tell her my own personal technique, which every tillerman has his own approach and this was mine back when I tillered six, eight years ago: "Steer from the bottom of the wheel when you're backing up and the top when you're going forward."

"Simple enough," she says, and I'm thinking, Yeh, it's simple enough when you say it, but catching on to the knack's something else again. If you don't keep the whole rig in a straight line, then it's not so simple. Like Neal the Eel Steicher, the ladder loot, one time the driver up front turned a corner and Neal the Eel cut too sharp with the tiller and wiped out a whole row of parked cars and buckled the side of the rig. And still made loot! Goes to show the value of kissing ass.

I look down and the black kid's tugging at Tyree's shirt. "Can Ah set up there?"

"Hey, you a taxpayer, ain'tcha?" Tyree says, and lifts him into the cabin. The kid grabs the wheel and pretends to turn it, and he's making this humming racket with his lips: *"Brmm, brm-brm-brm, brmmmmmmmmmmmmm . . ."*

Then we walk to the watch office, and Tyree and I explain the squawkbox where the alarms come in and we give the standard speech on how the housewatchman don't set off the bells, they're activated right from the alarm office and then the dispatcher gives us the nearest street corner by radio followed by the exact address.

After a while the ladies thank us and everybody leaves and Tyree and I realize we haven't seen the black kid in five or ten minutes.

We check the apparatus floor and he's still up in the tiller cabin, going *brmmmmmmmmm.*

"Hey, home boy, climb on down outa there!" Tyree says. "Visiting hours is over."

The kid's face drops. I grab his skinny hand and walk him toward the front of the station. His fingers feel like pencils.

Tyree pushes the button and the apparatus door swings open. "Well, enjoyed meeting you, bubba," he says. "Come back and see us, hear?"

The kid smiles and nods, but he's still watching me anxiously. Then he looks back at Tyree and just sort of gapes. I guess he never seen a black firefighter before, let alone one with a built like Santa Claus.

"Hey, how come you're not in school today?" I ask, just kidding around. "Better look out, they're gonna put you in jail."

The kid's big black eyes open wide, and he starts edging away.

"What's wrong?" I says, but he's already broken into a run, and in about two seconds he's around the corner.

"What'd you go and do that for?" Tyree says. "Scairt him off."

"Do I look like a truant officer?"

"You honkies, you never understand. You *white*, man, that's scary enough."

Nordquist's lined up Ladder 10 and Fire 5 on the apparatus floor. He's prowling up and down in front of us, and his face looks like a cross section of beet. Every now and then he forgets that he drove to work and he takes the bus home, and he stays pissed at the world for days, like it's our fault. Maybe he done it again.

"Goddamnit, men," he snaps. "I got this VODG from Chief Slater." VODG means "Verbal Orders Don't Go." It's a memo printed on blue interoffice stationery and it usually means somebody's ass is grass. In this case, Cap's.

"Listen to this: 'Beds are sloppy on your shift. Please advise your men to use their hands, not pitchforks. Somebody's shoes are marking the watch office floor. Remember, it is unadvisable to apply polish to the soles. On three separate occasions this month, the ramp had oil stains an hour after wash-down. The underside of Fire Five's pumper bore distinct mud streaks, and the wax was thin and worn in spots, placing the finish in extreme jeopardy. Last Tuesday morning the doors were shut on both rigs when I arrived without notice. Captain, you must be working with volunteers.'"

Cap looks up. *Volunteers!* The worst insult!

"'Let me remind you and your men, if you've forgotten your basic training: the doors on F.D. apparatus must always be kept open, in our relentless quest for speed out of the house. Your rating this month is eighteen.' "

Eighteen out of a possible hundred! No wonder Nordquist's steaming.

Ordinarily Friday is brass day, Monday is window day, Saturday is yard day and Sunday is wash-down day, but Cap says we're gonna do it *all* today, and we're not gonna forget the daily stuff, either: cleaning the crapper, emptying wastebaskets and ashtrays, neatening up the lockers, polishing the rigs and a half dozen other details.

For the rest of the day we run around like a bunch of gallery slaves. Finally we're ready for house inspection. "Wait a minute!" I says just before we call the captain. "Who's in charge a the apparatus floor?"

"Me," Sonny Wicker says. "B-b-beautiful job, huh?"

"Forget anything?"

"Nope. Spick-and-span."

"Open the rig doors, Chrissakes!"

Nordquist goes up and down the ranks, checking our uniforms, checking our shines and haircuts. Then he goes over the house and the rigs with white gloves, and when he finishes, his gloves are as white as he started, except for a little paste-wax. "Okay," the old man says, "now one more thing. When you're relieved by the next shift tonight, whattaya say?"

" 'Hot damn, the chickenshit's over for another day,' " Plummer says under his breath.

"Whattaya say when you're relieved?" Cap repeats.

" 'Fireman, you're relieved,' " Les says.

"Right," Nordquist says. "I got a phone call on that. Who's the jerk-off been saying, 'Okay, baby, split!' "

I look at Ax and Ax looks at Plum and then we all look at each other. Nobody says a word.

We're all the jerk-off.

74

"Long shift," Ax says as we lounge in our airplane chairs in the bullpen and try to get interested in a training film where all the firemen talk like college kids and the officers like fruits.

"Too long," I says, and then we both hear Les calling up the pole hole from the watch office.

"Hey," he says, "she phoned again."

"Who?" one of the Ladder 10 guys asks.

"The . . . lady."

We all slide the pole into the watch office, and Ax says, "How come you didn't put it on the intercom?"

"She caught me by surprise."

I ask what she had to say this time.

"She said she bet I had a nice . . . A nice . . ."

"A nice what?" Ax insists.

"She wouldn't say," Lester says, turning as red as the house captain.

"She says she'll . . ." Les can't get the words out. Probably he's worried about his mother's picture in his wallet. "She said she'd—"

"Give you a date anytime of the day or night?" Mike puts in.

"Right!" Les looks relieved. "How'd you know?"

"That's what she promised the last time."

"What'd you tell her, Les?" I says.

"I just asked if she'd like to go sailing."

"Go sailing?" Mike Mustache says, glowering.

"Yeh," Lester says. "Get to know each other."

Plummer Brown's flabbergasted. "You asked if she'd like to go . . . sailing?"

"Yeh," Les says. "She asked my name. So I told her: Michael J. Mustacci."

"You fink!" Mike says. "It'll get back to Sally."

"Maybe it *was* Sally," Ax puts in, nudging me. "Hey, Les, did she sound Eye-talian? Did she sound like she's got a mustache?"

Mike fakes a rush and Ax pins his arms. "Michael me boy, ya know I love ya," he says. "I gotta love Sally, too, don't I?"

Mustacci smiles at Ax, which isn't a bad health hint anyway. "Friends?" Ax says, and offers his hammy hand.

"You know what I always say, Ax," Mike says, dropping to his knees from the shake. "You can screw my wife and shit in my face, but one a these days you're gonna go too far."

It reminds me of the time Sonny Wicker was making a glowing address about love and marriage and life in America, back before he intercepted the note to the milkman. He raved on, "I can't understand married guys that chase. To me, making love to my wife is a b-b-beautiful experience."

"Yeh," Plummer said. "We all agree on that."

If I'm counting straight, this is the third call of the week from the same sexy female voice, and we still haven't reported the problem to the P.D. We talked it over and decided we'd tough it out. Sure, it isn't easy listening to that satiny female voice coming on heavy, but everybody knows it's just talk.

Everybody except our sex fiend, Plummer. He's running around the watch office grunting and groaning in passion. "Oh, Jesus Christ, I wish I'd a been on watch. Ooooo, man, how'd I miss her? Goddamn, she won't get away from *me*, bet your ass."

This gives me an idea, which I talk it over later with Ax and Mike, and we let the other guys in on it, except the victim. This is gonna be one of our better zings of the season.

It's three nights later, and Plum's on watch downstairs. Ordinarily we wait till the lights go out at ten and the housewatchman gets comfortable on his cot and then we drop a cherry bomb down the pole hole, sort of a goodnight kiss.

Tonight, no firecracker. The obscene call's scheduled for ten-fifteen, and all our pointy heads are crowded around the hole so we don't miss what happens in the watch office below.

The phone rings right on time. We hear Plum say, "Station Twelve, Firefighter Brown speaking." Les flips on the squawk-box above our heads, so we're patched into both ends of the conversation.

"Is that *you*, baby?" a sweet female voice says. It's Annie Stemkowski, a file girl at the dispatch office, but Plummer'll never know.

"Right on, honey, it's *me!*" he says. Nobody has to teach Vincent "Plummer" Brown how to talk to an obscene caller, he's been one himself. "What can I do you for?"

"You got it backward, baby," Annie says slowly, breathing hard between words, the way we coached her. "I'm . . . gonna . . . do . . . you . . .!" Then she giggles nervously.

Mr. Cool says, "Tell me more, hon."

"Do you have a big . . . *er uh*"—I can imagine Annie looking down at her notes—"weenie?"

Plum's voice drops, and we have to strain to hear him over the small speaker. "How's six inches sound?" he says.

Annie says, "Ooooooh!"

"Well, that's just the width," Plummer says, snorting.

"Oh, my! Dying to meetcha."

"Say the word, cupcake. I'm off at eight tomorrow night."

"Oh, baby, I'll be waiting for ya. Say you'll come, you'll come. *Please?*"

"I will, I will," Plummer says. He sounds like he already is.

"You big stud," Annie says, making her voice sound real dirty, "what should I getcha?"

"A little wine, some music, and you, sweetheart. That's plenty. Hey, on second thought, you can leave out the wine and

77

the music." He giggles at his own joke. Man about town! Debonair!

"Ooh, I just can't wait," Annie says softly. For a skinny little thing with terminal acme, she really sounds sexy. I'm beginning to turn on myself. "Now listen," she says, "here's whatcha do. Got a pencil?"

"Sure thing," Plummer says. "Always prepared, that's my motto."

"I might be in the shower, hon, so just push right in. I'll leave the front door unlocked. The white wine'll be on ice."

"The address," Plummer says. "What's your address?"

"It's fourteen seventeen—"

*Click!*

Exactly the way we coached her.

It sounds like a riot down there. Plummer's stomping back and forth across the watch office, he kicks his rack and bangs his fist against the wall. "Cut off!" he's saying over and over. "We—were—cut—off! Fuck! Shit! *Fuckshit!*"

Ax calls down the pole hole. "Hey, whatsa problem, Plum? You woke me out of a sound sleep."

"It'll ring any second," Plummer says. "By God, it'll ring!"

"Whatchew talking about?"

"The broad. The anonymous caller? Says she seen me someplace, she thinks I'm good-looking and all that shit. Says she'd like to chew the eel first chance we get. She says . . . Wait, she'll be calling right back. She'll call. I *know* she'll call."

"Sure," Ax says, "but try to hold it down, will ya, pal?"

For an hour we can hear Plummer talking to himself. Once the phone rings and it's a woman that accidentally took a pill prescribed for her horse. "I'll look it up," Plummer says. "Hold on." Then he comes back to the phone and says, "Look, I got an important call. A hotel fire. Ten dead already. All it says is try a soapy enema, about four quarts . . ." He slams the phone down and starts mumbling again.

Around midnight we turn in. Plummer's still stirring. Mike Mustache is gonna throw the cherry bomb, but I tell him that'd be cruel and unreasonable.

Three guesses who can't sleep tonight, the first two don't count. Around two-thirty I give up on the capitals and slip into the scullery for a nice relaxing cup of instant coffee, and a couple minutes later Sonny Wicker comes paddling in after me. "Whatsa matter, kid?" I says. "Bad dreams?" I always had a soft spot for Sonelius, but all the more since his wife ran off.

"Make t-t-two cups," he says. Everybody bosses the cook. "I wasn't asleep yet."

I start to ask if he's healing, but I already know the answer.

I shake out cigarets for both of us, and he plops down like an orphan basset hound. Poor guy! I know exactly what he's going through. First he wonders what he done wrong. Then he pictures the milkman in his mind. What's that guy got that's so special? He sees the milkman day and night in his thoughts. One minute he thinks he'll kill the guy and the next minute he thinks he'll kill his wife, but what chance does he have of either, a guy that can't even butcher a rabbit? So it all comes down to one thing in his own mind: the milkman's a big macho, and himself's a big jerk. I know how that thinking goes, done my share of it. Look at him there, trying to find the answer in his coffee cup. Well, I won't bring it up.

I do a few leftover dishes while Sonny broods. The strip joint across the street is closed by now and there's not even a front-door fracas to entertain us. Besides, Cap already posted a warning on the subject: "Chief Slater advises there will be no more orgling of the Gay Paree night club and bar, there have been complaints. The binocular surveillance must discontinue at once. Do not sit in the scullery with the lights out. This constitutes orgling, and is very unprofessional." He come short of calling us volunteers. Once a year is about all we can handle of that particular insult.

"Well, g'night, Charly," Sonny says, getting to his feet like he weighs 618 pounds.

"Yeh, okay, there, Sonny," I says. "What you need's a good night's milk—*ar ah*—sleep."

Lately it's getting like a matrimonial agency around here. Maybe there's an epidemic, some bacteria's making the wives act squirrelly. Ax asked me could we talk privately the other night. "I dunno, Charly," he says, "I think Francine's trying to tell me something. Comes to bed wearing three layers of clothes. I fumble around, she says, 'Why *me?*' "

It's getting so bad on the martial front, the only time Fire 5 gets bred is the night of the double break, once a month, when we all go out and chase laundry, which is only a fifty-fifty shot at best, and not even that good when you get my age. Ax, he don't do any better, with that lumpy face with the chin falling away and the nose tacked on like an afterthought. Comes walking up to a female table in that typical big man's walk of his, all stiff-legged and heavy, like the Frankenstein monster in a wet jockstrap, and he says, "Excuse it, hon, can I have this dance?"

Well, these chicks don't come to this singles joint for the purpose of studying civics, but half the time they put him off. "I'm waiting for my boyfriend . . ." "Thanks anyway, but . . ."

81

And yet he's a real decent human being, one that any pickup should be pleased to meet. He's no Plummer Brown, full of fast talk and big-city bullshit. Ax, he's a simple soul. Likes to get drunk and bawl in his Feinblatz and say, "Aw, fuck off, why don'tcha?" Likes to race the engine on his Camaro and do the old mechanic's honk:

*Beep Beep-a-deep Beep.Beep Beep.*

Likes to tear down burning ceilings and chop holes in roofs and carry old ladies out and fan them. A simple soul. All he passed in training school was gas, but they eased him through. A lucky thing for the rest of us.

This is the guy that his wife, the former Francine Laderrière, I believe her maiden name was, is busting his balls, though I don't think she's running around, like Sonny's old lady. Ax'd kill the guy. "She tells me go out and get a decent job, decent hours," Ax was moaning the other night, just the two of us old cronies sitting in the rig for privacy. "She's been different ever since the prowler."

With firemen, there's two problems: we're gone too long when we're gone, and we're home too long when we're home. A lot of wives can't handle the schedule. Francine Bedrosian was alone one night when she surprised a prowler in her room. She screamed and he run, and ever since she's been after Ax to get a daytime job. "What daytime job?" Ax keeps asking her. "Chief? Mayor? Okay, I'll look tomorrow."

Some joke! Ax is thirty-three years old, he's got a phony high school equilavency diploma that he bought from the correspondence school on Crefeld Street. What's he suppose to do, run down to Chittenden Memorial and apply as a brain surgeon?

"Now she acts like screwing's dirty," Ax confided in me.

Well, that's the way it begins, that's the way they turn the knife. Moose Levin use to recite an old Jewish proverb at 17's.

"Marriage trouble starts under the covers." Where else? In the garage?

I asked Ax why the two of them don't just sit down and talk the whole thing out, the way Dr. Joyce Brothers says. "Can't you communicate, you and the wife?"

"She says I only talk nice to her when I'm trying to make out. Says I'm too obvious. Maybe she's right. It's been seven weeks now. And four days. And—"

"That's okay, Ax, I don't need the hours."

"And then she was like Irma the dummy."

"How about flowers? You tried that?"

Sitting there in the cab of our rig, Ax took a deep drag on his Camel, your average fireman don't bother with filters. "I sent her a half dozen roses. She said what was my real motive. I sat up talking with her till three in the morning, and when we got in bed, my foot accidentally touched hers. She jumped up and screamed, 'I knew it!' "

"The drive-in movie?" I suggested.

"Took her Saturday night. She says, '*Please*, I'm trying to watch the show!' Asked me did I think she was common. I says, 'Honey Buckets, we don't have to go all the way.' She tells me to take her home. I get a few highballs into her, start loving her up, she says, 'Now you won't respect me!' "

A story like that breaks my heart. I'd give anything if I could help, but what can I do? I got enough trouble handling my own sex life, I make out about as often as St. Vincent de Paul. Look at that one the other night, Evelyn the waitress. Jeez, what a close call! She says we can't go to her place, she's married to a four-hundred-pound wrestler.

"Oh, terrific," I says. "How nice for ya."

"It don't have to come between us," she says.

"I'll call ya," I says, breaking into a trot. "Maybe the six of us can get together some time."

83

I dry off the two "specimen jars" that Sonny and I used for our post-midnight coffee and get ready to hit the rack myself, but first I take a little constitutional. Somebody left a *National Star* on the table in the bullpen. I stuff it in the basket. There's a cigaret butt on the floor—what pogue did that? Probably a visitor. I make sure it's cold and dunk it in the toilet.

On the way back to the bunk room, I pass one of the pole holes, and I take a peek down at the apparatus floor, dim and shadowy from the seventy-five-watt red bulb in the corner. The doors on Ladder 10's rig are shut, and I wonder who's the idiot that shut them, after Slater's VODG on the subject. Somebody'll catch hell at roll call if I don't go down and open the doors.

I slide in my underwear, trying not to grab too tight with my bare arms, you're suppose to never touch a pole with your skin because it puts body oil on the brass and slows it for the next man. Even before I hit the rubber mat at the bottom I see owl-eyes peering out of the truck. Before I can react, something darts out the side door. "Hey!" I holler, but the door slams shut. Another mistake: the housewatchman is responsible for double-locking the alley door before he turns in.

I think of hitting the alerter button to get everybody up, but what's the use? They'd just be annoyed and we still wouldn't catch the dwarf or whatever he was. Maybe a ghost. That's all we need.

I climb into Ladder 10's cab and take a look. The seat's warm. Everything seems to be in place. The helmets are on the rack behind the driver's seat and the air tanks are in their holders.

What's that rule in basketball—no harm, no foul? Climb back up the steps. Some day I'm gonna invent a pole you can slide both ways, make my fortune.

I slip past Sonny Wicker's rack. Eyes shut, that's good. I know how it is, kid. That home cooking tastes flat till somebody else samples it, then it's pure caviar.

The capital of Arkansas is Little Rock. The capital of Illinois is Springfield . . . Marilyn use to taunt me with her boyfriends. "Met a doctor tonight, he drinks, but he can hold it. Not like a certain party." We were separated by then. Probably better she found somebody on her own level. Not her fault she married beneath her station. Her friends use to call me "the happy fireman." Well, what's wrong with that? Put it on my gravestone, go ahead.

Some guys get ahead, some guys don't. Nobody can say I didn't try. I still got the notice laying around somewhere, know the words by heart:

> To all who shall see these presents, greetings: Know ye that reposing special trust and confidence in the fidelity and abilities of Charly Michael Sprockett we hereby appoint him to the rank of fire lieutenant to serve as such from this day henceforth. He is therefore carefully and diligently to discharge the duties of fire lieutenant by doing and performing all manner of things belonging thereunto. And I do strictly charge and require all firefighters and civilian employes under his command to be obedient to his lawful orders.

They say the worst kind of officer is a brand-new lieutenant or captain on his six-month probationary period, but me—I was a pussycat, ask any of the guys back at 17's. I was so busy proving I'm a regular fella, I didn't give an order without adding, "If it's okay with you."

Well, the Lord giveth and the Lord taketh away, I'll never see silver bars again. Once that notation's entered in your jacket—"boozer" or "alcoholic," however they put it—you're written off as officer material, and it don't matter if the strongest drink you take for the rest of your life is Pablum.

They thought Kirkpatrick was nuts when he mustered me on Fire 5. Pull my weight, by God.

The capital of Louisiana . . .

Kirkpatrick at a fire, what a study. The smoke curls around him and he holds his mobile unit like he's on the phone ordering a cheese Danish, telling the alarm office in his flat monotone, "We got a fully involved house, two stories," and then giving orders in the same calm way: "Tyree, hit the hydrant. Ax, start climbing. Lester, lay your pre-connect." None of that rah-rah bullshit, the old college try. Hump a hose for Loo and the next time you turn around he's humping one for you.

The Sears warehouse fire, Mustacci and I beat our way on our knees behind the old Rockwood nozzle, and it's like the inside of a smokehouse in there, kid's toys smoldering and spare bicycle parts bubbling in their own grease, and we're beginning to wonder if the air'll ever clear. Then we see a tiny glow through the darkness. It's the loot grabbing a cigaret.

"Fellas," he says, "you wanna put a splash on that joist? It's still got fire in it."

Mike and I are sputtering and gagging. "That's it," Kirkpatrick says. "Good job." The Congressional Medal of Honor! We back down the line for a blow, Loo's still in the corner, cupping his smoke.

Well, he always admired Chief Stieglitz, modeled himself on him, and that old fart ate fire and smoke for breakfast. Don't know how a man can train himself like that. Me, first I throw up and then I choke. Can't help it. Somebody said they put Loo in the airtight room with the other recruits in his training class and pumped it full of smoke and when all the rooks came stumbling out gagging and coughing there was no sign of Kirkpatrick. He was standing inside, waiting for instructions.

That's the story anyway, they always get improved from station to station and year to year. I asked him about it once and he just laughed and said it must of been some other guy, but he'd say that if it was true or not.

I was at the Brant shipyard fire when he come off the fire ground with a frozen nose and stuck his face down in a pumper's exhaust, and one of the guys said, "Look, the loot's getting a breath of fresh air."

Well, didn't Stieglitz like to go into the fire room in that long white coat of his and stand erect while his men were dropping like sprayed mosquitoes? Somebody'd crawl through the smoke and bump into his boot, and Stieglitz'd say, "Stand erect, Fireman."

That was one of the toughest funerals. Loo almost bit his lower lip off. Cap Nordquist and Chief Grant had a hell of a time controlling theirselves, too, Al had to slip out of church early.

Deputy Fire Chief Johannes Stieglitz, R.I.P. The autopsy doc said his lungs looked like old baked shoe leather.

The capital of Illinois is Chicago. No, Springfield. Or is that Massachusetts? Boston? What the hell, another cup of coffee'll never hurt.

Somebody's breaking our ass. Three arson fires this week, four injured, two seriously. He hasn't hit any more firehouses, but he did manage to slip a flare into the 14th Precinct police station and start a fire that burnt up the night sergeant's new toupee, hidden in a box in his locker. "Three bucks down the drain," the sarge complained. "Thoughtless, just thoughtless."

We hear about it from Zacarelli, the cop on the beat. "Still can't figure how the Flareman got in," Z says over a cup of coffee in the scullery. He's using the newspaper words, they already dubbed the wino-burner "The Torch" and the other guy "The Flareman." Assuming they're two different guys, which who knows?

Zacarelli's a big slab of beef, built like Ax but softer. "Whole fronta the station's barred," he says, "windows, everything. There's a little grate over the basement windows, leads down to the lockup. But nothin' bigger'n an alleycat could get through there."

"Where'd the fire start?" Les asks.

"Crawl space," Z says, helping himself to another cup of coffee and splashing in about a half a pint of cream. "He slud that flare under. Must be part snake."

"Fire in a crawl space and you girls ain't got the sense to call us right away?" Ax says.

Zacarelli looks sheepish. "We was embarrassed."

"About what?"

"Gettin' sabotaged like that. Cops 'n' all."

"Well, hang onna your pride," Ax says. "The way I seen it in the paper, your pride cost the city about twenty G's. We coulda put that fire out with a Flit gun, you called us in time."

"Always beefin'," Z says.

"Fuck off, why don'tcha?" Ax says.

The cop chugalugs his coffee, puts on his hat and grabs his nightstick, even though it's daytime. "Check you later," he says, and walks out.

"Hey, Zacarelli," Tyree calls out, "I didn't hear no clink."

"Clink?" the cop says, sticking his nose back inside the door.

"Me neither," I chime in. "You walked right past the coffee clutch bottle."

"Oh," Z says, digging in his pocket. He pulls out a coin and drops it in the slot, sounds like a dime.

"Thanks, pal," Ax says.

"Yeh," Mike Mustache says, looking up from his author work. "That'll keep us in the black for a month or two."

Z walks out, smiling. What the hell, he's contributed his share, he's a regular pillow of the community now. Next year he'll put another dime in. It's only fair.

As he walks out I notice he's favoring his left leg again. He's been trying to learn to spin his nightstick like a movie cop for eight years, but he always whacks himself on the kneecap except once he hit himself on the elbow, don't ask me how. Another eight years he'll get it down pat. His daughter's a baton twirler in high school, they make her wear a helmet.

This morning we're suppose to go out inspecting for a couple hours, us and Ladder 10, but before we get started we hear the bells that mean the battalion chief's in quarters.

"I want everybody in turn-out gear," Slater says. He lines us up and chalks big numbers on our backs. Just before we climb into our rigs, I hear him tell Captain Nordquist, "I want plenty of hustle today."

*I want, I want.* He sounds like a three-year-old kid.

We're whooping it up in the cab, showing hustle, and Wally Fenstermacher's standing on our tailboard, screaming, "Faster, faster!" He's just out of training school and on three months' probation. We like to have him around, he's cheaper than a dishwashing machine, but I wish he wouldn't holler "Faster, faster!" when the apparatus doors haven't even opened yet.

Turns out the marshals laid a pretty good drilling fire in an abandoned building on the outskirts of town, and it's plenty hot by the time we arrive. As we pull up from one side, Ladder 10, Engine 25 and Ladder 3 pull up from the other, and Slater's already spouting orders into his bullhorn: *"Fire Five, take the hydrant. Engine Twenty-five, take a two-and-a-half and an inch-and-a half off Fire Five and go in. Ladder Ten, get up on the roof and cut two holes, four by six. Ladder Three, get inside and ventilate. C'mon now, move! Hup two! On the double!"*

Everybody takes off hup two on the double. Hustle, hustle, hustle. It sounds like a college football game, enough to make you cringe that you're suppose to be an adult human being, a professional. "Come on, guys, *move it!*" "Awright, awright, aw-*right!*" "Beautiful, *beeyoo*-tee-ful!" Everybody's ranting and raving except Loo, he don't go for that rah-rah. Off to one side H. Walker Slater's writing on a clipboard, that's what the numbers on our backs are for, so we can be graded. Ninety percent and the company passes. Eighty to ninety, we drill again. Mess up real bad and we can even get docked.

Ladder 10's lieutenant, Neal the Eel Steicher, he's running around like a hamster in heat. He's another Slater, they both remind me of something I read about the Nazis, "They're at your throat or your feet." When the big brass are around, Neal the Eel says, "Yes, sir, Yes, sir," and practically gravels in the dirt, but to his own men it's "Get your ass over here" and "Who the hell you think you're talking to?" His men claim he don't know his ass from a manhole cover. I seen him stand right at the door of a burning building and holler, "Get inside! Get inside!" and then he'll slip just behind the door so the chief thinks he's penetrating with his crew.

You can imagine how we feel when Slater booms out, *"Ladder Ten and Fire Five, switch officers!"* They been doing this lately at drills. Fire officers are suppose to be interchangeable, so are the men, but not if we got to work under a guy like Steicher.

The first thing he does, he comes up behind Tyree at the hydrant and says, "Come on, boy, a little hustle." Tyree's about to turn the stem, but he hesitates for just a fraction of a second, and Neal the Eel grabs the wrench out of his hand and says, "Forget it! Get inside!"

Tyree and I grab a couple bundles of inch-and-a-half and start to stretch them into the building, and somebody hollers, "Irma's in there!" Irma is a 250-pound dummy the marshals throw into burning rooms and we got to go in and find her and save her life. The longer it takes, the fewer points you get, the chief's chauffeur times you with a stopwatch. "Up Irma's!" Tyree says, and I can see he's steamed.

The fire's extending along a second-floor corridor and biting into empty rooms as it goes, two or three rooms are involved. We bank one down with the inch-and-a-half, but there's no Irma inside.

Just then Steicher appears at the top of the staircase, breathing hard. "What's this, teatime?" he says. "C'mon, let's move! A little hustle up here!"

Tyree and I start to yank on the inch-and-a-half, but it won't budge.

"Sprockett!" Steicher calls out. "Advance that goddamn line!"

"We will, Lieutenant," I says calmly, "as soon as you quit standing on it."

Steicher mutters something about not talking back. I swear, him and Slater, they're *never* wrong! If you say they're wrong, they'll make up charges against you.

Twenty minutes later the fire's darkening down but we still haven't found Irma, then we hear a falsetto voice screaming, "Help, help, Mr. Fireman, save me!" It's Plummer, pretending he's trapped on a ledge. It isn't bad enough we've lost the dummy, the chief has to lay a silly rescue problem on us.

"Keep your panties on, lady," Mike Mustache hollers. "Stay insipid." Today's new word from the *Reader's Digest.*

"Oh, please, Mr. Fireman, hurry!" Plum calls out. "It's burning my public hairs." He's sitting on a window ledge with his pants rolled up and his bare legs dangling. The aerial's just underneath him, and two laddermen are on their way up to make the rescue. Plum sees them and screams, "Don't let them savages touch my nature."

He disappears in a tangle of arms and legs and helmets and I go back inside.

"Where is she?" Steicher's hollering, running around the fire rooms. He knows it's his ass if we don't find Irma. She may be only 250 pounds of asbestos and stuffing and sash weights, but in this exercise she represents a live female victim, and if we don't save her it's the same as losing a citizen at a fire. "Hey, boy," he hollers at Tyree.

"Hey *who?*" Tyree says, straightening up.

"Yeh, you. Now listen, take—"

"My name Firefighter Amerston D'Arcy. Not 'Hey, boy.' I'm nobody's boy except my mumma."

"Listen here, goddamnit," Steicher says, turning red to match his helmet, "you find that fucking dummy! *Where's that dummy!*"

"Onliest dummy I know is the one I'm looking at, man."

"Move your lazy ass!"

I'm standing alongside quietly taking mental notes for the firefighters' union, because sooner or later we got to make a formal case against this idiot, but when Tyree shoves him back against the wall, I jump in the middle to cool things down. Mike Mustache drops a bundle of hose and helps me drag Tyree off.

"Listen, you jive turkey, stop wolfin' at me!" Tyree yells. "One more word, I'm gonna jump right up your ass!"

Steicher flies down the staircase two at a time, holding his belly and muttering something about putting the whole god-damn Fire 5 on charges when we get back. That'll be fun, his word against four of us, and a racial matter to boot, the kind the F.D. hates and detests with a purple passion.

"Hear that?" Tyree says, upset with himself now. "I got us in the shit."

"Yeh, well, might as well have the game as the name," Mike Mustache says, and the rest of the guys gather around and we all agree it's time to take a job action, based on an old principle. The old principle is that when a firefighter screws up, it's his ass, but when a whole platoon screws up, the officer gets the blame.

"Hey, here's Irma!" Les Dawson hollers, dragging the dummy out of a broom closet. Plummer and Tyree pick up the smoldering victim and give her the heave out a front window, where the battalion chief'll be sure to see how gracefully we rescued her. She bounces twice.

Then Plummer and I go outside and begin shoving a ladder up against the side of the building with tormentor poles. We make sure the spurs are pointing up instead of down, and when Steicher runs over and shows us our mistake, Plum says, "Oh, gosh darn it gee whillikers anyway!" and we turn the ladder around and put it against the wall backwards. The chief's scribbling away on his clipboard.

Up on the roof we can make out Tyree and Mike Mustache, laying tarps. They throw one out and forget to hold on, and the tarp sails through the air like a magic carpet. Two more flutter down the same way.

Les and Sonny Wicker show up in a second-floor window with pike poles slung over their shoulders, and Sonny turns too sharp and slams his pole through a window. Les turns to see what's happening and pokes out the other window. They must of rehearsed. The Two Stooges.

Back at the station that night, everything's quiet. Lieutenant Kirkpatrick's pacing up and down in front of our TV, and every now and then he calls out, "Why? *Why?*"

"Hey, Loo," Plummer finally says. "You're okay, right?"

"What?"

"You're okay with the chief? You didn't get wrote up?"

"No, I was working with Ladder Ten. But Neal Steicher's in bad trouble. Chief says he lost all control of you men. I don't understand you guys."

"Yeh," I says. "We're all just sick about it, Loo."

So far our probie's holding his own. Wallace Fenstermacher, probationary firefighter second class, a tall skinny carrot-topped kid that's always got his nose buried in the manuals, or else he's giggling. I guess he's gonna try for lieutenant before he makes firefighter first class. The main thing is, does he fit in? We got to find out.

"Hey, Recruit," Plummer Brown calls out, "I can guess your weight within two pounds."

"That's awright," the kid says, grinning and turning another page in that big best seller "Hose Techniques."

"Come on," Plum says. "It's a tradition. Sit on the floor there so I can get my arms under your elbows. That's it! Now if I don't guess right, I gotta buy ice cream for the shift."

Plummer lifts him about a foot off the floor while Mike slips the egg under the kid.

Ten minutes later Tyree D'Arcy reminds the probie that all recruits have to learn how to balance a quarter on their nose. While Wallace Fenstermacher's trying to master the trick, Tyree slips a funnel inside his belt and Ax pours a quart of warm water down his crotch.

"You guys!" the probie says, snickering. He goes into the bunk room to change. He acts like we're all having a terrific time together.

"Nothing seems to phrase him," Ax says.

"Oh, yeh?" Plummer says.

When Wally comes back in the bullpen the guys pretend they don't notice him. "Poor Irma," Ax says loud. "Six years and she never got her sox charred. Till that probie come along."

"He's a jinx," Plum says. "We gotta do something about him."

The kid looks thoughtful. He knits his brows. He opens "Hose Techniques" again and reads. Once in a while he puts the book aside and peeks around at the rest of us, sitting there orgling Jayne Mansfield on the TV. It looks like we might be getting to him.

At ten-fifteen the probie's studying downstairs in the watch office. Plummer slides the pole and says, "Hey, kid, you seen the cableman?"

"The who?"

"The cableman. The guy we lower into the fire on a cable. You seen him?"

"Hey, c'mon, Mr. Brown. I gotta study." He giggles once or twice.

"Listen, kid, this is serious!" Plum says in his smooth con-man style. "There's a grain elevator burning out in the North End, Cap said we might need the cableman."

"Sure, sure." He's not gonna fall this time.

Two minutes later I slide the pole. I'm wearing long underwear, a T-shirt, swimming trunks, sneakers, a blanket around my neck like a cape, and Dawson's old ski mask that covers everything except my nose and eyes. "I'm the cableman," I tell the probie in a fake voice. "Where's the fire?"

I hurry out to Nordquist's command car and climb in. "The house captain'll be going too," I yell back. "Tell him the

96

cableman's ready and be sure'n bring the cable."

I run back to the second-floor pole hole just in time to hear the kid talking to Nordquist on the intercom. *"Er uh,* Cap'n, sir," he says, "the cableman's ready."

Cap snorts in his native Albanian or some foreign tongue. As usual, he's been asleep. "Says be sure and bring the cable," Wallace Fenstermacher rambles on.

"Be sure'n do *what?"* Nordquist says. "Wait there! I'll be right down."

The discussion that follows does nothing to show Cap's good nature, so I prefer to leave it out. "Those A-holes are needling you, son," he says at the end, and heads back up the stairs to his third-floor nappery. "Don't let 'em bend you outa shape. That's what they're looking for."

"Right, Cap," the probie calls out.

"G'night yourself," Cap answers.

So now we got to pull out the old Cecil B. DeMille. We wait a few shifts till Cap's gone inspecting, it's a warm night in the firehouse, maybe eighty degrees, and we send Tyree down the pole hole naked.

"Oh, hello," the probie says, not looking up from his studying.

"How they hanging, man?" Tyree asks, taking the extra chair in the watch office and crossing his hairy black legs.

"Okay."

The kid still don't look up, so we send Plummer down in his birthday suit, which this time the kid sees him and lets out a gulp. "Hey, what's this?"

"Oh, nothing, kid," Plum says. "We got orders to wear the ultra-light gear tonight, it's so warm out."

"What's ultra-light gear?"

Tyree stands up in his naked glory. "You looking at it, baby."

97

The probie checks back and forth between the two of them, chocolate and vanilla. Then he giggles and says, "You're kidding."

"Listen," Plummer says, "it's a godsend on a night like this."

"Where's your turn-out gear?"

"On the rig," Tyree says. "Boots, pants, coat, helmet, what more ya need? You don't put out fires with your jockstrap, man."

"No," Fenstermacher says, frowning. "I guess not."

I slide the pole bare-assed. "You too?" the kid says.

"Personally, I don't like it," I says in a businesslike voice. "Too cold against the skin. But orders are orders. Chief says the ultra-light'll improve our efficiency on hot nights."

"Sure worked good in Cleveland," Plummer says.

"That's where they first tried it," I says helpfully.

"Hmmmmm," Fenstermacher says. He's almost hooked.

At ten o'clock a bare Sonny Wicker relieves the kid on watch, and we all go to bed buck-naked, including Fenstermacher. He don't dare to be different, not during the probationary period.

Now it's just a matter of patience and timing. At eleven-fifteen we get word that the chief's coming through on night arson patrol, wants to look at our logbook. Ax slips from bed to bed, passing the word. When Slater steps into the watch office, we flip the light switch and somebody shakes the kid awake. He jumps up, sees everybody whirling around in their birthday suit and dives for the pole hole. *Zzzzzp!* He's on the apparatus floor, running for the rig. Fastest naked fireman in the west.

H. Walker Slater comes out of the watch office to see what's going on, and Lady Godiva's up on the tailboard fumbling around with his gear. He's got his helmet on nice and neat, and when he spots the chief back-lighted against the watch-office door, he knows he's been zinged. That's when Wallace Fenstermacher shows us something. Instead of fussing and fawning around and telling the chief it's all our fault, he pulls the helmet down over his face and sprints for the back stairs.

"Hey, you!" Slater hollers.

Wally takes three and four steps at a time, and when he gets to the second floor he dives into his rack and skitters the helmet halfway across the floor. "Not me!" somebody says, and slams the helmet away like a hockey puck, and then a couple more guys whack it till it winds up against the wall. Nobody wants that telltale helmet near his rack.

Ax douses the light about three seconds ahead of Heinrich Himmler himself puffing up the stairs.

We're all dead to the world.

Slater's heels click slowly as he walks up and down between racks. Mike Mustache lets out a superhuman snore, Tyree farts and moans, and I roll over and grunt like the heat's getting to me. Sleeping Beauties one and all.

Pretty soon we hear the chief back at the top of the landing. He mumbles something and walks downstairs.

This kid Fenstermacher may work out after all.


"Now listen to me," Captain Nordquist is saying in a low voice. We're all sitting around the back table at Joe's Bar & Grill. Every member's there, the whole "B" shift of Fire 5, even including Les Dawson, which he don't usually sing and dance and take a chance. "Either you stick together on this, or he'll transfer the whole platoon, I guarantee you."

"Cap," I says, "who'll transfer who for what?"

"Slater found out about the booze in the booster tank."

"Whoo-ee!"

"We're dead!"

"Up the ass without a cundrum!"

"Hold it," Cap says. You can read off his flushed face that we got a Code Red. "When it first happened, the loot and me give you a pass 'cause it didn't seem like much." We all lean forward to listen. "Stuff woulda gone down the drain anyway. But the chief's hot. Says you stole liquor."

"We didn't steal a goddamn thing," Ax Bedrosian says in a loud voice.

"Hold it down," I says, seeing that the house captain is on edge and fiddling around with his hearing aid and shooting glances toward the door. Slater's got everybody jumpy.

"Chief says he's gonna make an example. Says he knows Bedrosian was behind the whole thing and he'll start with him and then transfer the platoon, man by man."

Ax starts to say something, but all that comes out is spit and jibberish. I touch him gently on the forearm, and Plummer says, "What can we do, Cap? You tell us."

"You gotta hang together. He'll be calling you in one by one."

"We don't know nothing," Mike Mustache says, scratching his cue-ball dome.

"That's the way it's gotta be," Cap says, looking around again.

"How'd he find out?" Ax says.

"That's easy," I says. "Everybody's mouth's been flapping. The whole Ladder Ten knows the story, for one."

"Sharing secrets with Ladder Ten," Les Dawson says. "Storing water in a sieve."

Nordquist says, "You men together on this?"

"On everything," I says. I raise my bottle to thank the old boy. He takes a sip and ducks out, and I notice he's barely touched his Feinblatz.

He must of had good information, because the next shift we get grilled by Slater one by one. He calls me last, and by the tense look on his face when I walk in, nobody's cracked.

"All right, Sprockett, let's not mince words," he says in that basso profoundo of his. "The men of your platoon stole three hundred gallons of bonded liquor. You know it, I know it. I have a full statement drawn up right here. Sign at the bottom."

"Stole three hundred gallons of *what?*" I scrooch up my face like a congenial idiot.

"I know you did it, and I know Bedrosian was behind it."

"Good, then you don't need me, Chief."

He sits there quiet for a second, blinking at me. "Will you cooperate?" he says finally.

"Anything you want, Chief."

"Sign here."

He slides over a piece of paper that says something like we the undersigned members of Fire 5 "B" platoon do attest to the following facts blah blah blah and this theft was entirely conceived and carried out by Fireman First Class Burton Bedrosian etc. and so forth.

Very handy. The rest of us can get off by fingering Ax. That way the chief makes his point without admitting that a whole platoon screwed up, which wouldn't look too good on his own record.

I slide the paper back.

"You won't sign?"

"How can I sign, Chief? I don't have the slightest idea what this's all about. Are you sure I was working that day?"

"Get out of here," the little man says, standing up behind his desk.

I walk out the door backward. My old dad taught me thirty years ago, never turn your back on a hungry man or a maniac, let alone somebody that's both.

Where's Gasoline Gomez now that we need him? The worst thing for a firefighter is boredom. All's we been out on for three straight shifts is a couple Dumpsters and a car fire and about forty-seven service calls. I don't know what happened to the Flareman asshole, you'd think he'd learn his trade. Hits and quits, hits and quits. The Torch hasn't visited Skid Row lately either, the bums are starting to walk the streets openly again. Lurch the streets, anyway. All the firebugs must be off to the French Rivera, breaking some other F.D.'s chops. What they got to learn is be more dependable, give us a harmless little arson fire maybe once or twice a week, we won't complain.

At eight o'clock in the evening we roll on a single. A rubbish fire in Skid Row, we dump the booster tank on it. The dispatcher calls and asks us to wind the box at Ninth and Pender. Sure thing. Fascinating assignment like that, we're happy to help out.

We're cruising back to the station on a Code Yellow, obey all traffic rules, when I see a guy down an alley waving at us. "Hey, wait, Plum," I says, and he hits the brakes.

I run over to see what the man wants. He looks like a cadaver, he's got bandages all over his head and one foot in a dirty cast and a thin brown sack in his hand. "Fire," he croaks, and he raises one hand and dangles it like a puppet's arm in the general direction of north. Poor winos, they're no good to themselves or anybody else. I look north, nothing in sight except the broad side of a dilapidated building. I believe the poor soul's having optical delusions.

"Take care of yourself, old-timer," I says, and jog back to the rig.

Then I smell smoke, and no mistake. I got a Ph.D. degree in smelling smoke, you better believe it.

I jump aboard and Loo's already on the radio. *"Fire Five. Any alarms around Skid Row?"*

*"Negative Fire Five,"* the dispatcher says.

Well, there's a fire someplace. We can all smell it good. Skid Row hasn't turned in an alarm, no, but then Skid Row is stone-drunk.

We're hemmed in by buildings on the narrow street, can't see much, and Loo tells Plummer to drive around the block and head north. We go two blocks and turn into High Street and everything's bright orange. A flophouse hotel's burning like a Roman candle, the flames are shooting halfway across High and all the way up to the roofline. Very little smoke. Your basic blowtorch fires don't smoke much. It's arson if I ever seen it.

*"A two-eleven fire at Nine and High,"* Lieutenant Kirkpatrick reports in that calm voice of his, like he's ordering a sausage pizza. *"The Tivoli Hotel."* Plummer floors the gas pedal and we all lean forward for a better look out of the cab.

*"Affirmative,"* the alarm office says. *"We just got the first call."*

The closest we can stop is about fifty feet away. Somebody in the cab lets out a Texas-type yell, *"Ya-hoo!"* and we all spill out on the street raring for action. Then we see people huddled at the windows, back-lit by flames, and all of a sudden we got an "oh shitter," the kind of fire where you just keep saying "oh shit" and never get to enjoy yourself.

A body drops five stories and splatters in front of us. We all wanted a good fire. None of us wanted this.

*"Fire Five make that a three-eleven,"* Loo says.

*"Whattaya got?"* the dispatcher says.

*"Five-story hotel, fully involved,"* Loo says, cool as ever.

The dispatcher starts sending out the signal, *"Three-eleven alarm, three-eleven. Engine Ten, Seven, Eight, Ladder Ten, Battalion Four. Nine Avenue and High Street. This is a three-eleven . . ."* He'll get all the companies rolling and then he'll start calling out the move-ups. *"Engine Nine to Ten, Engine Six to Eight, Engine Fourteen to Twenty-seven's . . ."* All over the city fire companies are filling gaps, moving from station to station in the night.

"Make your lay," the loot says. Mustacci and Wicker are already dragging our full complement of hoses off the rig, we'll need every inch, no use futzing around with the booster tank on a body of fire like this.

There's a hydrant thirty yards away, and Loo sends me and D'Arcy with Plummer. The fire's whooshing out the windows like a Bessemer converter, but we can still hear the screams and the cries over the roar. "Don't look up!" I tell Tyree as he runs to the hydrant while Plummer and I chock the wheels. A firefighter's got to tend to business, there's no time for sympathizing. The body that fell in front of the rig when we pulled up, it's still there, guys are stepping around it. That's the job. A fire like this, if you stop to save one person, six others die of inhalation. The army calls it Triage.

Mike Mustacci has the two-and-a-half-inch pipe with Wicker and Dawson humping for him, and they disappear straight into the lobby of the hotel. Mike's jerking at the nob like he can get water out of it by sheer muscle.

"Hurry up, Tyree," I holler at the hydrant. "They're going in with a dry line."

"Sumpin' wrong," Tyree says. He's already taken ten or twelve seconds with the wrench. I run over and help him twist the cap on the three-and-a-half-inch port.

"Look out!" I holler, but it's too late, the heavy cap flies off like it's shot from a cannon and knocks Tyree flat.

"Already charged," he says, grabbing his leg. Some goddamn idiot street cleaner forgot to turn down the main stem when he finished filling his tanks, now we have to crawl back and shut off the discharge gate so we can make the connection all over again. Up above us, people are screaming.

I look around and see the first hose crew, Mike and Les and Sonny, they're stumbling back out of the front entrance like they been pole-axed. Their faces are streaked with carbon and the snot's dangling a foot out their noses. "You black asshole!" Mike screams. "Where's the fucking water?"

Another jumper hits the street just as Tyree gets the supply hose connected to the engine port and charges the lines. Mike and his crew disappear inside the lobby behind a heavy fog.

I run to help and Loo motions me back. "Get in the rig," he says. "Call in ambulances, all they got."

Somebody's already talking to the alarm office when I pick up the hand mike. *"It's really bad,"* he's saying in a shaky voice. *"Fire's going up the stairways and out the roof."*

It's Slater, he must of just pulled up on the other side. I wait a few seconds for him to ask for medical help, and then I punch the mike button myself. *"Fire Five,"* I says. *"We need all the aid cars and ambulances we can get."*

*"Medic One's on the way, plus two ambulances."*

*"All you can get,"* I repeat. *"Twenty won't be too many."* Up at the windows, a dozen people lean out while the fire licks up the walls toward them.

I drop the mike and run back to the street. Lieutenant Kirkpatrick's huddled with the chief. "Get back to your rig," Slater tells me. "Coordinate the radio."

It's not my job, but you don't argue with panicky chiefs. By now engines and trucks are coming from all directions. Lines are beginning to spaghetti up on the fire ground, and there's new noise to go with the sound of the flames and the screams: big diesels pumping water and short-wave radios set on full volume.

Down the street I can see three different engines pulling up. Seventeen's is already charging the standpipe. My old outfit, they look like a bunch of kids. A couple of ladder companies are raising their aerials and beginning their rescues. I see Wes Egan start up Ladder 10's aerial, but by the time he goes two floors the flames slip under him, and he comes down faster than he went up, sliding the rail, with his coat steaming.

Another ladder crew stretches a thirty-five-footer to the fourth floor, but they make a mistake and lay it square in front of a window, and before it touches the sill a woman in a flaming nightgown jumps four feet through the air to grab the tip. The ladder spills over backward and clatters down against the truck, and the woman's twitching on the street. Terrible! You never put a ladder right up to a window, you put it six or eight feet to one side and then slide it over. That way a jumper can't tip it over.

The radio blares in my ear. *"This is Portable Three inside. The main stairway's beginning to collapse. We can't make any headway."* It sounds like Loo. *"Can you get us some help from the other side!"*

*"Stay put!"* Slater says, he's running the show, but not for

106

long. A body of fire this size, the superchief'll be here to take over any minute.

*"We'll just have to work from the windows,"* Loo says. *"These stairs are going any second."*

*"Stick with it till I tell you,"* Slater repeats.

I punch my own button quick. *"C.Y.A.!"* I says. *"C.Y.A.!"* Cover your ass. Fireman's Rule No. 1, 2 and 3. Slater don't care, it's not him on that burning stairway.

Outside it's mass confusion and getting worse. The superchief pulls up in his street clothes and his white helmet, looks like he must of come from a banquet, and orders ladder pipes and deluge sets right away. We're already putting oceans on the fire, but it don't seem to have any effect. Flames spew out the roof twenty feet high. Nobody ventilated, nobody could last up there more than a second or two. The fire must of broke through and ventilated itself.

Thirty-one's unleashes its Stang water cannon at top volume, four hundred pounds of water a second, and the fire just spits back steam. There's bodies laying on the pavement, I can see three or four myself. The aid men are running wild, but there's just too much work for them, too much for anybody.

After a while Les Dawson staggers into the cab spitting teeth, the nob broke loose and caught him flush, and without even thinking how he's gonna be able to talk on the radio, I says, "Les, take over for a while," and jump out of the cab.

I ask Slater what I can do.

"Get a crew and find Kirkpatrick," he says. "Can't raise him on this thing."

"Is he Portable Three?" I ask.

"That's him. Tell him not to cut off like that. Goddamnit, I don't care what he's doing—I want contact!"

As I walk through the gutted lobby, hot water drips on me. Two floors above my head, it looks like somebody's opened the door on a locomotive's firepit, it's nothing but flame and glowing coals.

Mike Mustache and Sonny Wicker come stumbling along, their line's abandoned, they're trying to reach the outside without getting drowned or scalded. I can see by their pop eyes they're through for the night.

"Where's Loo?" I says, and Mike waves toward the back stairs. The points of his mustache are gone, his eyes are like agates. I try to shore him up from the side, but then Sonny slumps down and I can't handle the two of them. They start to crawl toward the door. I can see Sonny's bare hand is getting poached in the puddles of steaming water.

Two aid men take over and I pick my way toward the rear of the lobby and the staircase. It's smoky, but I can see the remains of the stairs hanging in space, the bottom half must of burned away. There's a closed door behind the old stairwell, and I get down on my stomach and shove it open with my foot, hoping the backdraft'll go over my head, but nothing comes out except a smutty cloud of blue smoke. I try to go in, but the hot air hits my lips and I quick cut off my breathing. One deep breath and you're finished, I seen a hundred cases.

As I'm backing away, trying to figure what to do, I hear a conversation coming out of a radio somewheres inside the room. *"Deputy One to Portable Two, are you up on the inside now?"*

*"Roger, we're on the fourth floor. We're making a little headway. If you send anybody, watch out for the stairs. They're weak, some already give. Over."*

I wonder if the portable radio could be Kirkpatrick's. Firemen don't abandon expensive mobile units. Somebody's got to be inside this burning room or the radio wouldn't be in there, crackling away.

"Loo!" I call out.

108

No answer.

I run back through the lobby, bump into somebody and knock him sprawling, and keep right on running till I'm out in the air. I grab the first mask I see, out of an aid man's hand, and strap it on with fumbling fingers. An old saying keeps running through my brain, "Firemen are dumb guys that run into buildings that other people run out of . . . "

My air's flowing pretty good by the time I get back to the smoky room, and I crawl right through the door on my belly. I can't hear the radio any more, but it's got to be in here someplace. I'm breaking rules, you should never go alone where you can't see, you should always have a line with you or some means of protection. But Loo might be burning to death.

Now I'm through the door, I'm crawling around the baseboard, at least I'm observing one of our rules, always search clockwise. A line from my old drill instructor comes back to me, "When you're in a smoky room, I want you either touching each other or talking to each other. *No exceptions!*"

Talk to me, Loo, talk to me! "Loo!" I holler. *"Loo!"* But the sound's muffled inside my mask. Where's that radio I heard before? Maybe it's burned up. Hope not. Need help with my directions, a reference point.

Something must be burning dirty in this room, a couch or something, it's putting out a blue-black oily smoke, you can almost feel the hot greasy particles in the air.

Might as well close my eyes, I'll see just as good. Goddamn job, you're always in the dark. Not like those phony movie fires, all flame and bright and light.

How far've I gone? Maybe ten feet from the door. Here's the corner. Keep following the wall, feel your way. Touch it, *touch it!* Don't get lost.

God*damn!* A floor-joist, still smoldering. Crawled right over it. Hope my turn-out pants didn't burn through.

*"Battalion Four, Battalion Four . . ."* That abandoned radio again. Seems to be in the center of the floor. Jeez, I hate to leave the wall, I'll lose my bearings worse.

My helmet bumps into something, feels like a big table. No, it's part of the staircase. Must of fell right through the ceiling.

Grope around in the center of the room. Nothing. The radio's quiet again, probably the battery's wet. What's that crack Plummer made when he turned in the wet radio? "Diagnosis: Death by drowning." *Where's the wall?*

Can't find it.

Crawl faster. *Bang!* There's the wall, I found it with my head. Where am I now, on the near side or the far side? Where's the door? It's got to be there, I just come through it.

What this room needs is Ax Bedrosian, pulling the ceilings with his pike pole. Tear the burning debris down, let the smoke whistle out like a flue. Too late for that.

Where's Loo?

I start crawling faster, come to another corner. Jeez, I must of gone the wrong way. How could I? I wipe my hand across the plastic mask on the Survivair, but the blackness is in the air, not on the faceplate. Can't see an inch.

*Oooooh.* Funny feeling in my stomach. Don't panic.

Claustrophobia's welling up. Keep control. Swallow hard. Think about the loot.

I know the goddamn door's there.

*Where?*

I crawl over another patch of baking hardwood. The varnish comes up in a tacky froth and tries to stick my gloves to the floor. The hair on my neck's sizzling, my knees are smoking.

I shake my hands in the air to cool them down. A loose board bounces hard off my helmet and a spurt of scalding water slips through the neck of my coat all the way to my shorts.

How long've I been in this room? Too long. These Sur-

110

vivairs, they'll give you thirty minutes if you're taking it nice and easy, otherwise it's closer to fifteen. The bell'll go off any second, and then I'll have a few minutes left.

"*Portable Six . . .*" The radio again.

Sounds like it's over against the other wall. Jeez, I've lost my bearings. Nothing to go by.

I drag myself across the room just as the bell starts in my ears. I'm at sea in a fog. I bang up against the wall and begin crawling toward the door I come in.

No feeling left in my hands.

"Loo? Where you at, Loo?"

The radio squawks again, it's closer this time. I can hear somebody ordering move-ups. My warning bell's ringing in my ear, my air tastes stale. Somebody's *got* to be in here, no fireman'd leave his portable unit. I come up against the door and reach around.

Behind the door. A body.

I went clockwise when I come in the room. If only I'd of went the other way . . .

Part of the collapsed staircase pinches across his middle. The radio's around his neck.

I reach up and feel for the head, and my hand draws back a sticky mess of hot goo. The plastic from the helmet's melted around his face like grilled cheese. Don't be Loo. *Don't be Loo!*

The plastic's red.

It's a lieutenant.

I grab for the radio. "*Code Ten, Code Ten!*" I holler. "*Fireman needs help! South end of lobby.*"

What a joke! Who don't need help at a fire like this?

The bells peter out, I'm breathing my own CO2.

Now my goddamn mask won't come off. I reach up, but my shaking hands won't make the connection. *Pretend it's a pussy.*

I yank it off and gulp a mouthful of hot air. Smelly but not superheated. If it was superheated, I'd already be dead.

I reach down and lift him by the armpits, but he won't budge. Must be a ton of stairs draped over him. The smoke's ripping into my eyeballs and the snot starts to flow from my nose in long cloudy strings. I make another tug, but he's not gonna come unless I tear him in half. I take a closer look. It's Loo.

I throw my coat across him and run across the lobby. Outside, the smoke's clearing.

I grab the first guy I see. "The loot's trapped!"

"Compose yourself," the guy says. "Now what is it?"

I can see he's a captain, he's got the yellow hat and a radio. I tell him what's happening and he calls the manpower chief, and three or four guys with clean coats come in with axes and masks and I lead them back to the room. They drag Loo out and an aid crew takes over, and the last I see is he's being put on a stretcher and loaded into an ambulance. The plastic helmet's still melted around his head like a skullcap.

Three hours later we drag-ass back to the station, and the dispatcher's already ringing the signal. Twenty bells at slow cadence. A firefighter killed in action.

If only I'd of went the other way.

*"Fire Five out of service."*

*"Okay Fire Five."*

Plummer hangs up the microphone and parks in front of St. Timothy's. I lock the rig, this is a bad neighborhood to leave a fire engine untended, or anything else of value. Loo lived here all his life, and when he got promoted he didn't run off to the suburbs, like a lot of guys. Wonder what his wife'll do. Bad place for widows.

I check the rig before we go in for the service. Streamers of black crepe hang along the sides, and there's a black curtain across the tailboard. We've unloaded two-thousand feet of line. Line isn't what we'll be hauling today.

The priest says something in Latin, then he talks about the only begotten son, he talks about how much God loved the world, he mentions the need for a spiritual awakening, he talks about everything but Weldon Kirkpatrick. By the time he finishes sprinkling holy water, he hasn't mentioned Loo once.

The church is packed with firemen on the off-shift and a couple dozen brass, guys that worked with him at other stations, guys that only knew him by reputation, but we already arranged that Fire Five "B" platoon will bear the pall, no assistance required. With our probie, Fenstermacher, there's seven of us, if you count the walking wounded.

Tyree D'Arcy, the poor guy's got a bruise the size of a grapefruit on his upper thigh where the hydrant cap hit him, about a quarter inch from the family jewels, and he's just kind of limping down the aisle with one hand on the coffin, not really carrying any weight. Les Dawson's face is swollen from where the two-and-a-half banged him in the mouth, but at least he's not flashing his new ice-hockey smile. Sonny Wicker's hands are bandaged where he blistered them in hot water getting out of the lobby.

The rest of us do the main humping, with me and Ax in front, him scrooching down to keep the coffin level. It looks real nice, there's an American flag on the top and red white and blue rosettes at each end, too bad Loo can't see it.

But the fuss, he'd hate that. He must be embarrassed, laying inside that box while we walk it through an honor guard of fifty firefighters with crossed pike poles. Ethel, she wanted a simple ceremony, followed by cremation, but we persuaded her out of it. Loo left no instructions, I guess he thought he'd live forever, but I reminded Ethel of one thing, I said, "Listen, honey, the last thing any fireman wants is cremation."

We reach the end of the honor guard and move into the crowd, two hundred, three hundred people, all of them trying to see . . . what? The top of the coffin? They're sure not gonna get a look at our loot—the undertakers said there's no use even trying to fix him up, just dress him in Class A's and wrap him in the flag. His plastic helmet's still melted around his head.

We slide the coffin on the skid load nice and smooth. Plummer goes back inside to drive and Tyree goes with him. The rest of us stay in the back for Loo's last run.

The first time I ever took a good look at a fire engine coming out of a station and seen the three guys standing in the open just behind the cab and three more lined up on the tailboard, it put me in mind of a bunch of trained monkeys with their

114

funny hats in place, hanging on to the bar. I thought to myself, Look at the trained chimps running off to a fire, I wonder what the human beings think when they see 'em. Never been completely able to shake that feeling. A little ashamed, I guess.

Not today.

On the tailboard, Sonelius Wicker takes a stance like a Marine D.I., bandaged hands and all. Mike Mustache holds the brass bar with one hand and rests his other on top of the coffin. Les and me stand in front of the box at a stiff parade rest. Ax is behind the coffin, sniffling.

"Can it!" I says out of the corner of my mouth. Ax bites his lip.

Plummer eases the Kenworth down the block and the church bells fade out behind us until all's we can hear is the dull plunking of our own bell, with the clapper taped. There must be twenty-five cars in the cortage. Loo had a lot of friends.

"Now remember," I says as we bump along about ten miles an hour and the engine spits and snaps from going too slow, "just a few words. Nothing fancy. Just—"

"We know, we know," Ax says. His face looks like a character actor with pure white make-up. The rest of the trip everybody's quiet. Rehearsing in their own head.

Loo's open grave's just off the main driveway of the cemetery, so Plummer goes about fifty feet beyond and stops, and the thought comes to me that he's showing Loo three exposures, near side, full front and far side, exactly the way we do at fires. We hump the coffin back and rest it on four flat boards over the hole. I'm glad it's not raining.

The priest says a few more words in Latin, and then I walk up to the coffin and motion for attention. I'm the oldest of our shift.

"Ladies and gentlemen of our audience," I says, a little too loud, so I repeat softer, "Ladies and gentlemen." There's an

115

ice cube in my throat, but I already made up my mind I'm not gonna screw up. "Before we lay Lieutenant Kirkpatrick to rest, each of us members of 'B' shift of Fire Five Special Engine Company would like to say a few well-chosen words."

I start out by telling what Loo meant to us, how much we miss him already. Then I come right out with how he saved my life by getting me off the bottle, plus saved it plenty more times when walls were falling down and backdrafts firing all around us and the visibility was minus.

I'm half finished and I still got a lot to say, but nothing's coming out. My mouth's open but the air won't pass my throat, the ice cube's too big. I nod my head and sort of wave at the coffin, and then I look into the crowd and see Tyree limping his way to the front.

He tells how Loo never played favorites because of race, creed or size. Then Sonny comes up and says Loo never ordered us to go anywhere he didn't go himself, and Plummer says we'll all report back for duty at Station 12 but it'll be a different place now. Les spits a few remarks through his torn lips about Loo's professionalism, and Mike Mustacci says Loo always had a good word for everybody, he'd rather others got the credit. Even the probie makes a little speech, he tells how Loo give generously of his time, even to recruits.

Ax hangs back. He's the one I'm worried about, he's gray around the gills. He stumbles over to the coffin and stands there looking at the sky, blinking, like he don't want to concede what's laying on the ground next to him.

He blurts his speech so fast only a few of us hear him. "Loo-was-a-good-man-I-can't-say-no-more." Then he walks fast toward the rig. I look over and the widow's daubing her eyes and one of Loo's big sons, Terence, he puts his arm around her back, and the ice cube's still in my windpipe but we got a few more things to do before it's over, and by God we're

116

gonna do them right, just exactly like Loo would of done them right if he was alive.

I nod to Tyree, and he slips his coronet out of its case and licks his lips. The horn points straight at the sun when he lifts it, the rays sparkle off the polished gold. Plummer looks nervous, but I know we got nothing to worry about. Tyree promised to play nice and slow, so his lack of rhythm don't matter much, and he said he could do the whole call without any complicated fingering. He ought to know the tune by now, he spent the morning in the cab rehearsing. The department wanted to send the police bugler, but I told them Fire 5 would handle it.

Tyree blows Taps, as clear and beautiful as the guy that blows it at the Arlington Monument. Never futzes up a single note.

We stand there saluting till the last note dies away, and I look over at Tyree and give him a smile for the great job he done.

Then Loo's twin daughters, Molly and Sara, nine years of age each, they step up to the side of the coffin and recite in their thin little voice.

> "Cut him out in little stars
> And he will make the face of heaven so fine
> That everyone will worship night
> And shun the garish sun."

You never know what kids'll come up with. When they courtesy, Plummer starts to clap, but I give him an elbow and he looks up in the air like he's bird-watching.

"C'mon," I says, and each guy grabs a strap. Sonny can't grip, so he just reaches over and touches the coffin one last time. We heave the tapes together and the caretaker slides the boards out from under the box one by one and we lower Loo while the priest mumbles something. When the coffin gets to

117

the bottom we each throw in a couple flowers and then we turn and head for the rig.

I climb up in front with Plummer, which Ax is already there. "I'm sorry," he says, snuffling. "I really—I really liked Loo."

I really liked him, too, you dumb ape. That's why I didn't cry.

I grab the microphone off the dash and push the button. *"Fire Five,"* I croak, *"returning."*

The way the schedule falls, this is normally our laundry night, when the whole shift goes down to the Bad Penny or the Hucklebuck and drink beer and orgle the broads and let our hair hang down. I'm against partying on the night of Loo's funeral, but Plummer makes a good point. "Look, it's important we do things the same way, not let this get us down. Look at Ax. Coupla beers'll do him good. Can't hurt the rest of us, either."

"You think the Hucklebuck's a good place for a wake?" I says. "With all a them chicks gyrating around to get picked up?"

"This isn't a wake. A wake's before the funeral. This is just . . . tradition."

"Some tradition," I says.

But Plum's been saving his best argument for last. "Got a flash for ya," he says. "This is the way Loo'd want it." I remember pro football once used the same point.

Five of us end up going: Ax, Plummer, Mike, Sonny and me. Tyree's gone home for a few shifts of sick leave, and Les—I don't know, chasing laundry never seems to interest him, especially now that his front teeth are missing.

The minute I hear the hard rock band, I know we made a mistake. Out on the dance floor, every loser in the county's trying to connect. The thing about a joint like the Hucklebuck is when you first walk in the females look like Bela Lugosi. It's not till you tuck away a few beers that they start improving, and pretty soon you can't live without 'em, you'll shoot yourself if she don't take you home and pour you a drink etc. and so forth.

What a sight, all those graduates of the Fred Astaire Dance Studio! There's Mavis Bush, the one with the lacquered hair that if you touch it'll shatter like the windshield of a car. She's shagging away in her party shoes, real fancy, with three-inch spike heels.

Across the way, Mae Dispacci's dancing with a swab jockey. We call her the pigeon, fat on top, skinny little bird legs and size-5 feet. Friendly broad, very agreeable. "Only puts out for her friends, and has no enemies," Plummer says every time we see her. *Every* time.

Ginger Lee's sitting at a table nursing a champagne cocktail. Ginger's got gorgeous reddish-auburn hair down to her kneecaps and a pair of legs that won't quit and the face of a sixty-three-year-old Irish washerwoman that's been in a plane crash. I wave hello, but she can't see me without her glasses.

We take the big booth in the corner and clutch for the first pitcher of beer, two bits apiece, and nobody says a word.

"Hey, Ax," Plummer says to break the ice. "Look at that one over there."

"Fuck off, why don'tcha?" Ax says, not even looking up from the suds.

We sit quietly for another five minutes.

"Hey, who's gonna dance?" Mike Mustache says half-heartedly.

"Who'd wanna dance with you?" I crack. Nobody even smiles.

I look over at Ax, he's gulping his beer and slumping in the booth.

"Fine b-b-bunch we are," Sonny finally mutters. "Lost our regular chief, lost our loot." Yeh, I says to myself, and our wife ran off with the milkman. Better keep sharp implements away from Sonelius for a while.

"Kid," I says, patting him on the back, "there's a Puerto Rican expression that covers it, and the sooner we learn it the better."

"What's that?"

*"Que sera, que sera.* Whatever happens, it happens, that's all."

Pretty soon we order another pitcher, and then another. I'm not drinking much, and I wonder who's slopping it up. By the fourth pitcher, I realize it's Ax. He's filling his glass and draining it and filling it again. Probably got two quarts in his stomach already. Trying to drown himself, I guess.

I'm talking to a waitress when I hear somebody hollering over the hard rock. I look up and Ax is weaving out in the middle of the dance floor, hollering, "Cut it! *Cut the music!* We're having a minute . . . minute . . . a minute of silence." The corners of his mouth are working.

"Siddown, ya drunk ya!" somebody hollers.

Ax takes a step toward the voice and almost falls. He looks embarrassed. The music stops with a last scratch of the brushes on the drumhead.

"A good man . . . a good man died," Ax says.

Plummer runs up and puts his arm around Ax's waist, and I grab him by the belt. "Come on, pal," Plum says, and we steer him toward the door.

"We'll get you home," I promise. The customers are quiet, watchful. In a corner, somebody giggles. Mike and Sonny follow along to the car. Just a bunch of drunken firemen.

All the way to Ax's house in my station wagon, he sits in the front seat and stares out the windshield. "You okay, Ax?"

120

Not a word.

He falls out of the car in front of his house and crawls up the lawn. He trips over the stoop and goes sprawling. The four of us drag him on the porch like a side of beef. Far as we can tell, he's out cold.

After about six minutes of ringing and knocking, Francine comes to the door and we haul him into his bedroom. I take a good look at Ax's wife in the light and I wonder my God what's happened to her, she's put on a hundred pounds, she looks like a Chinese regular in the Korean war.

Then I realize she's wearing three or four layers of bed-clothes.

Poor Ax. He could of used some consolation.

"Hey, Charly," Sonny Wicker says as I'm slicing tomatoes for guacamole salad, "I just heard N-N-Nordquist say something about calling you upstairs."

I rip off my gift apron—the one that has Executive Chef embroidered on it by Les Dawson—and in about eight seconds flat I'm in the housing above Ladder 10's fifth wheel and there's no way the cap's gonna root me out. I know what he wants. A flock of pigeons been roosting above his room lately and every day he gets somebody to wipe the ledge. I guess he thinks it's my turn. Well, I'm the cook, can't he get that straight? Your firehouse cook is excused.

I'll stay in here till he finds somebody else.

Jeez, I still got a sensitive pair from the physics teacher last night. She spends three hours harping on Boyle's Law, how it's something every fireman ought to know. The lights are dim, the music's playing Mantovani, and she's telling me, "Now repeat, PV equals P prime V prime, in which P is pressure, V is . . ." Who wouldn't of lost his interest?

Somebody's coming. Let 'em come.

"Okay, Charly, you can climb down now." It's Nordquist.

I don't make a move. The hatch swings open. "How old did you say you are?" Cap calls in. "Forty-one? Forty-one going on two and a half? C'mon, ya simple shit ya, climb outa there.

Come up to my office. I got a lollipop for ya."

No question, he's made me. Somebody must of ratted. God-damn, this hiding place lasted almost a year. Gotta suspect the probie. He's got big eyes, that Fenstermacher.

"Who finked?" I says, climbing out ass first.

"Who what?"

"Who ratted?"

"Nobody ratted, Charly. I know where alla you guys hide."

He does? "You do? C'mon, Cap, stop kidding me. Where's Bedrosian hide?"

"Who?"

"Bedrosian, Ax, I mean Burton."

"The big Armenian? He's usually behind the compressors."

"Mike Mustache?"

Cap thinks for a second. "Mustacci? Caught him once in the ash pit. Usually he's inside the fire door with his bunkers on. Who else you wanna know? Wicker? He stands on the toilet bowl, at least since he quit hanging himself in the hose tower."

"Okay, Cap, okay, I believe you."

"Huh?"

"*I believe you!*"

"Stop screaming at me. I got a new hearing aid. This one, I can hear a fly scratch his ass."

"Better turn down the volume," I says.

"Fine," he says, "except for my emphysema."

Who knows what he thought I said? He motions toward the stairs, and we clomp up toward his office, him first. His pants are so shiny, I can see my face. I hope he doesn't question me about Loo again. I already told him and everybody else at the Arson Board. Look, I said, it's one of them things, I turned left when I should of turned right. Inside I'll always blame myself, but the board ruled out negligence. The fire doc testified that Loo wouldn't of lived anyway, the stairs fell and crushed him and the flames opened up around him like an open-heart furnace and his lungs popped. The murderer's still walking.

"After you, Alfonso," Captain Nordquist says, holding open the door to his office on the third floor. I'm getting weird vibes. He never treated me polite before. Next thing you know, he'll be serving the condemned man's last meal. I hope I can cook it myself.

"What'd I do, Cap?" I wait for him to sit behind his old maple desk with the cigaret burns. The room smells like a warehouse for wet cigars and after-shave. Cap's always hacking at his face, shaving it to death and healing the wounds with witch hazel and toilet paper. He looks like he played goaltender without a mask.

"Charly," he says, offering me a Cigarillo, "we're in a bad way. There's nobody we can bring up, the budget the way it is and all. Superchief says we have to fill our losses by attrition."

"What's attrition?"

"Means no new hiring. Shift our personnel around and fill the vacancies. Chief Slater, he wants to bring Neal Steicher over to Fire Five and put Wes Egan in charge of Ladder Ten."

"Cap, Wes'd make a good truck officer, but Cap—*ar eh*—"

"I know," the old man says, pulling a file out of his drawer. "If Steicher goes to Fire Five, you'll all put in your papers."

I'm glad he said it, not me. A fireman don't like to knock a brother fireman, but in Steicher's case I would of made an exception.

"So it comes down to you, Charly," Cap's saying. "You're an acting lieutenant now. Temporary, of course."

I got to be hearing things. "Cap—"

"I don't want no argument. I spoke up for ya, now don't make me look stupid."

I'm dragging on my Cigarillo so hard the ash is an inch long and the heat's searing my vocal cords. The first thought that flashes through my head is a loot can't cook, can't jack around with the guys, can't really enjoy himself. But then I remember that a loot gets more money, he retires at a higher base, so I better not cut off my nose despite my face.

Cap can't keep from smiling, and then I catch on, he's been zinging me. Jeez, what a perturbed sense of humor.

"Cap," I says, going along with the gag, "there's one little problem. I haven't taken the lieutenant's test in ten years."

"So what? They're not making you a lieutenant, they're making you an *acting* lieutenant. First chance you get, run down and take the test. I guarantee you'll pass."

"How? I haven't studied that crap for years."

"Don't ask questions, Charly. Just take the test."

"But, Cap—"

He stands halfway up and points a stubby finger at me. My God, he's serious, he means business! "Listen, goddamnit, you see my new hearing aid? Well, I got it tuned so it won't pass no more bullshit."

"Cap, how can I pass the test—"

"Yes, it is," Cap says real loud. "A *very* nice day if it don't rain."

"They must be hard up for officers," I blurt out.

"Hard up for officers did you say? Funny, that's what the superchief said exactly. But you got a rabbi at headquarters. Chief Grant. He put in a good word for ya—more like a thousand good words. Whattaya got on him?"

I laugh at the idea of having something on Chief Grant. "I caught him screwing the exhaust pipe," I says. "Took a few Polaroid shots."

Nordquist laughs back. He knows all about Chief and me, how we entered training school on the same day and became fast friends till he started passing all the tests and I started boozing. But that didn't keep us from staying tight through the years.

Cap slides a plastic envelope across his desk, and there's two individual silver bars in it. "Here," he says. "Now try to show a little class, will ya? Next time I look for ya, don't be in the wheel housing, okay? Show some dignity. Hide in the crapper, at least."

"Cap, what about the Civil Service?"

"Let headquarters worry about the Civil Service. They fixed it up with the Mare. If the Mare can't handle the Civil Service . . ."

Then something occurs to me. "Leaves us short, Cap," I says.

"No, it don't. We're making Fenstermacher a regular. Can he handle it?"

"A lotta hustle, Cap," I says, remembering the night the kid ran up the steps when he was caught with his pants down and his shirt too. *A lotta hustle* . . . I sound like a fire officer already.

"Keep your eye on him, Charly. He's just a kid." The old man picks up a blue memorandum. "You'll be getting a new probie soon."

"Yeh? What's his name?"

"Huh?" He slaps at his hearing aid.

"The new probie. What's his name?"

"His name's Lulu Ann Tomkins."

Jesus Wellington Christ, the first firebroad! The situation puts me in mind of what Francine tells Ax in bed. *Why me?*

"Why me, Cap? I got a whole new job to learn."

Nordquist hoists his lumpy old black shoe up on the desk. "Don't bullshit me, Charly. You know the job backwards. Why, you oughta be sitting behind this desk right now, and you know it. So don't go singing the blues about the firebroad —the lady fireman, I mean."

126

"Cap, I don't know how to handle women. Ask my wife. My *ex*-wife."

"Treat her like any other firefighter. That's what she'll be, won't she? Second in her class at training school. Chief says she can do anything a man can do."

"Good, she can use our urinal."

"Talk to her the same way you do Wicker, Dawson, any of them guys."

"You mean tell her to shag ass, hump the fucking hose or I'll kick her in the nuts?"

Cap scratches the line of freckles that run across his forehead like ladybugs. "I think we can leave out the adjectives," he says.

"Maybe yes and maybe no, Cap. We're not the Methodist Sunday School, ya know."

"No shit? You ain't? Tell me about it, I only come on the department yesterday morning."

I start to get up, but the old man waves me back down. "One other thing. You got the best crew in town, but a couple of 'em's sex crazy, ya know what I mean?"

I don't let on.

"Especially that Vincent Brown."

"Plummer?"

"Right, Plummer. You tell Mr. Plummer to show some respect to this woman. Keep it in his pants at least for a week or so."

"Keep what, Cap?"

"You know what, Charly. Stop playing dumb. You been getting away with that act for twenty years. You're no dumber'n the rest of us."

Me, I can't believe there'll be a problem with sex. We showed a group of female applicants through the station a couple months ago, and they were worse dogs than the losers at the Hucklebuck. How can they *not* be? Like Ax says,

"Who'd want a broad that could pass our physical?" What kind of dainty femininity could hump eighty-five pounds of line up three stories and back in ninety seconds? Or lay to a hydrant, stretch two hundred feet of inch-and-a-half, put out a bonfire and uncouple all lines in four minutes?

The first firefem that passed those tests, I seen her up at 17's, the day the wives picketed, and she's got legs like telephone poles. She'd crush you if she rapped those pins around you, and from her short hair and her husky voice I'd swear she's a bull dagger, although they claim they're only hiring straights, no diesels need apply. But how're they suppose to tell? One or two of your lizzies is bound to creep in.

Sammy Giamfacaro's wife was carrying a sign that day, NO-BODY ELSE SLEEPS WITH MY HUSBAND, and the firebroad walks over to her and says, "Don't worry, honey, I got a boyfriend of my own, he takes good care of me." Rachel Giamfacaro, she says boy, that's some hutspa, whatever that means. Me, I don't speak Italian.

128

The guys act like a bunch of orang-utangs when they find out I'm an acting loot. "Excuse me, your royalty," Mike Mustache says. "Would you bend over so I can kiss the imperial heinie?"

Ax waltzes me around, and Sonny Wicker pours a bottle of water over my head, and then we all slouch at the long table and have a talk while Plummer slips an egg under my seat and Sonny gives me a hotfoot. All the latest routines from Las Vegas. Then they sing

"Hooray for Charly.
Hooray for Charly.
Hooray for Charly.
He's a horse's ass!"

"Faint praise," I says.

After a while Steicher comes in and shakes hands with me, and I feel like a hypocrite, but what're you gonna do? You can't pretend to be a leader of men and then snub a brother officer. "Next thing you'll be after my job," Neal the Eel says in that whiny way of his.

"Not me, pal," I says. "I wasn't after Loo's job, either. What I wouldn't give to have him back." I realize that's a dumb remark, but guys like Steicher always make me touchy.

Some of the guys' ears prick up when they hear Loo mentioned, he's only been gone a week. "I knew Weldon Kirkpatrick a long time and I admired him," the Eel's saying, "but he broke a rule and he paid the price. You can't brood about it."

"Broke what rule?" Ax says quietly.

"C.Y.A.," Steicher says. "Don't go single-O. You break a rule, you pay. That's what I'm always telling my men."

Isn't he the one with the answers? H. Walker Slater junior grade.

Ax stands up, Plummer and Sonny alongside him.

"Lieutenant Steicher?" Ax says, his voice real low.

"Yeh?"

"Get the fuck outa here."

"What?" The Eel looks like he's been pole-axed, but he turns toward the door.

"You got two seconds."

"Just a minute, Fireman," Steicher says.

I open the door quick. "Lieutenant," I says, "do what the man says." I can see Ax is ready to commit homicide in front of about eight witnesses, and if he don't, somebody else will. Maybe me.

"You'll hear about this," the Eel says as he disappears down the hall.

"Go fuck yourshelf, shumbitch!" It's Les, spitting through the hole where his front teeth use to be. First time I ever heard him cuss.

"Goddamn scumbag," Ax says after Steicher leaves. "Talking about Loo like that."

"Ax," I says, "for your own good whyn't you just ignore him? He's not in our company, he just lives here."

Before Ax can answer, Mike Mustache says, "The thing that

130

bothers me, Loo wasn't making a mistake at all, that's just not the way it evoluted."

"Evoluted?" I says.

"Yeh," Mike says. I can't keep up with him since he started his word-a-day routine. He starts running through the same routine he told the Board of Inquiry, how him and Sonny were halfway up the staircase, choking and lost, and Loo led them down. "That's when we run into you, Charly, remember?"

"I remember."

"We were out on our feet."

"Looked like a coupla wet noodles," I says.

"All I remember is Loo helps us down the stairs and then he heads right back up," Sonny says. "M-m-musta thought Les was up there someplace."

"I made a wrong turn," I says.

"Yeh," Tyree says. "We heard that the first forty times, Loo."

I notice Mike Mustache kind of hangs his head while Tyree's talking. They haven't spoken since Mike called Tyree a black asshole for not charging the hose quick enough, except that Mike tried to apologize that same night and Tyree turned him off. We were sitting on the bench in the emergency room and Mike said, "Tyree, I don't know what to say."

"Don't say nothing, man," D'Arcy said. " 'Cause it don't matter *what* you say."

"Lost my head, pal. Tail of my coat was burning. I didn't know what I was saying, Tyree."

Tyree grunted. He was still in bad pain from where the heavy hydrant cap slammed into his leg.

Mike said, "I just want you to know I don't think of you as a—you know." There were nurses around. "I don't even think of you as—you know—as a black anything."

131

"Do me a favor, man," Tyree said, clomping over to the other side of the emergency room. "Don't think of me as a nothin'."

Not a word between them since. It shows on Mike's face. He's usually in the middle of the jacking around, laughing the loudest when somebody calls him a Dago or a Wop. "My mom's Irish," he'll say, "so you're only hurting half my feelings." But that insult he laid on Tyree—that's heavy stuff around a firehouse, and Mike knows it.

"Okay, pussies," I holler, "let's start on the housework."

Everybody groans. "Ax, you wash the walls. Les, clean the windows." Dawson points to his injured mouth, like he's too disabled for housework. "Clean 'em with your hands, don't lick 'em," I says. "Tyree, you polish the fittings, that way you won't have to move around. Sonny, empty the wastebaskets and ashtrays and then help Ax. Mike, the bunk room needs dusting. Plummer, you clean out the lockers."

"Why don't we play pinochle instead?" Plummer says.

"Deal the cards," I says.

Everybody gets in on the game, playing or kibitzing, except Mike, we can see him on the phone, taking notes on one of his laundry boards. After a while he comes out and says, "Listen to my latest exercise."

Tyree looks pained and starts to get up, and Ax turns to Mike and says, "Fuck off, why don'tcha? I got a hundred aces and a run."

"Come on, listen," Mike pleads. "It'll just take a second." He reads

"Sometimes in the heat of firefighting, words are exchanged in the spur of the moment, as everything happens so fast and you do not always have time for the rules of Emily Post. But

132

firemen are proud, and they do not like to extend apologies or accept them, for it makes them feel childish and flaccid."

Tyree starts to limp toward the door, so Mike walks behind him and reads faster

"For instance, a firefighter of my acquaintance called one of his best friends an ugly name at a fire, which was very pragmatic as the tail of his bunking coat was on fire at the time and threatened to barbecue him."

"Hey, dig that!" Plummer calls out "Barbecue!"
"Read!" I says. Tyree's passing through the door.

"Whereupon the first firefighter said he would never speak to the second again as the name he called him was not true. So the second fireman said to him, 'Hey, listen, pal, I didn't mean it, for I was upset, the flame was crawling up my . . . '

Mike hesitates. "Buttocks?" I suggest.

" 'The flame was crawling up my buttocks. So I'm sorry,' the second firefighter went on. 'It's like I shot an arrow over the house, and hurt my brother.' "

Mike looks at Tyree, and Tyree's still frowning.
" 'Shot an arrow over the house and hurt my b-b-brother,' " Sonny Wicker says. "I like that."
Plummer says it's certainly a beautiful sentiment.
"So how about it, Tyree?" Mike calls out.
"How 'bout what?"
"How about calling off the war?"
Tyree walks back in slowly.
"Okay, brother?" Mike says, holding out his hand. "I apologize. I acted like a jerk."
"Okay, brother," Tyree says, and the two men do a thumbshake and pull apart quick, because God forbid any firemen

133

should act like they really like each other, the sky would fall and they'd be sent to prison as perverts.

Tyree laughs and says, "Whoo-*ee,* it feels good to hear you admit it."

"Admit what?" Mike says.

"You acted like a jive turkey."

Later on I take Mustacci aside and tell him the whole shift's proud of him. "That took balls, man," I says. "Sure, you were in the wrong, but how many guys would admit it?"

"Thanks, Loo."

"Great line you come out with. What was it? 'Shot an arrow through the house and hit my buddy'?"

"Shakespeare."

Oh, sure. "Shakespeare? They putting Shakespeare on the back of Frosty O's?"

"Got it from the librarian," Mike says. He explains how he called the city librarian and told her he needed a terrific apology, and she quoted him out of *Hamlet,* a play about a little village in England. A nice gesture, even if he did have to steal it.

Right after we finish the dinner dishes, a deputy fire marshal arrives for a briefing. We assemble in the bullpen, and the marshal puts up a screen and shows slides of the Tivoli Hotel, where Loo and twenty-three others died. "Pure arson," the marshal says. "Right from the nature of the burn-out, you could tell. Fires don't start in four different places."

"Four different places?" I says.

"Affirmative."

"Inside a hotel lobby?" Plummer says. "Who'd have time to set four fires?"

"It didn't make sense to us, either," the deputy goes on, "not till this morning." He's a young guy, maybe thirty, looks like he hasn't slept in a week. "Right before noon we got word the night clerk came out of his coma, and we went over and interviewed him quick, 'cause he's burned forty percent."

The marshal lowers his voice. "Fellas, what I'm gonna show you can't leave this room. The newspapers find out, the whole town'll panic." He stops and shakes his head like he's got the Western Hemisphere on his shoulder, while we sit there in the half-dark with our mouths open. A new picture flicks up on the screen, it's a diagram of the Tivoli lobby, and there's four X's on it.

135

"The clerk said he heard a noise at the front door, but before he could investigate, a man runs inside—that's this X at the entrance—and he's in flames head to toe."

"Oh, Jesus," somebody mutters.

"Not again," somebody else says.

"Subject staggers across the floor and a few drops of burning liquid fall on an overstuffed chair. That's this here X. He stays on his feet till he gets over to the window and tries to wrap himself up in a curtain, but by that time he's too weak and all he does is set it on fire, that's your third X. Then he falls against the stairwell and ignites the rug, here. Four different fires."

"Holy shit," Ax says softly.

"The clerk runs up the stairs to spread the alarm and the whole staircase goes up like a matchbox. Then he beat it back downstairs and out a side window."

"He musta been the only one that got down those stairs at all," I says.

"Affirmative. Everybody else either jumped or come down our ladders or died in their rooms."

Plummer says, "How'd the first victim get as far as he did, burning like that? He shoulda died on the spot, like a Buddha." "Buddha" is our word for a self-immolation, somebody committing suicide by burning himself up. A lot commoner than you think.

"Negative," the deputy marshal says. "Sometimes a dying man gets a burst of energy. This wasn't one of your older winos. Desk clerk said he recognized him, Indianapolis they call him. Liked to drink zinfandel and nod out on the front steps. Perpetrator musta doused him while he was asleep."

The marshal calls for the lights. "We held this back on the press," he says, tottering like he's about to fall asleep himself, "but we can't keep it from you guys 'cause we need your cooperation."

Everybody speaks up. "You got it." "Anything you say." "We listening."

"For a starter, we're extending the arson patrol to twelve hours a night—six to six. Watch for suspicious subjects carrying some kind of container. This psycho bastard's not pouring gasoline out his ears, it's gotta be coming from somewhere. Maybe he's got tanks strapped to his body, I don't know."

Normally we hate the arson patrol. From midnight to four you drive the station car up and down the back streets in the high-arson zones. Nobody on patrol has even seen a torch in the year and a half we been doing it.

The marshal says, "Take it in three-hour doses, so you'll stay sharp. Look *hard*. Hit the warehouse area, the projects, abandoned buildings, but concentrate on Skid Row."

"Witcha," Tyree D'Arcy says, and the other men nod their approval. I notice Tyree and Mike Mustache are sitting together. Scratch one war.

After the briefing I start to work up a new roster for arson patrol, putting myself in the rotation so it won't look like I'm gonna be another Steicher. Three different guys come in to tell me they want to take double-shifts.

Arson's no joke around here any more. Not since Loo. Mister Torch, your ass is grass. Fire 5 is on the case.

Many's the time I helped break in a new loot or house captain, but when you're on the butt end it's another story. The guys all know I have trouble getting to sleep but I always wake up like a cannon shot. I'm out of bed and into my gear practically before the bells, so they take advantage. They wait till I'm in a deep sleep, then four of them pick up my rack and move it a quarter turn. They flip the light switch on and I pull on my turn-out gear and run into the wall, blink my eyes and spin around and hit the wall again. Everybody's in bed laughing.

Then it gets to be a contest, see how far they can move my rack with me sleeping in it. They haul me into the crapper one night, Steicher wanders in and wakes me up. "What the hell you sleeping in here?"

I look around, take in the sights, and I says, "Well, I dunno. Evidently I hadda take a leak," which I calmly walk over to the urinal and shake off a few drops.

The next night Fenstermacher's on watch. He's a regular fireman now, no more probie, but there's still two or three tricks he hasn't learned. Four o'clock in the morning Plummer telephones him in the watch office and says, "Hey, this is the dispatcher. Your alarm busted?"

Fenstermacher says huh, he don't know, what time is it,

what's happening anyway, and Plummer snaps, "Hit the alarm button!"

Naturally the kid hits it, and naturally Lieutenant Charly Sprockett slides the pole and it's just me and the rookie standing in the dark watch office. All the other guys been tipped to ignore it, they just roll over and snicker.

"Well?" I ask the kid. "Where we going?"

"That was just a test, Loo," he says, like he's talking to some kind of amateur. "You weren't suppose to turn out."

"How the hell was I suppose to know it's a test?" I yells. But you can't stay mad at this kid. Always has that simple grin under that dumb tousled head of red straw, looks like Huckleberry Finn. I sit him down and acquaint him with some of the old dodges so he won't fall the next time and take me with him again. But I forget to warn him about the tarp drill, and the next day the guys call a tarp drill and wrap poor Wally in it and spray his balls purple. He don't care, he laughs and giggles like he's in his right mind. It's not like the time we're gonna paint Tyree's nuts purple, we de-pants him and discover they're already purple, so we wind up spraying them flat white, which Tyree takes it as a racist insult and reports us to the Black Firefighters Association.

"Might as well have our fun now," Mike Mustache says the day after they paint the rook. "Them firebroads come along, it'll all be dull around here."

"Yeh, how're we gonna initiate a fireginch, Charly?" Ax says. "Slip itch powder in her Modess?"

"Same way we did the others," I says. I'm busy writing a report. The goddamn paperwork is the worst part of being a loot, especially for we illiterates.

"Paint her purple?" Plummer says.

"How far's this bullshit gonna go anyway?" Ax says. "Where'll it end? We gonna have female loots, female chiefs?"

139

He shakes his big head slow. "We'll turn out some cold night and find the superchief can't come to the fire, she's having her ministration period."

"*Ad*ministration," I correct him. That's why I'm a lieutenant.

Battalion Chief H. Walker Slater wants the tiniest details to be perfect, but he screws up the big picture while he's working on the small. He's also a front-runner, which means he's the kind of officer that does a competent job on a fire if he's ahead from the first alarm. If the fire gets on top of him, he goes ape, runs up and down and screams, "Go out, goddamn you, go out!" There's all kinds of chiefs, but like I said, this is the first one I seen that thinks he can black down a fire with his mouth.

He calls me in after I been acting lieutenant for a month. "Siddown, siddown, Loo," he says, and slides a panetella across his desk. I leave it sit there. The last time I was here I refused to sign a paper against Ax, and I notice some changes have been made. He seems to be sitting above me, almost a head taller, which don't make sense as I'm five ten and he's a good three, four inches less. I look down and I could swear my chair's had a few inches amputated from its legs, while Slater's sitting on one of those adjustables you can raise to a high position. Also, he's painted his desk navy-blue and installed a light behind his head that comes in over his left shoulder and hits the visitor square in the face. I tell you, people hunt lions and start wars because they're short, it's the most dangerous physical disability.

141

"Sprockett," he says, leaning back in his chair and stroking his chin, "we didn't get off to a very good start, you and me, am I right or wrong?"

"What's the diff?" I says. "I got a job to do, just like you."

"Good, good! I like to hear a firefighter speak up. You don't like me, well, I feel the same myself."

"About me?"

"No," he says, leaning across his desk and scooping up the cigar, "about your whole goddamned platoon. Man for man, you're the biggest bunch of misfits I ever worked with. Look at your roster. You got Bedrosian that wears bloomers. You got Les—what's that fruit's name?"

"Dawson's no fruit."

"You got Les Dawson the fruit." He keeps right on talking like he don't hear me. "You got Vincent Brown that would attack a nun. You got that fat colored boy Emerson Tyree, or whatever his name is."

"Amerston D'Arcy. Nickname Tyree."

The chief blows a quivering smoke ring across his desk. "You got Michael Mustacci that's always in violation of the grooming regulations and Sonelius Wicker that couldn't keep his own wife in line and you got a probie that runs around naked and—"

He stops to take a breath.

"And we got me," I finish up for him.

"Right." He stands up and looks at me. "We got you." Then he launches into a long speech about how he thought he could trust me when he first made me an officer, but word's come back that I'm just as disloyal as the rest of Fire 5—I don't drill enough and I'm laxadaisical in the housework and discipline and I frequently make snotty remarks about the F.D. brass, and how can the men learn to respect their officers if one of them is a backbiter?

"Who told you all that, Chief?"

"I got my sources."

"Rats is what you mean. Chief, why don't you stop listening to Steicher? He can't hardly find his dick in the dark."

Slater looks at me for a long time, eyeball to eyeball, and I make damn sure he's the one has to break off contact. "Sprockett," he says in that booming bass voice of his, "if you want a transfer, I'll be glad to fix it up for you." His finger's shaking in my face, I'm thinking of biting it off.

"I'll stay," I says, walking toward the door. I didn't come in here to get screamed at, and I didn't come in here to talk about transfer. Fire 5's been like a family to me, I'm not about to leave on account of one Nazi in a white hat.

"You'll take my orders!" he hollers after me.

"Not forever."

Back at the station, I dummy up about the meeting. Maybe Slater's right about me talking too much to the men. I been an ordinary fireman for so long I don't know how an officer's suppose to behave, even if he's only an acting loot, which is about the same level as acting Pfc. in the army. The first time I hear something, I always take it to the men, it's second nature with me. That's the way it's always been on Fire 5. Social problems, business problems, martial problems, whatever. Sure, it's an unmilitary way to do things, but we're not the Coldstream Guards, we're just a bunch of firestiffs.

A few days later H. Walker calls me back to his office and makes me bring Tyree along. "Lieutenant," he says after he sits us down in those dollhouse chairs in front of his desk, "are you aware that the men on your platoon make a habit of flirting?"

"Sure hope so, Chief," I says, and Tyree flashes me a dirty look. He wants to cool the beef, whatever it is, and get out of here.

"I mean in the station, during visiting hours," Slater goes on.

He looks at Tyree. "Yesterday you spent ten minutes of duty time talking with a white woman."

"A *white* woman?" Tyree says, his eyes opening wide. "Everybody talk to women in visiting hours, Chief. They ask questions, we answer 'em."

"Everybody's not colored," Slater says. He sucks in his cheeks and stares down his bulldog nose at Tyree.

"Hey, back off a minute, Chief," Tyree says. I can almost see the steam coming out his ears. "Let's get straight on sumpin'. I'm not colored, I'm *black*. Now you might be colored, Chief. Your skin kinda orange."

"Never mind what I am," Slater says, turning even oranger. "Mess away from the white women or I'll write you up, and you too." He points at me.

"You write us up," Tyree says, "and the whole Black Firefighters Association'll run right up your ass with golf shoes."

"You threatening me, Fireman?"

"Do a hog shit on Tuesday?"

A couple of shifts go by and I'm called back. This time Slater hands me a copy of a letter. It's from a Miss Glory Jones and it tells how Firefighter Vincent Brown seduced her and she's pregnant and won't the department please force this vicious beast to do the right thing. I know the whole story. Plummer dropped the girl a couple of months ago and she's off the wall trying to get him back, she'll try anything. But there's no way she can be incubating a miniature Plummer Brown because, like Plum explained, "All she done was chew the eel." His favorite form of birth control.

"Chief," I says, but then I realize I can't tell the whole story.

"What do you intend to do about this dog in heat?" he says, his voice rolling across the desk like a shock wave. "Don't you men on Fire Five have any respect for your bodies?"

"Chief, this is a personal matter."

144

"Not any more it isn't." He punches a button on his desk. "Bring me Vincent Brown's jacket," he barks.

"Chief, this kinda thing, we can handle it better ourselves, down at the station."

"*Then why didn't you?* I'll handle it right here with ten shifts off and a notation in his jacket."

"Hey," I says, jumping up, "you can't gig a man for his sex life. He's a bachelor, he's a free man, Chief."

He passes the gig slip over to me. "Serve this on him today," he says. "Tell him to finish the shift and don't come back till the time's served."

"Chief Slater," I says, realizing that he's not kidding, "leave us men take care a this little matter ourselves. We can work it out, we always have before. No big deal, Chief. It's boy meets girl, ya know? The birds and the bees. It's not like he abandoned a hose line or something serious."

"You're dismissed," Slater says, his attention already on something else. "I got work to do."

A few nights later Ax is broke and needs gasoline money. He hits me up, he asks a few other guys, but we all got the shorts, it's the day before payday. So in front of me and Steicher and a couple other guys from Ladder 10, Ax says, "Hey, how about if I borrow a few bucks from the coffee-clutch money, pay it back Friday?"

"Why not?" I says. The other guys just kind of mutter. Who cares if somebody borrows a few dollars from the clutch?

We come back on shift Friday night, and the first thing Steicher does is he holds up the coffee box and he says, "Hey, this money's missing five bucks."

Nobody pays attention, so he calls out louder, "Hey! Somebody stole five bucks outa the coffee clutch!"

At the mention of the word "stole" the men look up from whatever they're doing. Firemen don't steal, it's our No. 1

145

taboo. Firemen walk right into your house or your place of business, you're at our mercy. A fireman with itchy fingers just can't be tolerated. Let a recruit steal a dime and he's canned the same day, and none of his buddies'll ever talk to him again. We had a guy back at 17's, Teets Dugan, he snatched half a pack of cigarets off the TV. He's now working at 27's. In Honolulu.

"Who stole what?" Ax says from the far end of the table. He probably hasn't heard a word till now, busy blabbing away with Plummer about something.

"There's five bucks gone," Wes Egan says. He's Steicher's biggest ass-lick, but not a bad guy when you can get him alone.

"Oh, that," Ax says, and he starts laughing. "I got it in my locker."

He comes back and tucks a picture of Abe Lincoln into the cup, but Steicher and Egan and another truckman, Larry St. Pierre, they keep giving him the evil eye.

"Whatsa matter with you guys?" Ax says. "I borrowed the money, now I paid it back."

"That's right, Steicher," I says. "I was here when he asked if it's okay. So were you. So were Wes and Larry, I'm pretty sure."

"Leave me out of it," Steicher says.

"Me too," Egan says, and St. Pierre says, "I don't know what you're talking about."

"Hey!" Ax says, stepping up to the three of them. "What's going on?"

I slide in between. If Ax gets the impression they're even hinting he stole money, he might send the three of them into orbit. "Hold it, Ax," I says. "They're only zinging you."

"That right?" Ax says, forcing a smile on his clown face.

The three truckmen turn and walk away.

"The next time you try to zing me," Ax calls after them,

"you better pick another sucker." Steicher turns and gives him a look. "That's right, Junior," Ax says. "You especially. Fuck off, why don'tcha?"

The next morning one of the secretaries down at headquarters tips me that formal papers are being drawn against Firefighter First Class Burton Bedrosian. The charge is theft. "Who signed the complaint?" I says.

"Chief Slater."

"Don't tell me the witnesses," I says. "Lemme guess. Steicher?"

"Right."

"Egan and St.—"

"Pierre."

The dirty son of a bitches! I run up to Cap Nordquist's room, but before I even knock on the door I realize Cap's too close to retirement to go to bat for Ax, it wouldn't be fair to ask him. Whatever Slater has in mind, Fire 5'll handle it.

The hearing's closed, and the three monkeys from Ladder 10 get on the witness stand and lie in their gums. All's they know is the money disappeared and Ax admitted taking it. The ancient hearing officer smiles and nods and then Ax takes the oath with a quivering hand and begins reciting his story. God knows it's simple enough, but he's so confused and scared he sounds like a congenial liar, I don't know if I'd of believed him myself.

Over at the prosecution table H. Walker Slater's sitting there with his blond hair slicked back and a cozy look on his pushed-in face. I have the feeling that Ax is really being tried for wearing bloomers, but since when is it a crime to catch the allergy? The poor guy, he's too dumb to put on a fancy defense. The hearing chief leans over and asks him, "Did you take the money or not?" and Ax admits he did.

I hear my name called, and I'm trembling as I walk up to the front. It's scary to be fighting the establishment.

"Lieutenant," the old chief says, "tell us exactly what you know."

I start to tell how Ax needed money for gasoline, but Slater keeps interrupting me with irrevelant questions, how long have I been on Fire 5, what's our tap record, how come I'm only an acting loot and not a regular at my age, all kinds of crap that makes me out to be pretty dumb myself. I look in the audience and see Neal the Eel and his two flunkies wisecracking behind their hats, and something snaps.

"Now you listen to me, Buster," I says, jumping up in the witness box. "I been here ten minutes trying to tell you what happened in this case and all you wanna know is my shoe size. Now listen here, goddamnit, this man didn't do a goddamn thing," I says. "There's three firemen here today that're lying their goddamn heads off. It's a wonder the good Lord don't send a bolt of lightning down here and kill all three of 'em!"

I turn to the trial chief and I says, "If you want me to point out those three son of a bitches, I'll be glad to. And the dirty bastard that put 'em up to it, I'll point him out too. He's got a lotta rank, but when he goes to a fire his knees shake, I seen him do it. Pees his pants, the yellow son of a bitch."

The hearing chief gets a look on his face like somebody's farted in church, and Slater's standing up trying to interrupt me, but I'm not about to be interrupted. "If I was Fireman Bedrosian," I says, "woe be unto your asses, brothers! I never knew firemen to lie about each other before."

"Immaterial, immaterial!" the hearing chief calls out. He's about Cap Nordquist's age, McGowan by name, been around since we used horses.

"I agree with you on that, Chief," I says. "It's the god-

148

damndest thing I ever heard in nineteen years nine months in the department."

"Who do you claim is lying?" he says.

"These measly-mouthed bastards sitting right out there," I says, pointing to the three truckmen. "They got their own reasons. Buncha goddamn scabs, they come in here and perjured themselves like they was cops or something."

"Sprockett," Slater says, yawning, "your opinions of the police are beside the point."

*"Beside the point?"* I holler. "Since when is perjury beside the point? Last I heard it was one-to-five in the state pen."

"All right, all right," the hearing chief says, trying to restore order. It's easy to see where things are headed, the fix is in up to the armpits.

"Okay," I says, trying to control my voice. "Go right ahead with your railroad job. Fire Bedrosian, do what you want. And when the case is over, him and me, we'll bring a little case of our own, we'll sue the jack-offs that perjured themselves here today. And we won't bring it in this closed hearing room, either. We'll take it right into Criminal Court, out in the open."

"Step down," Slater says, and I says, "Gladly. See you at the grand jury."

The hearing chief goes into private conference with himself and throws the case out. He may be a career fireman, but some fires are too hot to handle. The case goes back to the battalion level for disposition, and the most Slater can hand down is ten shifts off without pay, the same punishment he give Plummer. The whole Fire 5, all three shifts, we clutch together and put up every cent of the lost pay, so Ax winds up with a paid vacation.

He gets back one cool November evening, walks straight

149

into the locker room and slams Neal the Eel Steicher up against the wall. "You lying sack of shit," he says, and flings him on the floor. Then he hunts up Wes Egan, which Wes is almost as big as Ax, and Ax tells him, "You liar, you better get your ass transferred outa here. One of these days you're gonna go into a burning building and not come out. If there's just enough cigaret smoke around, you're gonna disappear!"

"But, Ax—"

Ax grabs Wes by the shirt front and pulls his face up close. "You open your mouth to me, even to say hello, I'll knock your teeth right out your ass."

Then he finds Larry St. Pierre and delivers a similar Thanksgiving message, and St. Pierre practically passes out.

"Ax," I says a little later, "it's nice to have your smiling face back. Say, Ax, I got the shorts. Could I borrow five bucks till Tuesday?"

The big man turns like he's gonna belt me one, then he clamps me on the shoulder and says in his gravelly voice, "No problem, Charly me boy. Get it outa the coffee money. Tell 'em Chief Bedrosian sent ya."

The Torch hits again on a Monday night, burning up a young wino in front of Sol's Sawdust Palace, and then he scores again on Wednesday about four A.M. in the morning, right after Les Dawson and Sonny Wicker come off arson patrol. The second case brings heat from the mayor's office. This time the dead man isn't a wino, he's a visiting businessman that's here for a pre-stressed concrete convention. Went slumming and had a few drinks too many, and when he sat down in a doorway to clear his head, the killer fricasseed him.

The next morning every brass hat above the rank of acting loot is called up to the mayor's office, and when old Nordquist gets back, he falls both companies in on the apparatus floor. "Pay close attention," he says. "The Mare says if something don't break soon he's gonna transfer every one of us."

There's a low grumble from the men, and Cap says, "Now wait a minute, wait a minute! I stood up for you, I said, 'Listen, Mr. Mare, it's your marshals and your arson dicks that're letting you down.' The superchief gets up and he says he transferred six deputy marshals into our district and that same night there was another Buddha. Remember? Mare says what good's it do to use the sniffers and the laboratory analysis and prove it's arson, we *know* it's arson soon's we see the body. Says what

151

we need is eyes in the field, *eyes in the field,* as many as we can get, and that means every man in this battalion."

"Unfair, Cap," Tyree says.

"Absolutely," Mike Mustache says. "A clear case of prejudism."

"Look, boys," Cap says, lowering his voice. "Try to understand. The whole town's on the Mare. Papers been screaming, TV, radio. Preachers been preaching about this torch, every do-gooder in town's been telling the Mare how to do his job. He's like a baseball owner. Things go cowshit, he fires the manager. He knows it ain't the manager's fault, but what's he gonna do?"

After the assembly Nordquist takes me aside. "Charly," he says, throwing his arm around my shoulder, "be ready."

"Whattaya mean by that?"

"The big chief knows you by name. He asked me who we got running Fire Five these days. I name you and the other two loots, and he says, 'Oh, yeh, Sprockett, he's been around a long time, ain't he?' I figure we got a week, Charly, maybe two. Then it's Fenwick Division for the both of us."

*Fenwick Division.* A nine-mile commute instead of a two-block walk to work. Nothing but industrial buildings and swamp and garbage dumps. I hope Cap's exaggerating, but knowing the superchief's problem, I can't be sure. The Robot, he'd transfer his own grandmother to Fenwick, he'd bring his wife up on charges. Superchief's beholden to the mayor, they're both political animals, they know how to keep their job.

Jeez, I hope I don't get transferred. I'd put in my papers is all. Somebody must need a security guard or a short-order chef.

I'm sipping a cup of Tyree D'Arcy's latest sheep-dip coffee in the scullery when I hear a commotion in the watch office, a bunch of guys talking at once, and I slide the pole and see the house captain's white head surrounded by firemen. "Get

152

your—get yourself right over here, Loo," Nordquist says. "Shake hands with your new probie. This here's Lulu Ann Tomkins."

I look around, but I don't see any Lulu Ann Tomkins. Where is she? Then somebody skips out from behind Nordquist, and it's a pigmy, a dwarf. She's been hiding behind a man that's only five eight himself. Dimunitive, I believe they call it, but she's got a handshake like a hod carrier.

So this is what's gonna back me up in fires? Not that I'd mind if she'd back me up someplace else, or even back up to me. She's at the most five three, five four, and she's got a little round micky face with freckles and a turned-up nose, bright blue eyes and a thousand red-brown wood shavings on her head, like a white Afro. She's wearing the pea-green suit that all probies wear, and the front of it's bulging. Trouble ahead. We don't have enough already? We got to get a probie with a built?

I mumble a few words and step back, and Ax moves in and says, "What's your name, honey?"

The probie looks at Captain Nordquist like he's her protector or something, and he nods. "Lulu Ann Tomkins," she says.

"Is that Miss or Missus?" Ax says. "No, wait. Why don't we just call you Lulu?"

"Why don't you just call her Firefighter Tomkins?" Cap puts in.

Tyree D'Arcy is introduced. "Hey, baby, what's shakin'?"

Lulu looks puzzled for a second. "Oh, you mean how'm I doing?" she says, and I notice her voice is slightly strained. "Fine, thank you." She's got a delicate accent, sort of like Jackie Onassis or Marilyn Monroe or an upstairs maid.

Sonny Wicker waltzes over and gets introduced and says, "Excuse me, m-m-miss, have you got a picture of yourself for the station b-b-bulletin? In a b-b-b-bathing suit?" Evidently he

153

forgot that Jumbo Esposito on "C" shift puts out the station bulletin, and our mimeo machine won't reproduce pictures.

"No, I don't," Lulu Ann Tomkins says, shaking her red ringlets, and old Nordquist snorts and says, "Of course she don't. Run a picture of Bedrosian's underwear."

Vincent "Plummer" Brown shows up, wearing a quart of Brut. "How ja do, honey?" he says, bowing slightly.

Lulu Ann's getting a little confidence, with Nordquist backing her up, and she snaps out, "Firefighter Tomkins, if you don't mind."

"Well, how do you *do*, Firefighter Tomkins," Plum says, his fangs dripping with Lavoris. "May I take the trouble to inquire as to your first name?"

"I was christened Lulu. Lulu Ann."

"Well, I must say you were well named." He turns around and leers. "Wasn't she, gentlemen?"

"Inevitably," Mike Mustache says, smiling like a bald baboon.

There's a tendency to diabetes in my family, and if I hear one more "I must say" or "Wasn't she, gentlemen?" I'm gonna puke. The probie's a hot little number, I'll admit it, but first and foremost she's a green pea and she's got to be handled like one or else we'll never get anything done around here, we'll all go off to Fenwick arm in arm doing high kicks.

"Firefighter Tomkins," I speak out as the loot on the shift, "if you'll come with—"

But Plummer's already stepped in front of me. "Allow me," he says, and he starts to heft her duffel bag. "What's in here?" he says, straining at the straps. "Silver service for the station?"

"I'll handle it," Lulu says. She grabs the bag by one hand and flips it over her shoulder and skips up the steps to the mezzanine, showing a dainty curve of ankle. Plum stands there in shock.

"Use to be a gymnast," Cap says. "They say she's tough as a buck."

"Good," I says. "She won't have any trouble humping hose."

"Or hosemen," Plummer puts in.

"She's here to fight fires," I says. "Keep it in mind."

"Hey, Cap," Tyree speaks up. "That chick ain't no five six. She's at least a inch under the limit."

"It's different for females," Cap says.

"How come? I thought the rules was the same for everybody." If there's anything Tyree hates, it's favoritism.

"We make exceptions for minorities," Nordquist says. "Otherwise you'd be out for being five two."

*"Five two?* Hey, Cap, I'm no five two!"

"Depends on how you measure," Cap says, tapping Tyree's gut.


Right after lunch the picketing starts, somebody must of phoned home. I look out the bullpen window and there's fifteen or twenty of them, pacing up and down in front of the apparatus doors carrying signs with painted messages. Would you believe it, there's Francine Bedrosian. Her sign says MY HUSBAND SLEEPS WITH ME NOT YOU. Well, there's no denying that. And she wears three sets of pajamas for the occasion, too.

Further down the line I see Theonia D'Arcy. Her sign says FIGHTING FIRES IS A MAN'S JOB. An award-winner if I ever heard one.

The guys crowd at the upstairs window and watch, and Ax waves a handkerchief and says, "Hi, Buckets!"

"Where's the probie?" I says.

"Doing what you told her," Plummer says. I guess he's taken

over as guardian angel. "Under the rig, waxing."

The house captain walks up to the window for a look, and I says, "Cap, what're we gonna do about this?"

"Do?" he says, like he's talking to one of the Jutes or Kallikaks. "Whatta you guys usually do? Play cards, eat, jack off."

"No kidding, Cap. We can't just let 'em walk up and down like that all day long."

"Why not?" he says. "They breaking the sidewalk or something?"

After a while the bell rings, one round of three. Les Dawson hollers up the pole hole, "Fire Five! Nine Avenue and the river." On the way out I push the acknowledgment button and we all hit the rig.

Firefighter Lulu Ann Tomkins is standing on the tailgate, completely suited up, with her turn-out coat over her green probie suit and her helmet down over her eyes. "Hey," I says. "Get offa there!"

"This is my assigned—"

"Get up in the cab!"

"But, Lieutenant, a probationary firefighter's supposed to ride—"

*"Ride up front in the cab!"*

I can imagine what's waiting for us when the apparatus doors swing open, with a pack of female rabble-rousers waiting for their shot. "Flog it hard," I tell Plummer. But our old Kenworth's been with the F.D. as long as I have, and it isn't designed for drag racing or running blockades.

We drive out of the station and the air's full of guided missiles, they're spattering off the windshield and ruining the new wax job. They're also ruining the three guys on the tailboard. I can see a stain running down Sonny Wicker's visor, and Tyree D'Arcy's shielding his face, and Mike's wiping his

156

mustache. All three of them look like we just flew through a herd of starlings. In a way, we did.

Plummer quick flips on the windshield wipers to spread some of the fruit salad. Very dignified. Fenwick, here we come!

*"Fire Five, Nine Avenue and the river,"* the dispatcher says. *"A barge."*

The Ninth Avenue wharf is where all the tooty-fruity cabin cruisers tie up and everybody meets for cocktails at eight and chases each other's wives around the poop deck. This time it's a service barge burning. There's petroleum products aboard, and it's swinging out in the stream by one hawser and getting ready to break loose and go bumping into all the other boats downcurrent, which could ignite them one by one and light up the whole damn marina. There's not much smoke, but from the squiggly refractions above the waterline, she's burning pretty hot below decks.

I can see this fire's got to be knocked fast, so I tell Tyree to drop the hard-suction line in the river and we'll go from there. Usually we prefer a hydrant, because river water's hard on equipment, but there's no time. I grab the charged pipe myself and tighten down the spray till we're dumping a pretty good load out on the barge, but most of it just skitters off the deck plates and into the river.

"We need an inch-and-a-half fog in the hold," Plummer says. Sure, but how're we suppose to stretch it? Three of the guys have been pulling on the hawser, but this barge must weigh five-hundred tons anyway, and it's not coming an inch our way, it's just swinging out in the current about six feet short of a Bertram boat that must go easy sixty grand.

"The hawser," a female voice says in my ear. "I can climb out the hawser." I halfway hear and halfway don't, I'm trying to figure how I'm gonna get somebody to dog-paddle out there

157

with an inch-and-a-half line. The current's fierce, the water's cold, and how's he gonna get up the slick side of the barge carrying a heavy hose?

"The nozzle!" the probie shouts again. "Let me take it out!"

I realize what she's suggesting, and I realize she can't possibly make it, she'll fall in the river and it'll be my ass for placing a recruit in unreasonable danger. But I also realize that this barge is about to ignite the whole fleet.

"Go!" I says. She grabs the inch-and-a-half and clips the nozzle to her belt and starts clambering out that hawser like a spider on a web. She's gone maybe twelve feet, not quite halfway, when another engine pulls up.

"Go, Lulu, go!" Plummer hollers, and a sharp voice comes back from the rope, "Tomkins to you!"

Two pulls and a heave and she's on the barge, shaking the nob. Sonny's so amazed he forgot to charge her line. "Water!" I holler. "She needs water."

The pipe jumps up in her hand—jeez, I hope she remembered to get a good grip—and she drops to her knees like she's wrestling a boa constrictor. Either they taught her or they didn't. We'll know soon.

She drags herself and the charged line six or eight feet and rams the pipe down a hatch. She must be hitting the fire dead-on because it banks down in about two minutes. The fireboat pulls up to finish the job, and Lulu Ann shinnies back on the rope. Ax gives her a hand up the side of the wharf and she calls out, "Lieutenant, this fire's tapped."

I turn around and see a dozen firemen standing there like guppies, opening and closing their mouths and nothing coming out. Live and learn, live and learn. Who'd like to be first to put the knock on the firebroads now?

On the way back I'm playing it cool. This fire department, it don't believe in stars, we don't recognize the hero concept, with ribbons and dingleberries all over your chest. Something like Lulu did, that's a day's work. But Plummer, he can't keep his mouth shut. "I don't believe it," he says. "Where'd you learn to be a nozzleman?"

"Nozzleman?" Lulu Ann says. "I'm afraid you've got me mixed up with somebody else." She dabs at her nose and squiggles over next to Plummer so she can make up her face in the rear-view mirror, and I'm halfway expecting him to drive us through a storefront any second, the way he's handling the rig.

"Well, you sure did a nozzleman's job today," the poor boob says.

Lulu Ann slides back to the middle of the seat and stares straight through the windshield. "A nozzleperson's," she says. "Try to get it straight."

It's just not the same around here any more. No, I'm not blaming Lulu. She does a good job, she don't lead the guys on, she stays in her private room off the mezzanine and studies her manuals, and when it comes to housework she can dust the ears off any of these jamokes. But she's still *here,* and it's flaking everybody out. Maybe things'll change in time, maybe the boys'll accept her as just another firefighter and settle down, that's what Cap and Chief Grant keep saying. Me, I doubt it.

Mike Mustache reads us his latest story for his author course, it's about a female fireman that saves the chief's life by pulling him out of a burning room. The story ends

> "After that, everybody respected her and stopped discussing her body, as her measurements were 36–18–36. She served a few more distinctive years and then married an explicit young firefighter named Michael Morenzi, the No. 1 man on the shift. They made a handsome couple and moved to a two-bedroom home at 413 S. London Ave. in the Maplewood section."

"Smash ending," I says.

"Thanks," Mike says. "I polished it up."

"Yeh," Plummer says, "it sure sounded Polish to me." I'm glad to see him join in the conversation instead of drooling

160

about Lulu Ann. Practically the sharpest fireman I got on the shift, and he walks around mooning and juning like a pimply-faced kid at the senior prom.

"Charly," he says to me, "I gotta have her. That firm little body. Those big jugs. Charly, she's killing me softly with her ass."

"Think of her in her turn-out gear," I says.

Plummer rolls his eyes practically out of their sockets and beats a fist into his palm. "Charly, that chick is better-looking in a bunking coat than Raquel Welch buck-naked."

"When did you ever see Raquel Welch naked?"

"Every night, man," Plummer says. I forgot about his dreams.

Later I'm laying in bed with my hands folded under my head, trying to remember the capital of Mississippi, when I hear these grunts and groans and a high voice mixed in with a low voice and I realize the wifes' worst fears have come true, somebody's got Lulu Ann in the sack. I sit up and listen. Plummer's going ooh and aah, and a squeaky soprano's saying, "Do it, do it, more, *more!*" Then she giggles.

I run over and find Plum in his rack alone, a neat row of sweat beads on his forehead. He's playing both roles himself. I wake him up before somebody throws a bucket of water on the two of him.

Then a pair of Lulu's pantyhoses disappear. "I know I didn't misplace them, Lieutenant Sprockett," she says to me. Never calls me Loo, like the rest of the shift. Keeps her distance. I imagine they advised her at training school.

"How d'ya know?"

"They were hanging on a line in my room."

"Who'd do a thing like that?" I says.

"Just about anybody, except maybe Wicker," she says.

"Thanks. You include the officers in that?"

161

She just taps her foot.

"Well, don't include me," I says, heating up. "I'm not your size."

"How about Firefighter Bedrosian? I hear he wears women's panties."

"Doctor's orders," I says. "How'd you find that out?"

"Plummer told me."

"Well, tell Plummer mind his own business." If there's anything we don't need, it's firemen telling tales. I can just hear him, he tags after her like a puppy. The other day she slides the pole, no big deal, and he slides right after her and calls out, "Hey, that's amazing! Where'd you learn to slide so good?"

Lulu says, "Oh, I just applied myself at training school, studied day and night, burned the midnight oil, read every manual I could get my hands on, and all of a sudden I could slide the pole." You can see she's onto Plummer's line of chatter. He starts to make some other clever comment, but she's already walking toward her private room, her little back-side twitching like a rabbit's nose.

The pantyhoses turn up under Sonny Wicker's pillow, and I call him in. "Look, Son," I says, "I know you got problems and I'm with you two hundred percent, kid, but this is no solution."

Sonny swears up and down he didn't steal the sox, somebody must of planted them there, somebody has it in for him because he's the only guy in the station Lulu likes, they're all jealous, etc. etc. and so forth. "Whattaya mean you're the only one she likes?" I says. This is big news to me, although I do remember she left him off her list of degenerates.

"On arson patrol the other n-n-night," Sonny says, "she told me."

"Told you what?" Jeez, could I be getting jealous myself? An old fart of forty-one?

162

"I'm not like the r-r-rest." He sounds half proud and half embarrassed.

I start to make a smart retort, but then I remember what Sonny's just went through, so I bite my tongue. Let him think he's a big hit with her. Let any of them think it, but for Chrissakes let's go back to being a fire outfit, not a singles club and matrimonial agency. Though like I said, I don't blame Lulu, it's everybody else that's to blame. Or maybe just human nature.

The other night she's on watch with Les, which she's answering the phones and he's supervising, since she's still in her probationary period. The phone rings and Lulu says, "Station Twelve, Firefighter Tomkins speaking."

The way Les tells it, there's a short conversation and then Lulu hangs up.

"What'd they say?" he asks her.

"If you must know, it was a woman," she says. "Asked me, 'You're a firefighter?' I said, 'Yes,' and she hung up."

"I think that solves the problem of the anonymous caller," I says when Les tells the story in the bullpen.

"That was a problem?" Plummer puts in.

"Hey, Plum," Mike Mustache says, "did she ever call you back that night?"

"If she did, ya think I'd tell you?" Plummer says. "Anyway, they got a probie at Twenty-one's that's screwing the whole shift."

"Yeh?" Tyree says. "What's his name?"

"And we wind up with the Virgin Mary," Plummer says.

"Listen, you guys," I says, "I'm getting sick and tired a this. Talk about something else."

"Yeh," Ax says, "fuck off, why don'tcha? All a ya."

Poor guy, he's been steamed for three days, but he's too embarrassed to bring up the incident, and we're too scared. He was asleep around midnight and the alarm rang and he wakes up a little late and realizes his pants and boots are gone. He's spinning around in his pink bloomers and looks under the racks and screams about how he'll pry the eyeballs out of the guy that snatched his stuff, and then he remembers he left it in the utility room.

By the time he recovers his gear, the Kenworth's halfway out the station. Ax figures he'll dress in the cab, only he can't quite catch the rig and we can't hear him hollering over the siren and he winds up chasing us down the middle of the street in his panties till he practically collapses.

A squad car rolls up and a cop says, "Can we help you, lady?"

Naturally the poor guy's spitting fire when we get back. "Buncha jerk-offs ya," he says after Lulu goes to her room. "Why couldn't ya slow, down?"

"We had to flog it, man," Plummer says, a twinkle in his eye. "That was an important service call we were making."

*"Service call?"* Ax bellows.

"Right," Plum says. "Some old lady stuffed the toilet at the train station. With her bloomers."

Ax makes a move on Plummer, but Plummer slides the pole and runs out in the alley. Poor Ax, he sniffs around for a few minutes and then stomps off to his rack.

I wait till morning to tell him he gets thirty gigs for missing the rig. A half a day's pay. I hate disciplinary chickenshit like that, but it's the lieutenant's burden. Rules are rules.

I tell him over the intercom.

The Flareman's revived his act, but not by popular request. It's not bad enough we got a psycho out torching winos and conventioners—twenty-eight bodies so far, including Loo—but we still got this weenie that throws flares into police stations and firehouses and anyplace else that people wear uniforms. The Little Sisters of the Poor is next, I guess. Last week he hit a National Guard armory, but your basic armory's just like your basic apparatus floor, there's nothing much to burn, so the thing just spluttered and flared out before 17's come in on a single.

Then last night he drops one of his flares down a grate in front of police headquarters, and the hot strontium flame burns off the jacket of a 7200-volt underground power line and the wire "takes off." The short circuit rips its way from building to building, sputtering and blowing the conduit and spewing out dangerous gases. Strictly a mask job, and even some of the guys in masks went down. When a buried cable takes off like that, you get terrific pressures that can buckle foundations, and all you can do is try to vent the gas till somebody kills the power. A few minutes before the electric company threw the master switch, the pressure blew a manhole cover six stories in the air, like a maple leaf. It come down near Chief H. Walker Slater, but the fire department got a tough break, it missed.

On the way back from that exciting adventure, we get special-called to a railroad warehouse in the freight yards, the place has been burning three hours and the upstairs is still pretty well involved. Engines 12 and 18 and Ladder 6 are there when we pull up, and Sonny Wicker and I put on masks because we been advised the firemen on the second floor are pooped.

We follow their inch-and-a-half up the stairs and tell them to take a blow. Sonny's got the pipe and we advance it into a room that's burning pretty good, looks like some of the fire load's still in the walls, and the ceiling's blazing hot and heavy. Sonny lays down a nice steady half-fog in a counterclockwise motion, hitting the floor and the ceiling, but mostly the ceiling, because then your water turns to steam and floats back down and puts out the floor. Double sudsing action.

Pretty soon the fire's blacking down, and Sonny and I are expecting to hear the warning bells any second, we been in our masks fifteen minutes. I step into the middle of the room and grab the nozzle and start spinning it around my head like a lariat, the water's spiraling out on all four walls and up to the ceiling like a backyard rotary sprinkler.

I begin hollering, "Yahoo! Yahoo!" underneath my mask. What the hell, there hasn't been much to cheer about lately.

Then I turn and see Sonny waving his arms over his head and I can hear the muffled sound, "Y-y-yahoo!" We keep this up until the warning bells, and as we're backing out of the room an ember slithers down the inside of my bunking coat and rests just above my bellybutton. I shove the nob inside my collar and douse it, but I'm a little late. I'll have a blister the size of a walnut.

As we leave, new guys from 12's and 18's move in, and it's only a matter of patience now, maybe an hour or so, and the fire'll be out. Chief H. Walker Slater's already told the dispatcher that it's tapped, which all our chiefs cheat on their tap times. This is for the benefit of the underwriters, keeps our rating up and our insurance down. Usually a chief'll call in that the fire's tapped, then turn to one of the captains or loots and say, "Okay, I got it tapped, now you put it out."

Some of the guys are ambling around the ladies auxiliary van, eating doughnuts and drinking coffee, so I run over to get my share, and I find Les Dawson being treated by an aid man. Les's face is blacker than Tyree D'Arcy's, he's scratched up, his nose is running like a deluge set, and his eyes look like a jack-lit deer.

"What happened, kid?" I says.

"Huh?" Les says. I can see he's spaced out.

"Porch steps gave way," the aid man says. "Fell in a burning coalbin."

"Porch give way?" I says like a dummy.

"Yeh," Les says in a fuzzy voice. Jeez, he's barely gotten over having his teeth knocked out at the Tivoli Hotel. Look at him: a man in constant search of an accident. "Hey, Charly," he says, wiping bloody snot with the back of his glove. "How late is it?"

"Two o'clock in the morning."

"Gee," he says, staring at the stains on his glove, "time sure flies when you're having fun."

One of the loots from 18's is off to the side talking to a deputy fire marshal, and I slidle over. "A squirrel," the marshal is saying.

"Gotta be," the loot says. "Hey, whattaya say, Loo?" he calls out when he sees me. "Thanks for helping." Not many officers bother to thank us when we're special-called, but this guy's an older dude like me, he's more interested in fighting fires than getting famous and rich.

I shake hands and meet the deputy marshal, and I says, "Which squirrel you guys talking about, the mayor or the superchief?"

167

They laugh, and the deputy says, "We were talking about the nut that set this fire. Look at that fence."

"Yeh," I says. The fence is woven wire, ten feet tall, with a three-foot angled overhang of barbed wire like a concentration camp.

"Way we figure it," the marshal says, "the perpetrator hadda climb over that fence, there's no other way."

"Why not just walk through the gate?" I says.

"This is a top security area," the marshal puts in. "Got it all sealed in. Been that way five or six months."

We stroll to a small blockhouse that's just inside the main fence and surrounded by another fence of its own, maybe seven feet high. "What's in there?" I says.

"Dunno," the loot says, "but—Hey, wait! Look!" The door's slightly open.

An old watchman comes puffing up and wants to know what's the trouble.

"Looks like you had a break-in," I says.

"Break-in?" He rattles the lock on the wire enclosure.

"Not there," the marshal says. "The inside door."

The guard opens the outer gate with a key, yanks the blockhouse door and pokes around the cinder-block building with his flashlight. "Whattaya keep in here?" the loot from 18's says.

"Dynamite, blasting powder, hot stuff like that."

"Anything missing?"

"Not that I can tell."

We crowd through the doorway and snoop around, nobody's nosier than firemen. Inside, boxes are stacked to the ceiling, they're marked "Dangerous" or "High Explosives," with big red skull-and-crossbones on some. I can see why the blockhouse is inside a fence that's inside a fence.

"Look!" the marshal says. He's over in a corner fiddling with a broken wooden box. "Empty," he says.

168

He holds it up and I take a look. The end's marked "Signal Flares, Emergency, FJX6. *Danger: Inflammable.*"

It looks like we found the Flareman's supply. Now all we got to do is find the Flareman.

I'm staring at the other loot and he's staring at me, but we don't say anything till we get back by the rigs. "You thinking what I'm thinking?" I says.

"Inside job?"

"Got to be. Who else could get through two fences like that?"

"Maybe a squirrel?" the loot says.

Right after we get back to the station, Nordquist calls me up to his room. He's sitting on the edge of his bed in his long johns, screwing his hearing aid into his ear. "Have a seat, Charly," he says. "Hear the latest?"

"Yeh," I says. "I was there when they found the empty box."

"No, no. I mean the latest Buddha."

"Tonight?"

"About fifteen minutes ago. They called me from headquarters. Cops found the guy in the basement of an abandoned house. Torched three or four days ago. Nobody even reported a fire."

"Holy balls," I says. I flop on the end of Cap's rack. "So we got two torches going full-blast?"

"Two? What makes you think it's only two? You know how these things work, Charly. One nut inspires another, pretty soon they're burning the whole goddamn town down."

"The domino theory," I says.

"Correct. Might be six, eight, ten nuts lighting us up. They had an arson fire on the 'C' shift last night, burned out a store. There's been three cars set off in the last week."

"The poor people's street opera."

"Yeh, only these cars weren't junkers. A brand-new Cadillac

169

Seville and a Porsche and a car from the Fish & Game."

"Any evidence?"

"A burnt-out flare in the Fish & Game."

"That guy hates anything in uniform, even cars."

"Hates it or maybe he loves it to death, who knows? Well, he's going good now. He won't stop till he's caught."

Cap turns out to be right, as usual. Within a week, three more fires start up with that same eerie red glow. A police car gets torched, a Coast Guard motor launch and then the craziest one of all. On the top of a weather station next to the Federal Building, thirty feet up a thin mast, the Flareman sets a fire in a little gray box that houses weather equipment, and it burns like a beacon before we can get it out. Who'd go to that much trouble? What kind of a fruitcake?

We're sitting in the scullery mulling things over, just the guys from Fire 5. Ladder 10's been keeping to itself lately, ever since Egan and St. Pierre were transferred out and word come down that Steicher's headed for a tour at training school. Give it another month, the whole damn station'll be just a memory.

"The way I figure it," Ax is saying, "no human could of shinnied that pole and set that fire. Had to be a bird, a large bird."

"A *trained* large bird," Mike Mustache says, looking up from his author work. "Hey, thanks, Ax, you just gimme the ending for my story. This guy, he's got a hard-on for the F.D., so he trains a falcon to carry railroad flares around and set fires where we can't get at 'em."

"No," I says, "it's a giant pheasant that got wing-shot by a fireman one time. Bears a grudge."

"I think you got it!" Mike says.

"Yeh, and you better get it treated," Plummer puts in.

170

"I still say it's a bird," Ax says. "Trained by one of your all-time great firebugs."

Wallace Fenstermacher pipes up. "First he trains the falcon to break into a railroad shed to steal the flares, then he teaches it to climb through the crawl space at the 14th Precinct and set one off, and then he trains it to throw a flare on our apparatus floor when you guys're out at a fire, and then—" He stops for breath.

"Look up a story called 'The Murders in the Rue Morgue,' " Les Dawson tells Mike. "That'll give you your ending."

"By Edgar Allan Poe?" Mike says. "Man, he's sure a magninimous writer."

Les looks up from his knotting and picks at a Band-Aid on his chin. "In the Rue Morgue," he says, "people kept getting murdered in odd places, like locked attics. They finally figured it had to be an ape."

"Yeh, I remember," Mike says. "Turns out there's one missing at the zoo, and—"

Ax interrupts, his eyebrows are beetled together. "You think a gorilla's setting these fires?"

"Let's go down to the zoo and do some interviews," Plummer says, stringing Ax along.

"A juvenile delinquent's more like it," Les says.

"Sure," I says. "A kid three years old, a war vet, hates authority ever since the sergeant bawled him out for messing his diaper."

"We'll check every nursery in town!" Tyree says.

Firefighter Lulu Ann Tomkins enters the scullery for her evening cup of coffee. Walks like a queen. Goddamn, she looks tasty even in a probie suit. "Hi," she warbles, and everybody grunts except Plummer.

"Evenin', may-am," he says in a fake Southern accent. "We

all is mighty honored by you all's company."

Lulu pours herself a cup and walks out without a word. "Gonna study some more?" Plum calls after her.

She nods and disappears down the mezzanine steps, and we hear her door close gently but firmly.

"I think you're getting to her," Ax says.

"No doubt about it," Plummer says, rubbing his palms together. "But I'm taking it slow."

I says, "Another fifteen, twenty years she'll be eating outa your hand, Plum. 'We all is mighty honored by you all's company.' Sound like a riverboat pimp."

Everybody giggles except Plummer. "Got a flash for ya," he says. Him and his flashes, he'd have a flash for Walter Cronkite. "A little more time's all I need, then—*wowwwwww!*" He makes a fist and screws it into the air, straight up. Such tenderness.

"Remember what I told you," I says sharply. "Don't probe the probie. The chief's dying to get something on us, the least little thing. Wouldn't surprise me if he sent Lulu Ann as a decoy."

I could bite my tongue. I promised myself not to knock senior officers in front of the men. Very unprofessional.

"Whattaya mean by that, Charly?" Ax says.

"Oh, nothing," I says, and head for my rack.

That Lulu's got us all acting weird, she brings out the beast. I wonder how long it'll take the guys to get back to normal. A year? Ten years? *Forever?* Well, it's not her fault. She's dead serious about firefighting, I learned that from my old pal Allan Grant.

"Had a long talk with your probie the other day," he says. "I wish all your guys cared as much as she does."

"About what?" I says.

"About the job. Doing things right. Making sacrifices."

"Shee-it!" I says. "What sacrifices did she ever make except sit up every night over the manuals?"

Grant laughs. "When she first applied, she was five two. A full inch under the female limit. Slept on a bare floor for a year to stretch herself out, then she came in and passed the physical. Her husband hated the whole idea."

"Husband?"

"Yeh, she was married. Broke up."

"I'm not surprised." I make a note to keep this titbit to myself. All that gang of hyenas need to know is our probie's a gay divorcee.

"Talk about motivated," Allen says.

"Yeh. I wonder what it is with her."

"Her motivation's in the genes, Charly. Her maiden name's Stieglitz."

"Stieglitz? She's the old chief's—"

"Granddaughter," Grant says.

Now I get the picture. Old Stieglitz's granddaughter. That's what they call breeding.

●

Two A.M. in the morning. The capitals aren't putting me to sleep, better switch to the presidents.

George Washington, 1789 to 1798. No, 1797. John Adams, 1797 to 1801, Thomas Jefferson, 1801 . . .

Goddamn, we got to get our ass in gear and catch us a firebug, at least make some progress. Wonder how many there are? Two, for sure. The Flareman and the Torch. They can't be the same guy, they got entirely different M.O.'s. One's trying to clean up Skid Row and the other's trying to repeal the law of gravity, crawling in and out of slits and up skinny poles.

Let's see, who came after Zachary Taylor? His girlfriend's husband? Jeez, I'm getting silly. Where's my watch? It's 2:08.

What's that noise?

I sit up in bed. Somebody's moving around in the hall. "Sshhh!" I says. Then I hear a snort. I tiptoe out and there's Plummer and Ax peering down the pole hole in their underwear. "Chrissakes," I says, "what're you two zanies up to now?"

"Aw, nothing, Charly," Ax says. "We was just—"

"Telling jokes," Plum says quick.

Something don't smell right to me. Who stands by the hallway pole to tell jokes?

174

"Yeh, just a little humor," Plummer says, talking out of the side of his mouth as usual. "This guy bought a new four-hundred-dollar hearing aid, and the other guy asks him what kind is it, and the first guy says quarter to three."

By now I can see Plummer's hiding something behind his back. A bottle, probably. What next? These two guys never had a drinking problem before. At least why don't they go down into one of the rigs or back in the compressor room like I use to do? Why stand out here in the open?

"Hand it over, Plummer," I says, trying to keep my voice low.

"Go ahead," Ax says. "He seen it."

"Seen what?" Plum says, backing into the wall.

I grab him by the shoulder and spin him around and snatch what's in his hand. It's the butt section of a fishing rod with a big Penn reel attached to it and a full load of monofilament.

"How they biting?" I says.

"I just bought this outfit today. I was showing it to Ax here."

"At two o'clock in the morning?" I says. "Where's the tip section?"

"Oh, the tip wasn't on sale."

"Not on sale?"

"He's going back when the tip's on sale," Ax puts in.

"You bought half a rod?"

"Can't resist a bargain," Plummer says.

I take a good look at the outfit. The reel's scarred and the wrappings are starting to unpeel. "Some bargain," I says. "This thing's been used."

"Used?" Plummer says, grabbing it out of my hand. "Well, I'll be dipped."

"They seen you coming," I says, taking it back. "Maybe it still works okay." I grab the handle, but it won't turn. Then I notice that the monofilament's stretched tight through the

175

pole hole and down to the apparatus floor. "What the—" I says, and I give the reel a hard crank.

A siren begins to moan.

"Cut it out, Charly!" Plummer says.

I crank harder, and the siren whines.

"Now you done it," Ax says. "Chrissakes be quiet!"

"What?" I says.

Plummer yanks the rod out of my hand and reels in about forty feet of slack line. Then the two of them lay on their bellies and peep down at the apparatus floor, and I flop alongside to see what they're looking at.

A sliver of light comes from the room on the mezzanine and a shadow moves fast along the far wall. It's Lulu Ann Tomkins, turning out in response to the siren. She's pulling her suspenders up over her bare shoulders as she goes down the short flight of stairs, and I catch a flash of white as she pulls on her bunking coat and jumps on the tailboard of the rig.

"Hot shit!" Ax says.

"Shut up!" Plummer says.

The probie looks as puzzled as I am. She backs off the tailboard and walks around the cab. Nobody's inside, so she marches along the aisles between the rigs and then reaches up and touches the siren. She takes a peep into the watch office, where Les is dead to the world, and then she pads back to her room.

"Okay, folks," Plummer says, standing up. "That's our show for tonight."

I steer the two of them into the bullpen by the elbows and shut the door.

"Plummer's idea," Ax says.

"You helped," Plum says.

Turns out these two kindergarden kids have worked their

176

trick twice now, and Lulu Ann has fell both times. They tippy-toe downstairs after her light goes out and wind a few turns of the fishing line around the exposed axle of the siren, then reel it back through the pole hole. Makes just enough noise to turn her out, she figures she missed the bells and the rig's starting to roll.

"Sure," I says. "Perfect. Terrific idea. But why? *Why?*"

"Didn't you notice, Charly?" Plummer says, grabbing me by the arm. "Didn't you see that gleam when she come down the stairs?"

"What gleam?"

"That was tit, man, bare tit! She comes down the stairs with her coat half off. Last night, man, we seen—"

"*The whole thing!*" Ax says.

"The whole thing," I says, flopping back against the wall. I can't believe my ears, I must be having a nightmare. "Why, ya coupla psychos ya. The chief was right. You're sick, you guys. *Sick!*"

"We didn't mean nothing," Ax says, hanging his clown head.

"Just jacking around," Plummer says. "What the hell, she's a probie, isn't she? We can't paint her balls, can we?"

"Look, you coupla turkeys," I says. "Slater's laying for us, right? Tried everything but the kitchen sink, right? Suppose he comes around some night and finds you assholes fishing through the pole hole?"

"We'll explain—"

"You'll explain nothing!" I says. "He'll take one look and send for the butterfly net. Me, I'm incline to write you up myself."

"You wouldn't do that, Charly," Ax whines. He's right, I wouldn't. I only said I was *incline* to. That's another argument

177

against late-blooming lieutenants—they got too many cronies. A good fire officer would break somebody for a banana nut bread stunt like this.

I confiscate the fishing outfit and put it in my locker. "Now if you're good little boys and don't look up teacher's dress," I says, "I'll give it back in a few months."

"Relax, Charly," Plum says. "You're beginning to act like a brass hat. We don't know you around here no more."

If I thought he meant it, I'd be pissed. But it's just that he feels stupid, it's tough to be exposed as a sex fiend and a peeping Plum. "Climb in your baby cribs now," I says. "Tomorrow I'll buy you both a dirty comic book."

"Fuck off, why don'tcha?" Ax says, but not very loud.

I look at my watch: 2:30 A.M. Another night of deep and restful sleep for the acting lieutenant.

I snap off the bullpen light and go out in the hall, can't resist one final peek down the pole hole. Who knows, Lady Godiva might be up and around. I'll have to talk to her in the morning about snapping on her bunkers before she leaves her room. Let's see, how'll I put it? *"Ar uh,* Firefighter Tomkins, the men'd appreciate it if you'd cover your knockers when you turn out." Not too diplomatic, no, but then I didn't ask to be a fire officer, let alone have to deal with the sexual stirrings of kiddies. Next thing we'll be having a panty raid . . . Against Ax.

Thought I heard something downstairs. A rat, maybe? Damn things been coming in from the alley in herds. Ought to set a few traps.

*Hey, wait!*

That little vent between the apparatus doors, it's . . . it's opening.

I'm punchy, I'm seeing things.

*There!* Another inch or two. What . . . ?

I slide the pole as quietly as I can, but my bare skin squeaks

178

where my underwear don't cover. I walk over to the doors. The vent's maybe ten feet up. As I watch, it opens a few more inches.

*Something dark's beginning to poke through.*

Can that be a head? I press against the bottom of the panel, trying to look up. If the head don't look down, it won't see me.

It don't.

Pretty soon he's through to his waist and I can make out the silhouette of a kid, about as thick as a hose line. Watching him squeeze through that opening is like watching a woman deliver a baby, except that he's stone-quiet the whole time.

I see him dip into his shirt front. A match flickers.

I slam the door as hard as I can with my open hand. "Get down offa there!" I yell, but the kid starts to squiggle back through the opening.

"Get down!" I holler, stomping my bare foot. He's slowly disappearing the way he came. I jump to grab him, but I come up short.

I'm trying to figure out what next—my brain don't percolate too fast at three in the morning. Then I see a blur out of the corner of my eye.

Something's streaking across the apparatus floor in a nightgown.

She uses the front fender of the rig for a springboard and flies through the air like Nadia Comaneci.

The next thing I see, she's bulldogging the kid back inside and the both of them are wriggling around on the floor. Her nightgown's shredded, but she's got the kid in a hammer lock. Tell you one thing, she's a legitimate redhead.

"Break!" I holler, like I'm a referee. I jump on top and pry them apart and sit on the kid's chest. He's still heaving and twisting like a beached tarpon, but he can't weigh more than ninety pounds and Lulu Ann's got him by the ankles.

179

I take a good look. He's black, he has one of those close-cropped hairdos that blacks use to wear when they were colored people. He looks familiar as hell.

By this time the guys are sliding the pole, trying to see what the commotion's about, and when they spot Lulu half naked, they reel back as though paralyzed. I mean, we all knew there was a pair of large economy-size tickets under that green-pea probie suit, but we didn't know till tonight that she's got a bustline on her like the lady we pulled out of the bathtub a few months back. She must wear those bras that flatten and diminish, rather than the kind that enlarge and enhance. Not a bad idea if you're the only woman in a firehouse.

The last man to slide is Plummer, and when he sees her he loses his powers of speech. He goes Puritan on us, takes off his pajama shirt and throws it over her. Good. Now we can look at the kid.

He seems to realize he's licked and stops squirming. When he stands up, with a fireman on each arm, I can see the railroad flare sticking out of his back pocket.

"Hey, man, that's—that's—" Tyree D'Arcy's stammering. "That's—the kid we showed through the station, Charly."

"What kid?" I says.

"This kid right here," Tyree says. "Don'tcha remember? Stood in the tiller cabin for a long time, said *brmmmmm?* Come in with a couple teachers and a buncha little girls?"

"Was that you, son?" I says.

He nods his head. He's not very talkative, I remember from his earlier visit.

Les Dawson's on watch, we get him to call the marshal's office, and while we're waiting Tyree questions the little punk. "You stole them flares and started a lotta fires, didn'tcha?"

The kid nods his head about a quarter inch.

"Where's your mumma and papa?"

Mumbles.

"Huh?" Tyree says, grabbing him by an ear. "Speak up!"

"Said they gone," the kid blurts out. The way he says "gone" it rhymes with "bone."

"Gone? How old're you?"

The kid turns up his hands. His education's been sadly neglected, he don't even know his own age.

He flinches when Tyree grabs the other ear. "Try again!" Tyree says, squeezing. *"How old're you?"*

"Eight. Twelb."

"Eight or twelve?" Tyree says, his voice cracking. "What kinda answer is that?"

The kid juts out his lower lip and stands there. His black eyes are rolling at the apparatus door. Fat chance he has to get away. Lulu'd be on him before he got around the corner.

"Where you live?"

"Junkyard." His voice shakes, he's trembling.

*"Junkyard?"*

The kid nods.

"Ain't nobody live in no junkyard."

"Ah does."

"Don't jive me, home boy," Tyree says. The kid starts to bawl.

"Get him a robe or something," I says. "He's shaking." It's unheated on the apparatus floor, cools down to fifty degrees at night, and the kid's wearing a thin short-sleeved shirt suitable for Rio de Janeiro, a pair of chino pants with maybe a dozen holes and rips, and high-top sneakers with both soles flapping. The rest of us are wearing even less, but we're not shaking like him.

"So that's the mighty Flareman," Mike Mustache says.

Les Dawson wraps a regulation blanket around the kid, and Tyree starts in again. I guess this is one of his specialties, grilling black kids. "Whatchew think you was doing, starting all them fires?"

"Playin'."

"*Playing?*"

"Yassuh."

"Where you come from, trash?"

"Done tol' ya. The junkyard. Got me a car to live in."

"You live in an old car?"

"Yassuh, me and my rat."

"Yo' rat?"

"Got me a rat."

"Where you live before the junkyard?"

"Down Souf'."

The marshals arrive with guns drawn. I guess Les forgot to tell them we had the suspect surrounded. "There's your man," I says. The deputies can't believe it either.

"Who made the pinch?" one of them asks me, pulling out a notebook.

"Tomkins," I says. "Probationary Firefighter L. A. Tomkins."

A dainty voice calls from the mezzanine. "Make it Fire Five," Lulu Ann says. "Just Fire Five's enough."

"How'd she do it?" Sonny Wicker whispers to me.

I point up to the vent. "Caught him crawling through that hole," I says. "Jumped up and grabbed his ass."

Sonny looks at the vent high on the front wall and turns to take another peek at Lulu Ann coming back down from the mezzanine in her green-pea suit. "S-s-sure," he says.

I look around at the guys. Two or three are in pajamas, the rest are wearing standard firehouse sleeping gear: long-john bottoms, Jockey shorts, fading boxer trunks and one in pink bloomers. "Chrissakes," I says, "let's all go upstairs and get dressed and make some coffee. This place's gonna be crawling

182

with marshals and chiefs and reporters and everybody else."

For the rest of the shift I'm up to my eyeballs in reports and explanations in triplicate. The main complication is trying to explain what Lulu Ann was doing at three in the morning watching the apparatus floor. "I knew somebody was zinging me," she says when I question her, "but I couldn't figure out exactly how they were doing it. Two nights in a row the siren went off just loud enough for me to hear. Well, I had to turn out. You know how it is when you're a probie, Lieutenant."

"Yeh," I says. A probie turns out if somebody burps. Missing the rig's thirty gigs when you're a regular firefighter, but when you're a recruit, it's the end.

"So I turned off the lights in my room," she goes on, "and moved my rack over by the door and watched."

"You must of seen me slide the pole," I says.

Lulu Ann laughs that musical laugh of hers. "Oh, yes," she says, and claps her hands in front of her face. "I thought to myself, *Now* I'll find out how they're doing it . . . Tell you the truth, Lieutenant, I was surprised to see you."

Naturally I got to play dumb. "I was just checking around," I says. "Thought I heard a noise."

"Then you walked over to the apparatus door and I looked up and there he was. Poor little thing, I feel sorry for him. Did he say he lives in a junkyard?"

"Yeh. Where'd you learn that jump?"

"The flying vault off the rig? Oh, that's basic stuff. I'm a gymnast, you know."

"Yeh, but ten feet in the air?"

"That's not much," she says, laughing again. "In high school we had a human pyramid. I had to vault fifteen feet off a slantboard to get on top."

"We could use some of that at fires. Climbing roofs and stuff."

"I'm available."

Later in the morning Cap Nordquist calls us into the bullpen. "Just got the Xerox from the marshal's office," the old man says, looking down at some papers. "Kid's eleven years old, small for his age, name's Jasper Lee Haymon. Run away from home coupla months ago."

"Where's home?" Tyree asks.

"Tupelo, Mississippi."

"Can't blame him much, a black kid in Mississippi."

"Anyway, they're trying to find his people, but he swears he don't have any," Cap goes on. "Got thrown in a juvenile home in Natchez, climbed through a drain and hopped a freight and never looked back. Been living in a junked Buick. Juvenile authorities picked him up here, too, held him a couple weeks till he run away again."

"That musta been why everything was quiet for a while," Mike Mustache puts in.

"You were right all the time, Les," I says, slapping Dawson on the back and making him drop a knot.

"How's that?" Cap asks.

"Les said it had to be a kid."

"A kid, a falcon or a gorilla, one," Ax puts in.

"Why'd he do it?" Tyree says.

"Oh, yeh," Cap says, "I left that part out. He liked uniforms. Crazy about fire engines and firefighters. Not much else to do around the junkyard, I guess."

"Did anybody ask him why he threw a flare in the station?" Plum says.

"Let's see, it's down here some place." Cap turns a page. " 'Subject was asked why he tried to incinerate Station Twelve. Answer: 'Cause you all drove away.' "

Jeez, I'm thinking, it's great to be loved.

For two, three days, there's a big hoopla in the papers and the TV news shows, but naturally no mention of the kid's name, since he's a juvenile. But there's plenty of mention of H. Walker Slater. His picture's on the second page of the *Herald.* CHIEF WINS MAYOR'S PRAISE. The local Eyewitness News does ten minutes on the case, and half the time's spent interviewing Slater on how he created the patrols that led to the capture. He didn't create them, Chief Grant did, and in the second place the arson patrols had nothing to do with catching the Flarekid, he waltzed right into our arms. Right into Lulu's, anyway.

Some of the coverage really puzzles me. "The juvenile was apprehended when he tried to enter Station 12 in the pre-dawn hours." Not a word about Lulu's vault, not a damn word. There's got to be a reason. Somebody at headquarters is holding back. *Why?*

Better put it out of mind. Pretend it's the army again. The dirt soldiers win the battle and the general gets promoted. *Que sera, que sera.*

I mean, I don't like the idea of female firemen any better than the next guy, but you got to give credit. What a vault!

Could of come down and cracked her ass. What an ass! Should of took a better look when I had a chance. That stupid Plummer comes running in with his pajama top. Standing in front of her like knighthood's still in flower. If she only knew the real Plum . . .

My date with the lady vetinarian don't take my mind off things one bit. Turns out she's interested in Ladder 10's Mexican hairless Pomeranian Chihuahua that sometimes clogs up our intake hose at fires. She says why don't they get a Dalmatian like the other firemen, they're a historical breed and very disease-resistant.

"Yeh," I says. "Eighteen's and Twenty's got Dalmatians. Ladder Twelve had one too, but it wasn't disease-resistant."

"Oh? What did it succumb to?"

"It succumbed to Charley Gallagher backing the rig over it."

"Horrible!"

"That was the Dalmatian's impression."

When I get home from the alleged date, I snap on the TV, and what hits me right in the eyeballs but H. Walker Slater being interviewed on a midnight talk show.

"No arsonist can stand up to the kind of pressure we applied," he's saying. "All-night patrols, extra manpower flooding the area, constant surveillance of every block of Skid Row. I knew we'd smoke him out."

"Smoke him out!" the M.C. says. He smacks the chief on the back and laughs. "But seriously, folks," the M.C. says in a voice you could pour on waffles, "we owe the chief here a big vote of thanks," and the camera sweeps over the audience and they're all jumping up and clapping. A standing ovation from three hundred old ladies with wigs.

"We'll bring in the other perpetrator, too," Slater promises. "The one they call the Torch." Everybody applauds again. I know I can sleep peaceful now. Whatever happens, H. Walker Slater's on the job.

I hope the Torch isn't listening. If there's one thing I know, it's never challenge a psychopath.

Mike Mustacci takes a call on our hot line. "Ax, it's for you," he hollers, and comes back to the apparatus floor with a funny look on his face. It's our second shift of the month, so we're polishing the rig—two and a half hours of ball-busting work with old-fashioned orange wax that the purchasing agent must get a ninety-cent kickback on the dollar.

"Whatsa matter with you?" I ask Mike.

"That was the anonymous caller, I'd bet on it. What's she doing asking for Ax?"

"Search me," I says.

"I was waiting for her to make one of her suggestions, ya know? Like meeting me later? But instead she just says, 'Excuse me, may I speak to Firefighter Bedrosian, plee-uz?'" Mike looks annoyed, we're supposed to share.

A couple hours later the hot line rings again, and this time I take the call and it's her for sure. I'd know that voice if it was coming up out of a mine shaft, we practically been around the world together on the telephone. "Oh, hi, hon," I says.

"Excuse me?" she says, the soul of dignity. "I wonder if I might have a word with Mr. Bedrosian?"

This time Ax talks to her for twenty minutes. "Well, what'd she have to say?" I ask when he gets back to the scullery.

188

"What's that suppose to mean?" Ax says, picking up a towel and worrying a saucer to death.

"Wasn't that the anonymous caller?"

Ax just wipes all the harder.

We go out on a false alarm and a trash can, and by then it's seven-thirty at night, the last half-hour of the long shift, and we're lounging around the bullpen in our surplus airplane seats. Plummer comes back from taking the lieutenant's exam, he's been trying to make the eligible list for two years, and now he acts like he passed.

"Did you tell 'em you're a sexual degenerate?" I says. "You get bonus points."

"I'm a fireman," Plum says, smiling at me. "Don't that cover it?"

"I dunno," I says. "At least, I knew a few firemen that wouldn't screw a sports car. But you—you'd give it an honest try, anyway."

Plummer just laughs. I can see nothing's gonna upset him tonight.

"What'd they ask you on the oral?" Tyree says.

Usually it's some silly question like what would you do if you responded in a ghetto section and the rig was shot at. Oral lasts fifteen minutes, and it'll wipe you out. I knew some guys would score ninety on the written, damn near hit a hundred on the physical and then draw a blank on the oral, just stand there and slobber while the three examiners try not to laugh. Then it's back to the drawing board for another year. Happened to me twice.

"They asked me to discuss why people become firefighters," Plum says.

I'm not surprised. Lately the oral questions have been getting peculiar.

"What'd you t-t-tell 'em?" Sonny wants to know.

"Oh, I told 'em it's eleven twenty-five a month, good job security, a nice uniform and—" He interrupts himself and clams up.

"And what?" I says.

"I didn't know how to put it in words," Plummer says, acting like he still don't, "but it's the feeling—like if people see you're a fireman, they figure—they figure you're okay."

"How little they know," Les Dawson says in a dry voice.

Mike looks up from his latest laundry board and says, "Hey, Plummer, did they ask you how come you're so different from the others?"

The buzzer goes off and we shuffle into the locker room to dress for home. I'm kicking off my Class "B" shoes and thinking, What would I say if they asked me a question like that on the oral? Why did I become a fireman, anyway? The money? Jeez, I can count, I'd of made more money waxing cars for twenty years. Was it the glory? Ask Ax, the night he saved thirty retarded kids and his wife wouldn't even wake up to hear about it. What drives us poor fools, anyway?

I remember one time I was chauffeuring Chief Allan Grant, back before they kicked him upstairs, and Al was saying he seen where a bunch of psychologists studied five-hundred firefighters and found out they almost all had trouble with their parents. "We were unloved," Chief said, "so we go through life trying to impress people with what good guys we are."

"You believe that psychological bullshit?" I asked him.

"What do I know? I'm just a worker like you, Charly. Gotta admit, the shoe fits a few guys I know. Always seem to be saying, 'See, Mom? See, Dad? See the rescue I made? See the fire I put out?' "

190

"Yeh," I said, "I know a few."

Al was quiet for a while, you could practically hear him mulling it over while we drove. Then he said, "Okay, Charly, let's check in. Drive nice and safe and I'll give you a cookie."

How I wish he was back at Battalion! But who don't?

I'm walking out the door when I hear a "Psssst" and see old Nordquist standing to one side in his civvies, looks like he just mislaid the winning ticket on the Irish Sweepstakes. "Hey, Charly," he says. "How about a beer?"

"Cap, whatsa matter?" I got a date, fool that I am, but there's always time for a brother officer, especially if he looks like he just climbed out of his own grave and shook off the dirt. He tries to smile, but his pink face winds up crooked. "Come on, Charly," he says, grabbing me by the arm, "we'll go to Joe's."

Cap's not suppose to drink or smoke, either one. Usually he goes straight home after a shift and sleeps practically around the clock and fiddles with his stamp collection till it's time to climb out of the sack and come back on shift. Anything to keep his heart pumping till he finishes out his years.

"Gimme a seltzer with a little bitters," Cap tells Joe, "and take care of my father here."

"What'll it be, Charly?" Joe says. I got a temptation to tell him a pousse-café with a zombie chaser, but I'm too puzzled about Cap to clown around. "The usual," I says.

"Lookit this," Cap says, passing me a slip of paper. It's been creased and recreased and fingermarked and splattered with

192

coffee and walked on by a team of draft horses, but it's dated today and it says across the top *From the Desk of H. Walker Slater, Battalion Chief.*

"Uh oh," I says, and start to read

Certain officers are not turning out for all fires, or loitering on the fire ground while their crews are penetrating. *This is absolutely contrary to department regulations.* With the personnel problem as severe as it is, no battalion can afford passengers.

Nordquist reaches across the paper, and his pudgy finger trembles as he points out the word "passengers." "That's me," he says. "Along for the ride."

"Cap—"

"Read the rest."

"Cap, you can't be turning out every fire, you're not a well man."

*"Read!"*

From this date, all officers will make a point to personally supervise their crews on all fires including singles. This does not mean loitering behind fire apparatus or remaining in the station.

"Cap," I says, "don't worry."

"Read the P.S."

It's scrawled across the bottom in oversize bold handwriting. "House captain chores are supplemental. Combat firefighting takes precedence. H.W.S."

"That's for my personal benefit," Nordquist says, sipping at his drink and spilling a few drops.

"Cap," I says, "I don't understand some of the things been going down lately."

"Well, I do, Charly. It's pressure stuff, politics. This Slater's an office pol from way back, he knows the routine, the sensitive nerves, he knows where the skeletons're hiding."

"Cap, haven't you got a rabbi at headquarters?"

"My rabbi was Chief Stieglitz, God bless 'im." He looks upward.

"Now listen, Cap," I says, not knowing what to say, "just leave everything to the rest of us. We'll take you inside the door, just out of sight. The way Steicher use to. We'll take care a you, Cap—"

"Goddamnit, I don't want anybody taking care a me!" the old man explodes, blinking his faded blue eyes. "I been in more goddamn fires than that punk Slater ever heard of."

"I know, I know." I'm trying to calm him down.

"I ventilated the Sentinel Hotel," he says, banging his hand so hard on the bar that Joe starts fixing a couple of refills. "I was inside when the Texas Building blew, I went through the roof at Morningside Gardens, I drug Middleton and Warner outa the Coliseum dead. Why, Charly"—he takes off his rimless glasses and wipes the sweat from above his eyes—"I spit hunks of my lungs all over this goddamn town fighting fires." He lowers his voice. "The wife's not well, Charly. I just wanta finish my pension time."

"I know, Cap."

He takes a deep breath and blows the air out in a narrow stream. "It's funny," he says. "Ya know who broke him in?"

"You?" I says.

"Down at Eighteen's," Cap says, shaking his head grimly. "Ten months I had him under me, when I was a truck lieutenant. I got his number, don't think he don't know it."

I'm surprised to hear Nordquist talking like this, but he's panicked, the poor old guy. Like he admitted to me one night, he could kick off right now. *Zip!* Lights out. A guy like that has got to face the truth every second, he can't go around kidding himself.

"Knew it when he come in as a probie," Cap says, leaning

an elbow on the bar. "Knocks on my office door, wants my advice on which manuals to study. Whoa, I says to myself, we got a student in the outfit, I wonder can he fight fires? I soon found out. He kept coming off the fire ground with his face all streaked, his gloves dirty, but nobody ever seen him in a fire room."

"He wasn't—"

"Faking it! My mother's grave! Rubbing dead coals across his face so he'd look like a fireman. Boys took it for a while, then they shoved him into a burning room and shut the door. Pissed his pants."

I've heard stories like this before: captains that're nervous climbing a ladder, chiefs that're scared to death inside, but I always put them down as malicious gossip spread by losers. But Cap's a straight shooter, always has been. He may be feeble and hard of hearing, but that don't make him dishonest. "Cap," I says, "the guy must of had talent somewhere."

"Oh, sure," Cap says, tilting his head to the side as though he's trying to remember. "He had potential, you could see that. And ambition. The American dream, ya know? Work your way to the top. Christ, you couldn't keep him home. He'd come in on the off-shift, polish the rig till you could shave in it. He did everything like it was life or death, ya know?"

"Except go into fire rooms?"

"Well, I'm not sure he could help himself. Some guys are sick, Charly. We all got our little problems." I think about my claustrophobia. When it hits, there's nothing I can do about it, no amount of guts or logic'll beat it back. Cap says, "I must of had him in my office ten times trying to help him out. 'Look, kid, relax! Don't be so pushy, Rome wasn't built in a day,' I use to tell him. He says to me one night in the watch office, 'Loo, I got one speed, dead ahead.' I says, 'Keep it up, son, and that's exactly where they're gonna find you.'"

195

"But, Cap," I says, "he musta done *something* good to make battalion chief."

"Listen, Charly, I got a spot on my bedroom ceiling I just about wore through, laying there thinking about it. Tests, yeh. Best test-taker we ever had. Hit ninety-eight on the written, ninety-five on the oral, made lieutenant in two years."

"The minimum?"

"The record. Nobody ever done it that fast."

"But as a combat firefighter?"

"Strictly below par."

"Why didn't somebody blow the whistle?"

"About laying back? You know the rule, Charly. Y'ever know a fink fireman?"

"Not many," I says, thinking about Steicher and his cronies. "How'd he do as a loot?"

Cap screws up his face. "Pure cowshit! Use to stand outside a burning building and holler, 'Come on, you guys! Get in there! Let's go!' I actually heard him holler, 'On the double!' "

What a joke. If you hollered "On the double" to Fire 5, you'd just slow us down. Our normal pace is on the triple.

"One night a truckman got fed up, Gerry Cohen, he says, 'Goddamn it, Slater, we put these fires out before you got here, man. Calm down, get ahold of yourself.' Slater transferred him out, and I transferred him back. Maybe that started the resentment, I dunno."

"Funny guy."

"Charly, he was a laughingstock! But he kept getting high marks on the tests, and he kept getting promoted, and he still does."

"Peter's Principle," I says.

"Guess so," Cap says, holding up two fingers for a third round. "We use to have an old Seagrave V-twelve, the most gutless wonder you ever seen going up a hill. Slater'd press on

196

the siren switch and drain off engine power till the rig was hardly moving. You'd look out the window and guys in wheelchairs'd be passing us on both sides, and the driver'd holler, 'Loo, take your foot off the siren, we're not gonna pull the hill!' Slater, he'd keep right on pressing. Ya know why? Because the manual says the siren—"

"—shall be sounded en route to all fires," I quote.

"No mind of his own," Cap says. "No guts either."

"Oh, he's got guts," I says. "I beg to differentiate on that one. Look how he's been going after Fire Five. Takes guts to be that dirty."

Nordquist's busy scratching his belly.

"At first I thought he had a hard-on for Ax," I says. "You know, a personality thing? But now I think it's the whole company. We just seem to aggravate him is all."

"You never seen the picture, did you, Charly?"

"What picture?" I says.

The old man turns and looks me straight in the eyeballs, like he's trying to check if I'm playing dumb.

"Walker Slater wasn't brought in to lead Fire Five," he says after a long pause. "He was brought in to kill it, to put you gung-ho guys outa business. Why d'ya think they put you in charge instead of bringing in somebody—bringing in somebody that was—"

"Qualified?" I says, knowing that Cap would never say it.

"You know what I mean, Charly," he says, laying his hand on my forearm. "Some hotshot with a big future. Not that you don't have a future, Charly, but—"

"I know what you mean, Cap. I wondered myself."

"A lotta guys hated the Fire Five concept from the beginning, you knew that, didn't you, Charly?"

Who didn't?

"I mean, right up to the Mare's office it was a political

197

football, am I right? Superchief never liked the idea, it was foist on him by the Mare, and everybody knows it. Now the superchief wants to dump the whole Fire Five, all three platoons, but he's gotta have an excuse, and the excuse is gonna be the system's not working."

"Worked pretty good the other night," I says. I'm beginning to feel defensive even though I know Cap is just quoting other people. "We caught the Flareman—*ar eh*, the Flareboy."

"Oh, yeh? Better check the official report on that one, Charly. All it says about the capture is, let's see, 'Suspect surrendered at Station Twelve.' "

"Jeez," I says, taking a long sip of ale, "maybe Slater's the Torch, j'ever think of that? Trying to make us look *real* bad?"

"Don't kid around, Charly. That sumbitch'd roast his mother if he thought he could get a promotion. He's not the Torch, he's the Hatchet. He was one of the first guys at headquarters that attacked Fire Five, said it'd cause backbiting and jealousy."

"Most of it by him."

"He'll bury you, my boy. Mark my words. Long after I'm dead and gone, he'll still be on your ass. That's the nature of predators, Charly." He shakes his head slow, mumbles almost to himself. "You don't know what it's like to watch a guy like that come up through the ranks, catch you, pass you, then one morning you climb outa your rack and he's your commanding officer. Helpless, Charly, helpless! Christ, I can hardly move around any more. I got pains in my chest, my arms."

"Angelina pectoris?" I says. That's what I heard.

"Yeh. And a touch of emphysema, a spot on my lung, the heartbreak of psoriasis. I got every thing but the berry-berry." He laughs at himself.

"Who told you? The fire doc?"

"You kidding?" he says, laughing louder. "I can't go near the fire doc. He'd retire me in a second. No, Bess has a nephew graduated from medical school, he gimme a complete work-up, EKG and all. Says I got five or six more years if I take it easy."

"How long if you don't?"

Cap shrugs his shoulders and slugs down his Shirley Temple. "Now, Charly, I got no call to complain. I'm almost sixty, I done plenty. But Bess, she's got the arthuritis so bad she can hardly pick up a fork. If I go on full pension, she's set for life. If I don't, she's gotta scratch around, and in her shape—" He runs his finger across his throat.

"No insurance?"

"All borrowed out. Maybe enough to last her a few years."

I look at my watch. "Cap," I says, "I hate to see you upset like this."

"Sure, Charly, sure." He pats me on the back. "You're a decent guy, Charly." He pats me again, like he's trying to comfort me instead of the other way around.

"Well," I says, feeling disloyal, "I gotta be running now, Cap."

"Heavy date?"

"Yeh. With the department dietitian. Can you believe it?"

I walk him back to his car. It's only two blocks, but by the time we reach his old Ford Galaxie, he's breathing hard. "See ya next shift," he says, flopping down on the sprung seat.

"I hope so," I says under my breath.


The dietitian turns out to be a pip, I would of done better dating Cap. All night long she's telling me what vitamins E and C and B will do for me. "Vitamin B as in beer?" I says. "Personally I prefer Vitamin A as in ale."

199

"Oh, by the way," she says, "if you drink beer, make sure it's German. The German brewers retain the yeast, the Americans use chemicals."

No kidding? How can I tell her there's not a guy in the station that'd drink a foreign product. We'll start drinking German beer the day we put a German flag on the rig.

Then she gets off on some business about how zinc reconditions the prostrate gland, and older men should take a daily supplement. Get that. *Older men.* For a second there I thought she was talking about me. Then it turns out she *was.*

Arson patrol's different now, no more driving up and down the streets in the bright red F.D. car, showing the flag. Now we use our personal vehicles, fifteen cents a mile reimbursement, and most of the time we're parked, slouched down in the front seat seeing what we can see.

Which isn't a whole lot lately. Skid Row's been deserted from sundown on. The missions, the Salvation Army, places like that, they're crammed with scared winos through the hours of dark. Plenty more left town, just lit out on the first freight. What the hell, a man should be able to drink himself to death without getting sautéed at the same time.

Ax and I are parked in my station wagon at the upper end of Coulbourn Place, which gives us a neat four-block view along the rainy street, and I'm trying to focus the binox. The dispatcher's quiet, our portable unit crackles and snaps. Ax is scrunched down in the passenger's seat breathing hard, and I'm filling him in about a date I had with a Red Cross lady, blond and thirty-four years old and wears glasses but they don't distract from her looks. "We're wining and dancing," I says, "and then I waltz her to her apartment and she's got an upright piano against one wall. She pours us a drink and lights up a chemical log in the fireplace and starts belting out operatic arias."

"What's arias?"

"Songs."

"Then say songs, why don'tcha?" He sounds sleepy.

"So I sit next to her on the piano bench, sipping my San Sebastiani and listening to her sing, and after a while I notice she's developing an English accent and I'm developing a soft-on. She can hit G above high H, but only mice can hear it. Dizzy broad, she musta broke every wineglass in the apartment house."

"*Zzzzzz,*" Ax comments.

"I finally make my move and she says, 'Oh, not tonoit, dawling, Oi'm just totally exhausted don'tcha know but Oi do hope you enjoyed moi little recital?' Me, I figured the fire log and the wine was leading me on, right? An open invitation, wouldn't you say, Ax?"

Ax wouldn't say.

"Jeez, I dunno, it's getting like the fifties, you had to have a lock and a key to get in a broad's pants. I'm gonna have to give some real thought to the priesthood."

I look over. Ax's mouth is wide open and I can see all the way back to his gold crowns.

"Ax?" I says.

Usually he's picky about where he craps out, but lately we been making so many arson patrols, the whole station's got the sleeping sickness.

"Ax?" I give him a nudge.

"Huh? What time is it?"

"Ten after two." I spot something moving. "Hey, take a look. The next block. The alley past the Harbor Light Mission. What's that sticking out?"

Ax pulls himself up in the seat and adjusts the binox. "God-damn," I says, "you got to change the focus every time?"

202

"You're going blind, Charly."

"Bullshit," I says. Maybe he's right, lately I've had trouble seeing in the distance.

"Yeh, it's . . . something," Ax says. "A rock. No—a foot. Charly, it's a—oh, shit!"

The flame shoots up yellow and blue like somebody's lit a bonfire. It's about a fifteen-second drive, and Ax grabs the hand extinguisher and jumps out of the car before we stop. I alert the dispatcher and run after Ax. Nobody else is in sight, there's a short alleyway in the back, but it's empty.

He puts out the fire in a couple of seconds, but the clothes are already burned off the poor guy. I throw a coat on him, it's cold and rainy, he's quivering. *"Ba ba,"* he says. *"Ba ba. Ba ba."*

Slobber comes out his cracked lips, his face is covered with reddish sores, his hair's gone, if he ever had any. It's maybe thirty-five degrees out and he's barefooted, his feet look like blue lumps, the toenails are curled up and split. He reeks of booze and gasoline.

I lean my head down close. *"Ba—ba,"* he says. "Ba—Ba—Bible." Pathetic old wino, he wants his Bible. Poor man, he knows he's done for.

The aid car pulls up while a crowd of derelicts watch from the windows of the Harbor Light, too scared to come out on the street even when it's crawling with men in uniform. Paramedics slap oxygen on the victim and load him into the ambulance.

Everything's under control, so I take a little stroll down the alley to see where the Torch made his getaway. There's nothing much to see—the whole alley extends maybe fifty feet into Plains Street. All the guy had to do was run out the far end and hop into his car and he'd be nine miles away by now. I guess

203

the marshals and the cops realize it too. There's a couple of them checking the alley, but their heart don't seem to be in it.

Wait a minute! I was wrong, this alley don't exit into Plains Street, I was thinking of the next one over. This alley dead-ends at a brick wall.

Jesus P. Christ, we had the guy trapped! Me and Ax! We had the guy that killed Loo and all the others!

Don't say anything, don't let on. Besides, what were we suppose to do, let the victim burn up while we chased the Torch?

Some would say, Yeh, right, you should of. H. Walker Slater, for one. Except if we chase the Torch, then we neglect the victim. How can we win?

I check the back doors that open on the short alleyway. There's four of them altogether. Two are padlocked, warehouses probably. One leads down three or four moldy wooden stairs into a subbasement of a sporting goods supply house, Patry's.

The door's already a few inches open. I pull it back and step inside. It's black down there, and somebody's breathing, I can hear it plain. "Don't move!" I yell. My voice cracks like a kid.

"Calm yourself," the voice says. "It's me. Troski." A deputy marshal.

"I know, I know," I says, trying not to sound too stupid.

"You thought I was the Torch, didn't you?" Troski says. "What were you gonna do, Charly, hit me with your purse?"

Always was a smart-ass, even when we were at 17's together.

"Anything in here?"

"Nope. It's a loading basement. Empty. The inner door's locked tight."

I go back outside. There's one more door in the alley, and

204

it leads into the Harbor Light Mission. A waste of time checking there.

*Hey!*

That Torch disappeared awful quick. Where'd he go? He couldn't get out the end of the alley unless he's a lizard that can climb walls, he couldn't go through two padlocked warehouse doors and he can't be in the subbasement of Patry's because Troski checked down there.

Where else?

He escaped into the Harbor Light!

He's a wino himself!

"Hey, Troski," I holler, running back to Patry's just as the deputy marshal's climbing outside. "I got it!"

He listens patiently while I tell him the Torch has to be a wino that's got it in for the other winos. Maybe he's not even a legitimate wino, just pretending to be one.

"How ya figure?" my old friend says.

I tell him my door theory, how there was only one door the Torch could of escaped through, but Troski interrupts me. "There's one other way he coulda escaped," he says. "Right down Coulbourn."

"With me and Ax coming at him the whole time?"

"It's a dark night, Charly. You can't watch everything at once."

I know better, but what's the use? If a mouse moved down that street, Ax and I would of seen it. Wouldn't we? The Torch went into the Harbor Light, I'm sure of it. *He's there right now.* But what do I know? I'm just a stupid fireman.

By the time we get back to Station 12, Battalion Chief H. Walker Slater's arrived, his blond hair mussed, skin flushed, collar open, like he just finished a marathon. He's pacing up and down the scullery cursing. "Goddamn it, somebody'll pay for this! Where was Nordquist? Where was Fire Five? Who can I depend on around this goddamn place?"

"We were there in seconds, Chief," I says. "The Torch got away, that's all."

*"The Torch got away,"* Slater says in a female-type voice, mocking me. "Well, why didn't you do something, you—"

"Easy, Chief," somebody says.

"Chief?" Ax starts to put in, but Slater struts right past him.

"I'm putting this company on notice," he says. "The next time an arsonist hits in this district, I'm shipping the whole outfit out. *The whole goddamn outfit, ya hear me?"* He's practically screaming by now, his bass voice is up to Irish tenor. "Fenwick's not far enough," he says. "I'll ship you guys so far you'll beg to be transferred to Fenwick."

"Chief," I says, "take it easy."

"Done what we could," Ax mutters.

The other guys are lurking around, trying not to be seen.

They don't dare go back to their racks, even though it's four in the A.M. Nobody sleeps when they know the battalion chief's in quarters, especially when the battalion chief's yowling like a maniac.

"Chief," I says, trying to keep my voice moderated, "we're not fire marshals."

He don't seem to hear. He flops down on the bench and puts his head in his hands. "More goddamn fire loss than the whole rest of the city," he's saying. "Buncha pussies."

"Chief—"

"Be quiet when a chief's talking!" He jumps up and shakes his white hat at us. *"Pussies!"* he screams.

I want to tell him, "Chief, you're overwrought, you're not *well.* Chief, you need help, you need a doctor," but I don't dare. The shape he's in tonight—I know I'm suppose to hate his guts, but instead I'm feeling sorry for him.

At the staircase, he turns to look back. His face is twisted, his light hair's messed up where he's been running his hands through it. "I know what you're doing," he says, looking around the room. He seems to be making an effort to hold down his voice. "It won't work," he says. "I got means, I got means . . . " He goes down the steps and out of sight, still muttering.

"What's that all about?" Cap Nordquist says, coming out of the crapper.

Before anybody can explain, Mike Mustache calls up the pole hole from the watch office, "The wino's dead."

Christ, I says to myself, so's Fire 5.


The story's splashed on page one, and if Skid Row had the jitters before, the place is epileptic now. I guess the public figures there's no way to stop the Torch, not if he can strike

207

right under the nose of two firemen. Cops are walking their beats two by two and three by three, some with dogs, and there's so many undercover cars crawling up and down the streets, they almost create traffic jams at dawn, and still an old man dies.

Two days after the Torch's latest murder a wino runs into the station, hollering, "It's him, it's him!"

I'm talking to Ax in the watch office, and we grab the guy and steady him down. He's wearing sneakers and no sox, he's got half an ear, and he's holding a bottle in his trembling hand.

"It's who?" Cap says.

"Torchman," the wino says. "Right down the block. Tried to get me, dirty bastard!" He points a shaky finger. "There!"

Ax is out the door like a scalded giraffe, I guess he figures he's gonna make up for the other night, and I'm right behind him, I guess for the same reason. There's nobody in this house that wouldn't knock down a mother superior to catch this crazy nut.

We run up to the Torch. He's another wino, maybe thirty-five or forty, it's hard to tell when they're so wrecked. One lens on his glasses is cracked and taped. "Up against the wall!" Ax says.

"He's already up against the wall," I says. The guy's so up against the wall he looks like he's part of the bricks, slumped there with his pants dangling loose in sprung suspenders.

"Oh, right," Ax says. Haven't some of the union guys argued from the beginning that firemen aren't cops and cops aren't firemen? We don't even know how to make an arrest without making fools of ourself.

"Where's the gasoline?" Ax says, sticking his nose up against the wino's and then quick drawing back.

"Hey, man, spare a quarter?" the guy says. His head's wobbling like it's on a spring.

Our informer comes lurching up. "That's him," he says. "That's Torchman."

"How d'ya know?" I says.

"Stopped me when I passed by," the old man says, standing like the leaning tower of Pisa. "Sez gimme a match."

"Fer my fuckin' cig'ret," our prisoner pleads. His pupils are rolling upward into his head.

"He wanted a light?" Ax says. "That's all?"

" 'At's when I run," the older wino says.

"Jesus Christ," I says, and Ax and I sprint back to the station. If the alarm had went off while we were gone, it'd been both our ass, especially mine.

That afternoon we get a V.O.D.G. from the superchief's office. "Every firefighter in this command is under an obligation to apprehend the perpetrator," the message says. "We *will* apprehend the perpetrator." He don't even bother to say what perpetrator he's talking about, you'd have to be blind, deaf and dumb not to know.

Looks like everybody in town's flipping his gourd, except one man, old Mr. Perpetrator himself. He flipped his a long time ago.

The next night, with "A" shift on duty, the Torch broadens his operation. He goes to a hustler's room in a seedy hotel, breaks a lamp over her wig and burns her up with gasoline. In the resulting fire, three others die—an elderly saleslady, a Filipino cook and a police sergeant's widow. That brings his known victims to thirty-four, counting the Tivoli Hotel.

While "A" shift's working the fire, somebody drops a note on Station 12's apparatus floor.

209

The Son of man shall send forth his angels, and they shall gather out of his kingdom all things that offend, and them which do iniquity; and shall cast them unto a furnace of fire . . . Matthew 13: 41-42.

Beware of a Torch quoting Scriptures.

A chief's drill usually lasts an hour, maybe an hour and a half, but we been out in the snow and ice in front of the station for two hours already. I wouldn't mind if it was a dry hose drill, but we got almost every inch of line laid and charged, our ladders are off the rig, we even got a deluge set going. If we catch an alarm, it's gonna take us a good three minutes to recover enough equipment to roll.

The underwriters'd pass out. They got a rule, never lay more than half your hose in a drill. And that's dry hose drill. With wet, you shouldn't lay more than a third, a quarter, because it's harder to recover if you got to go. Me, I don't think we should bother with wet hose drills in the first place. Just lay your line, check your couplings, make sure everybody's in his right position and pretend to turn the water on. What's the difference? Then you don't have a half a mile of soggy line to dry out in the tower.

Tyree clomps past me carrying a bundle of hose. "My fault, Charly," he says as he passes.

"Negative," I says, loud enough for Tyree to hear but not Chief Slater.

Right at the start of the drill, with the chief looking like he's retaining an enema, he'd jumped Tyree hard. "Goddamn you, D'Arcy, can't you tighten a coupling?"

"Chief, I'm not in this evolution."

"Don't talk back!"

A few minutes later he orders us to recover our line. Fenstermacher and Lulu Ann hump a thousand feet of inch-and-a-half back on the hose bed, but he makes them so nervous they put it on with the couplings backward. When the last flake's in place, Slater points out the mistake, jots something on his clipboard and tells them to start over.

After a while we settle down, we're drilling smooth, everybody's doing his job, and I figure the chief's got to give us an approval any minute. It's after two o'clock and the shift should of ate lunch two hours ago. I never knew a chief to deliberately drill you through lunchtime, but when I bring up the subject Slater says, "Sprockett, fires don't start at your convenience." I don't get the logic.

At two-fifteen he struts over to me and says, "You people need a lotta work, a lotta work."

"Who people?"

"Whole goddamn outfit." He heads back inside the station. "I'm going upstairs. Keep drilling."

We go for another half-hour in the cold, and every once in a while I see that slicked blond head up at our scullery window, sipping coffee and watching. I hope he's warm and cozy. I'll have to remember to hit him for the clutch money.

All of a sudden I'm drowning, a defective coupling worked loose at the pumper. Nobody's fault, but we got to shut down the hydrant and fix it.

Turns out the washer's shot. Ever since the budget cuts, we been using equipment a bunch of volunteers would be ashamed of.

I look up at the window. Slater's scowling. He looks like a British general reviewing barefooted gerkins on the late late movie. Instead of standing up there like Mary Queen of Scot, why don't he go out and get us some decent equipment?

Lulu Ann comes by, humping about eighty-five pounds of wet line. "This is so much fun!" she says. She heaves it up on the hose bed and runs back for more. I'm watching her little backside do its Turkish belly dance underneath her green-pea probie suit when Fenstermacher jumps out of the cab and hollers, "A run! A run!"

I peek at my watch: 2:27.

"Let's go!" I call out. It's 2:31 before we recover enough line to roll.

The fire's six blocks away, in the industrial section. It don't look like much when we pull up, but there's a problem. The building's a long two-story tire warehouse, the fire's square in the middle, and we only got two narrow exposures to work from, the front entrance on Hanaway Boulevard and the loading area a block through on Oxford. Buildings like this are outlawed by the city fire code, but they still get built. It's like fighting a fire inside a tube that's only burning in the exact center.

"Ax, you and Les hit the roof," I yell. "Everybody else mask up." Tyree and Sonny Wicker are off at the hydrant, about forty yards away, and we get pressure quick. Out of the corner of my eye I see Cap Nordquist hurrying along, a mask covers his pink face. He must of come in his own car or the station's —it's been a long time since I seen him in action.

"Cap," I says, "we can handle it."

"I'm going in," the old man says.

Plummer and Mike Mustache hump the inch-and-a-half with Cap directing them, and Tyree and Sonny drag the wet two-and-a-half with me on the pipe.

By the time we push through the door, thick smoke's rolling across the floor. We're in an office, but there's no open flame. Then we burst through another door and into the main part

213

of the warehouse and a blast of hot air almost knocks us down. Out ahead, I can see a scarlet glow, so I motion Tyree and Sonny to the deck and go to work with the big nozzle, sending a long plume of water in the direction of the fire. Our other crew sets up alongside with Cap.

"We're not reaching it!" Tyree yells through his face-plate.

Cap Nordquist calls out, "It's easy another hundred feet." He's breathing hard. "We're gonna move up!" Sure, Cap, sure. Before I can say a word, he's headed into the smoke with Plummer and Mike. They're throwing out a fog from the Elkhart nozzle, you get a little extra oxygen that way, but not a drop's hitting the fire source.

"Come on!" I says, and we chase after Cap's crew with our two-and-a-half. It's elephant duty dragging one of those big lines when they're charged, plus our ordinary turn-out gear weighs maybe thirty pounds and the air tank and mask another thirty, so we're each hauling an extra sixty pounds dead weight. I can see the strain on Tyree and Sonny as they pull at the hose straps, and I try to help as much as I can, but there's a limit to how hard you can work in a mask. It seems like hours before we pull up behind Cap and Plummer and Mike and start throwing water.

We still can't see the flames. The smoke's billowing out and somewhere ahead of us there's a dark reddish tinge, but the rest is pitch-black. No matter how bright the sun's shining, it's always four o'clock in the morning in a fire room. To add to the fun, my radio quits cold. I can't transmit, can't receive. More of our top-grade equipment.

Jeez, it's boiling in here! One by one the guys rip off their masks and sprawl over their lines. Not worth the work to run back for new canisters. Better to breathe the smoke and try to bank the fire down quick.

But it's no pussy, this fire. Sparks shoot off the walls and up

214

ahead a pillar of flame jumps out of a pile of tires and licks clear up to the roofline. The visibility's getting better but the fire's getting worse. That's the firefighter's curse, you usually have one or the other. Tires are burning, hundreds and hundreds of truck tires. Not easy to ignite, but twice as hard to put out. And the stink! Christ knows what gases we're breathing. In this jammed warehouse there's gonna be plenty of incomplete combustion, and that means carbon monoxide, colorless, odorless and tasteless, the sneaky assassin.

I take a good look at my crew, check for the cherry-red complexion. Everybody looks healthy, even Cap. His mask's off and the sweat's pouring down his round face and he's breathing hard, but he's smiling. "Hey, whatsa matter with this fire, Loo?" he calls out.

I know what he means. Usually when you hit a fire with a two-and-a-half and an inch-and-a-half at once, it gives up pretty fast, but this damn load's getting fatter and fatter, we don't seem to be gaining an inch. It's like a big fat heavyweight fighter that don't give when you hit him, just stands there and keeps ducking. These high-powered hoses create a draft of their own that pushes flame out ahead, but this fire's blasting right back in our faces no matter how much water we throw.

"Keep slugging," Nordquist calls out, and I says, "What else?" and we're all sprawled on the floor wrestling the lines and throwing Niagara Falls. Five minutes goes by, ten minutes, and the smoke starts up again, so thick I can hardly make out Cap's yellow helmet right next to me. Without thinking I beat at the smoke with my hands and I see Cap dragging the pipe up toward the source, with Plum and Mustacci humping for him.

"Cap," I holler, "let me!" But he don't even turn, and they disappear.

"Hope they don't get outa range," Tyree says.

"Somebody's gotta m-m-move up," Sonny complains. "All

215

we're doing is t-t-teasing it." Typical Fire 5. Never happy unless their ass is on fire.

We stay huddled on the floor for another three, four minutes. Tyree relieves me on the pipe. He straddles it in a kneeling position, and Sonny and I pinion it down with our full body weight. I never seen so much water do so little good. Once in a while there's a whoosh and the smoke opens up and the flame flashes back over our heads. Must have something to do with the way the tires are stacked. Flue effect, maybe, the fire heats up in the middle of the stack and blows out the top like a geyser. Faintly in the distance I can hear eight straight blasts on an engine horn, somebody's starting up a Stang water cannon, that's the signal. Probably damping down the roof.

"What next?" Tyree yells.

"Keep working," I says. "I don't know what else." We penetrated, we're putting water on the fire, that's all you can do. Elementary.

*Goddamn!* I rested my hand on the floor, now it's scalded. Our own water's boiling back at us.

"Look out, Loo!"

A blazing joist flops a foot in front of us. Tyree drenches it with the hose and then raises the nob toward the fire. "It's right over our heads n-n-now," Sonny says.

"Choke down a little," I says to Tyree. "Aim straight up a minute."

Tyree points the nob at the ceiling and drills a hole in the smoke, and we can see flames licking along the two-story ceiling. Another joist's about to tear loose.

I'm baffled. Why's this fire bearing down on us? Fires don't travel up water, they travel away from it. This is against nature. Right down our lines! I try to give an order to back up, but no sound comes out, my voice box is as dry as a prune.

Up ahead I can make out the dim silhouettes of Cap and

Plummer and Mike. The old man seems to be in some kind of trouble, they're yanking at him, and the inch-and-a-half's swishing around, ruptured, spraying in all directions. Just in front of them a wall of flame's coming like a steamroller. The whole crew's on their hands and knees when they finally get to us.

"Shut down our line!" I croak to Tyree. The way this fire's moving, we'll be lucky to save our ass, let alone the hose.

"How's tricks?" I croak to Plummer. He can't talk either, his face is dark from rubber soot and he jabs at his throat with a gloved finger.

Mike stands up, the tips of his mustache gone again, nothing new for him, and he says, "We're okay, we're okay."

The five of them crawl toward the exit door and I drop to the floor to follow down our lines. The smoke stinks and hurts, it's oozed right down to floor level. I take a deep breath and feel it in my toes. I get back up on my hands and knees, the fire's all around me now, it's driving along both walls and the ceiling like somebody's pushing it with a big bellows.

I retreat ten or twenty feet down the line and then bump into a body.

"Cap!" I says.

His yellow helmet jerks around.

"You okay?" I says.

I get a good look at his face. He looks frazzled and snotty, like the rest of us, but he has a silly smile. "Keep crawling," I says, motioning toward the street. "That's it, Cap, keep moving." I follow along behind, keeping him in sight in the heavy smoke.

Just before we get to the office door, Cap takes a bellywhopper. His mouth's wide open, he's breathing like a beached porpoise. "Get up, Cap, get up!" I'm yelling, but not much sound comes out.

217

I try to pull him, but I barely got enough strength left to haul my own weight.

He raises himself up on his hands, like he's trying to do push-ups. Then he slumps flat.

*"Get up, Cap!"* I says, yanking at his belt. Things go black, then red, then the whole world's a Christmas tree.

I grope for the line to get my bearings, if I can't follow it by sight I'll follow it by feel. Cap's stranded in front of me. Gotta crawl around and get some help.

I blink my eyes hard, water pours out of them and out of my nose and all the fluids from my eyes and my nose join what's dribbling out of my mouth.

I feel my stomach start to contract. My head's heavy on the warehouse floor, I'm gonna inhale my own vomit.

*Where's Cap?* He's got to be just ahead. I raise up and start crawling, I'm swimming the sidestroke. I kick and shove with my feet. Am I moving?

Then the smoke clears a little and I can see the flames licking over my head, and I can't budge, it's taking all my strength to keep from blacking out. Maybe I'll burn to death, but by God I'll stay conscious.

A hand clamps on my arm and I'm dragged outside like a rag doll.

I open my eyes and see Ax. How much time's passed? Where's Cap?

"Where's Cap?" I says, trying to get up and falling back.

Ax leans over me. "What?" he says.

*"Chrissakes, where's Cap?"* I scream, but my vocal cords aren't doing the job.

They prop me against a wall, somebody mops my face with a towel, and I look up and see Cap kneeling there, big as life, dousing his sweaty white head in a leaky line. Old firedog! Last I saw him, the angels were warming up for a Requiem Mass.

218

Very beautiful, only somebody forgot to tell the guest of honor.

"How'd he . . . get out?" I croak.

"Crawled," Les says.

"Old fart's tougher'n home cooking," Ax puts in.

Cap wobbles over and looks at me through red eyes. If he don't watch out, the Torch'll get him, thinking he's a uniformed wino. "Through for the night?" I says weakly.

"Maybe you," Cap says. He turns away and coughs, and it sounds like he's gonna pitch up his lungs.

I hear a siren. Slater's lime-yellow command car careens around the corner, he must of been working the other entrance.

"Goddamnit, get in there!" he hollers, seeing us. "C'mon! Hustle! *Hustle hustle hustle!*" He claps his little gloves together.

I start to explain the situation, but all that comes out is spit.

"Get inside!" Slater yells again, gesturing wildly.

I manage to get on my feet and look where he's pointing, straight inside the building. Back through the partition that separates the office from the main warehouse, there's a white-hot body of fire, it's like looking into a spot-weld.

"Can't get in, Chief," Mustacci says when he sees I can't talk. "We lost our lines."

"Lost your lines?" Slater says, ripping off his helmet and slamming it against his palm. *"Lost your lines?* I don't want any goddamn excuses. Pull off more hose and get in there!"

"Chief," I blurt out, "we—"

"No more excuses! C'mon, c'mon, a little hustle!"

*A little hustle?* This isn't a drill, this is a genuine twenty-four-carat oh-shitter, the whole building's involved by now, any volunteer can see that. We'll be lucky if we can contain it, protect the surrounding properties, cover our own ass. "Chief," I says. My throat feels like it's bleeding on every word. "We need help, bring some more companies around this side."

Sonny Wicker starts to pull off the pre-connect to the booster tank, I imagine more for something to do than anything else. That 325 gallons won't make a dent in this fire, it'll be like taking a leak in a volcano.

"More companies?" Slater says, looking at me like I'm the mental case, not him. "We got four already. Now come on, move!"

Nobody moves.

Sonny drops the pre-connect as though he realizes it's no use.

"Move, I said!"

The only thing that moves is eyeballs.

"Cocksuckers!" He's screaming now. *"Cocksuckers!"* He slams his helmet on the street.

He runs up to Tyree and grabs him by the shoulders, but Tyree stands like a mahogany statue.

"Get inside!" Slater screams. "Move, ya goddamn baboon!"

He lets go and turns toward Mike just as Tyree cocks a fist. Ax pins Tyree's arms. Physically resisting a fire officer at the scene of a fire—that's like insubordination on the field of battle. Ax knows it if Tyree don't. They'll practically shoot you for it.

The chief's stomping like a wild moose, running from face to face and screaming orders. He jerks around so hard he almost slips and falls on the wet street. He walks up to Sonny and slaps him across the side of the face. Sonny don't even rub. Pure Fire 5, that guy.

"Nobody's going in?" Slater hollers. "None of you yellowbellies?" We stare back at him. "None of you *elite?*"

Tyree farts, that's the only answer.

"Cocksuckers! *You goddamn yellow fucking cocksuckers!*" There's civilians standing just beyond the barricades, they

220

can't miss hearing him. I wonder if the public ever seen a chief flip out before?

He yanks off his gloves and flings them down. "Get in, *get in*, GET IN!" he says. He's drooling, his blond hair's flopping like a wild man of the jungle.

Cap Nordquist speaks up in a soft voice. "We'll do what we can from out here, chief."

Slater's eyes bug out a half inch, a vein throbs in his temple. "Negative, *negative!*" he says, waving his arms around. He juts his bulldog chin into Cap's face.

"We'll—" Cap struggles to say something. His face seems to twist sideways from the strain. He reaches up with his hand and rubs his jaw. "We'll—" he says again, and then he walks over to the rig and slumps on the running board.

"Suspended!" Slater yells after him. "You're *all* suspended!"

I notice Les's face is twitching. He's looking back and forth between Slater and the fire, I wonder which he hates more. Then he grabs the pre-connect and runs through the front door. "Get back!" I call out, but it sounds more like a gargle.

Les opens the nozzle to full fog and advances the line toward the burning back wall of the office.

The spray turns to steam as it impacts, but he keeps moving. We can see him crouching over the knob, back-lit by the fire.

Then the wall comes down and the whole scene lights up like a fireworks display.

Before I can move, four guys run past me into the flames and drag Les out. All their coats are smoking when they get back to the sidewalk. "Les," Ax says, "you okay, man?"

I lean over him. It's a miracle. His face don't even look burned, and he's laughing. Then I notice his legs. They're facing two different directions, opposite.

"His knee," Plummer says. "It's crushed."

Les isn't laughing, he's moaning.

221

Slater barks something into his portable unit. Tears blind me. I start to go over and drag him down—a sick jackal's still a jackal, you got to remember that.

But then I stop.

What I feel like doing, it'll take some time.


Back at the station after dark, we add up the damage.

Les is in the hospital.

Ax has a gashed hand, six stitches.

All of us have burned throats, but we'll be okay after a few suds.

Fire 5's lost 220 feet of inch-and-a-half and 200 feet of two-and-a-half, which means I'll be up to my ears in triplicate for at least two weeks.

And Cap—

"Where's Cap?" I says. Lately I been making a career out of keeping up with the old coot.

"Dunno," Sonny says. "Drove himself b-b-back, I guess. Then went to his room."

I hurry up the stairs, with Ax and Plummer behind me. Cap's door is half open, he's laying on the bed in his underwear. His face is still streaked from the fire, funny he hasn't washed up.

"Cap," I says, "how they hangin'?"

He gives me a lopsided look. "Whatsa matter with your face?" Ax says.

Cap opens his mouth, but all that comes out is a low "Aaaarghhh . . ."

"Lemme look at your throat," I says. I tilt his head back in the light, it moves stiff. I notice there's dried spit at the corner of his mouth.

"Wait!" Plum says, shoving me aside. "Don't touch him!"

Plum worked aid cars three years, he can practically do brain

222

surgery. "Cap," he says, "give us a smile. C'mon, Cap, a big smile now!"

Cap's mouth twists like a rubber man.

"Thought so," Plummer says. "Lay back, Cap. Here, Charly, lift his feet." Plum slips a pillow underneath. "Ax, call an ambulance," he says real low, like he don't want Cap to hear.

"What is it?" I says in my raspy voice.

Plum puts his mouth right next to my ear and whispers, "I think he's had a stroke."

Far into the night the hot-line telephones ring and firemen exchange information. Jungle drums. I myself talk to a lieutenant at Engine 12 and an old pal at Engine 18, two of the companies that fought the tire fire from the other side. Ax talks to a couple of laddermen he use to work with, and Lulu Ann picks up some titbits from a dispatcher she use to date. By early morning we can reconstruct the crime.

Slater pulled up at the Oxford side about the same time we were reaching the Hanaway Boulevard entrance a block through the building.

He sent Ladder 6 to the roof and Engines 12 and 18 inside, and they ran into thick stinking rubber smoke that blocked them from the fire source.

He called Fire 5 on his portable unit and talked to Fenstermacher on the rig and found out that we were already inside with Captain Nordquist.

At this point there's two groups penetrating from opposite directions, and he's got to pull off one or the other. If he don't, they'll drive the fire down each other's throat.

Slater gives everybody the same command: "Get inside and stay inside!" Who knows why? Maybe he thought the superchief was coming, and he wanted to show hustle. Never mind if a few firemen get wasted, hustle's the thing. It *looks* good.

So 12's and 18's kept pushing from the Oxford end, using everything from two-and-a-half-inch lines to a Stang water cannon, and Fire 5 kept penetrating from the Hanaway Boulevard end, and before long their superior water power overcame ours and they drove the fire down on us, and that's when we were forced to abandon our lines and get the hell out, lucky to be alive.

An elemental mistake, right out of the textbook.

Odd for a guy that knows the manuals backward.

Two days later we come back on shift and the rumor is out:

Fire 5's being bled out to regular companies.

I grab the phone. "Al," I says to my rabbi, "is it true?"

"Hold your water," Deputy Fire Chief Allan M. Grant says. "I'll be right over."

So it's got to be true.

I go back in the bullpen and somebody's stuck a funny drawing of Slater up on the bulletin board and marked it "Der Fuhrer." I rip it down. No sense calling names. Besides, some admirer of Adolf Hitler might sue us.

Grant arrives in his command car and motions me to climb in. "Go up and get yourself a coffee," he says to his driver, and I slip in behind the wheel.

"Al," I says when the chauffeur's out of hearing, "give it to me straight. We're gone, right?"

"I won't lie to you, Charly," he says. He won't and never has. Thirty-eight years old, three years younger than me, some say he has a shot at superchief in a few years, although he's Protestant and it's the Catholic turn, but maybe they'll make an exception. If Slater don't overhaul him in the stretch.

"What's the beef?" I says. "The tire fire?"

"Not just that. It's the whole picture."

"The whole what picture?" I says, raising my voice as much as I can without tearing my sore vocal cords. "What fire didn't we put out? When didn't we do our job?"

"Hey, hey!" he says, tapping my shoulder. "Cool down, pal. It's me! You're not dealing with Slater now."

"Sorry, Al," I says, feeling ashamed for barking at a guy like him.

"You don't have to sell me on Fire Five," he says. "I worked side by side with you guys long enough, didn't I?" Two years and never a harsh word. I guess he knows us, all right. "But Chief Slater, he sees it different," he says.

"How's he see it?"

"He says you guys act like independent operators. Says you're insubordinate, a bunch of hot dogs. Listen to this."

He reads from a paper fished out of his pocket. " 'This uncooperative attitude is inherent in the Fire Five concept. Any firefighters named to such a unique outfit would draw the same conclusion, namely, that they were a special group, and could act accordingly. The very notion of Fire Five undermines our traditional approach to firefighting: teamwork and cooperation among men and among companies.' "

"Who wrote that?"

"It's from Slater's original critique."

"When we were mustered? Two years ago?"

"Right."

"I get it," I says, trying to control my temper. "It's what they call a self—a self—"

"A self-fulfilling prophecy?"

"That's it."

"Slater hates improvisation, always hated it," Grant says, lowering his voice as though he don't want to be overheard talking about a fellow chief. "He knows the manuals by heart and he thinks we should follow them to the letter. Detests change. He's still annoyed we don't use horses."

I'd laugh, but my throat hurts.

"Al," I says, "can't you put in a word for us? I mean, before it's too late?"

"*A word?*" He looks at me like I'm flipping out, and maybe I am. "Listen, upstairs is sick of listening to me on the subject. Charly, gimme a break, I'm just one of three deputy chiefs. There's the assistant chief and the superchief above my level and they both got their minds made up. Slater worked close with the brass for years, he's convinced 'em there's a better system."

"Sure," I says. "Stand on the fire ground and order the fire to go out. Scream and holler and stamp your feet. That's his better system, I seen it in action."

"He wants us to designate high-density fire areas, reassign more companies from the outlying areas."

"Permanently?"

"Yep."

"Al, Chrissakes, the outlying areas're undermanned as it is. That's the whole point of Fire Five, rove around and help out where it's needed. Spread the manpower."

"Charly, don't tell *me!* I helped write your charter."

"That's probably another reason Slater's against it."

I wait for Al to comment, but he keeps quiet.

"Who's gonna cover Fenwick and places like that if we bring more personnel into the central city?" I says.

"Volunteers."

"Volunteers?" The wax must of stuck in my ear lobes again, I can't be hearing right. Volunteers is a dirty word to professional firemen. I mean, they're usually a nice bunch of guys, plumbers and dentists and clerks, but you'd never want your sister to marry one, and they're the *last* guys you'd want at a real fire.

228

"Charly, it's no help that the Torch's still walking," Grant says gently.

"Goddamn, Al, I get sick of hearing that. The Torch's the marshals' responsibility, the cops', you know that."

"Sure I know it, but try telling the boss. Slater's got him convinced otherwise. Claims you guys shoulda had the Torch the other night."

"Yeh, he's right, except we had a dying man to take care of and we never laid eyes on the Torch. He was gone before we pulled up. Nobody wants him more than us, Al. He killed our loot."

"I don't know, Charly, I just don't know," Grant says, slumping back in the front seat. "I'm laying my job on the line for Fire Five night and day and glad to do it. But you guys better prepare yourselves."

"For what?"

"Just be ready, that's all."

"C.Y.A., ya mean?"

"All the way."

The rest of the shift climb all over me upstairs. "What'd he say, what'd he say? What's gonna happen?"

"You wanna know what's gonna happen?" I says, stalling for time. "We're gonna keep on being the best goddamn fire company in town. That's what's gonna happen. If we fall, it's because we were pushed, not because we jumped."

I call an engine drill to get their minds off the subject. What I usually do, I usually take off some little part and put it in my pocket, and they have to diagnose what's wrong. This time I screw the idling control all the way down so the engine won't start.

Lulu's first, she disappears under the hood like a gopher backing down a hole, and in about six seconds she hollers, "The idling control's screwed down." She comes out with grease on her face, two black streaks under each eye, looks like a cornerback on a sunny day, if you can imagine a cornerback you'd like to take on a trip to Tahiti.

"Where'd you learn engines?" Plummer says.

"The engine manual," she says.

"Engine manual?" Ax says. "Is there an engine manual?"

Then when it looks like morale's picking up, the phone rings and it's the fire doc with a report on Les. He's just come out of surgery, his knee's broke in about four places and the cartilage and ligaments are so twisted he'll never be able to walk right, let alone fight fires. Guess he'll just have to go back to being a rich kid again. I have a hell of a time picturing Les with a cane.

Slater must be feeling pretty good, one down and one on the way. Cap's still in expensive care, and they penciled him in for an exploratory brain operation. The way he's acting, they think he might have pressure on one of the lobes, that's why he can't talk right. If it turns out to be some kind of malignancy, he's probably terminal.

Him and Fire 5.

"Okay, let's knock off," I says after I get the glad news.

I walk in the crapper and sit down and put my head in my hands. I don't really have the urge, it's just a way to be alone for a while. Sweet Jesus Christ, where'd we go wrong?

No matter how I figure it, the answer always comes out the same.

H. Walker Slater.

Grant should of taken care of him for us, nipped his bud. But maybe that's too much to expect. Maybe it's unfair, too. What's that line in Fire 5's favorite movie? "A man's gotta kill his own snakes."

230

Yeh, but listen, Kid Blue, what if the snake's your own battalion chief?

I hang around jawing with the next shift, and by the time I head for home it's almost nine o'clock. A half a block from the station I see an oversize man climb out of a little sporty car and look both ways and then shuffle toward the fire department parking lot. The car glides along the street and stops at a red light next to me. I snoop inside and the driver's a good-looking chick maybe thirty years old, big but not fat, maybe a hundred fifty pounds on a heavy frame, she looks familiar.

"Hi, Lieutenant," she calls out in a mellow voice. "I hear a lot of good things about you."

Before I can answer, the light changes, and she hollers "God love ya" and takes off like she's in a drag race with Don Garlits and they already split the first two heats.

I look back down the street. The guy that got out of the car's walking into our parking lot, and I can tell by the knock knees that it's none other than Ax Bedrosian. "Wait!" I holler, and I jog up the street to catch him. "Who the hell was that?"

"Who the hell was what?" he says, pretending surprise.

"Ax, never bullshit a bullshitter," I says. "The broad. You got out of her car and she knows me."

"Knows *you?*" He scrooches up his eyes. Mr. Innocence. He's no threat to Marlon Brando.

"Yeh. Said she heard a lot of good things about me."

"Goddamn it, I told her to dummy up."

"For what? Who is she, anyway?"

"Charly, Chrissakes, keep your voice down, why don'tcha?" He looks around, 360 degrees. "I ain't said nothing to Francine yet. It's a secret."

"Ax, let's you and me have a beer."

We stroll over to Joe's and the story starts to come out. He's been seeing this woman for several months, ever since—ever since— He can't quite seem to say it.

"C'mon, Ax, don't hold back on your pal."

"Well, a long time ago we hauled her outa . . . outa the bathtub."

I can't believe it. He's lying. "No way that's the bathtub broad I seen tonight, Ax," I says. "C'mon, now."

"She was our telephone caller, too."

Sure, and Marie Antonette and Tillie the Toilet at the same time. "Look, Ax, gimme a break, pal. I had a long day."

The simple idiot, he swears he's not zinging me. It started on the phone, he says. "Poor kid, that was the only sex life she had, calling up Fire Five. Weighing four hundred pounds and all."

"Sure, Ax, sure. I had one too, but the wheels fell off."

"Then she had her jaws wired and then the gland operation and dropped two hundred pounds."

"Only two hundred?" I says. I got to admire his imagination, stringing me along like this.

"Then one night she calls the station and I get on the phone and I figure what the hell, Francine ain't doing me no good, might as well have the old ashes hauled, and when I make a date it turns out she's no fat lady, she's a good-looking heavy-set broad—*ar uh*—lady." He throws me a nervous look. "Charly," he says, "you won't leak, will ya?"

"Leak what? That you been chasing laundry? What's new about that?"

"No, I mean don't tell that Margaret was the caller. I mean, them calls was never obscene, Charly. Just kinda flirty."

" 'Margaret?' "

"Margaret Winston de Boliver, that's her name. She's an interior decorator. Remember how nice her place was?"

232

"Yeh," I says. All's I really remember is a cowboy picture on the wall and the safflower oil.

"Charly, we're gonna get married."

A slurp of ale goes up my nose. *"You're what?"*

"Get married. M-a-r-r-y-e-d. Married."

"Hey, Ax," I says, twisting on the stool to see if the guy with the strait jacket's arrived yet. "You're already married, pal. Francine? Francine Bedrosian? Name sound familiar?"

"Francine ain't been a real wife for six months. Says it's degrading, what a wife's gotta do. Calls it 'performing.' 'Do I have to perform tonight? Oh, how trashy!' The lawyer says I got her by the balls."

"Sure, but—"

"Why d'ya think I was staring down the pole hole at the probie? You think I'm some kinda degenerate like Plummer? I was just naturally horny, that's all."

"So you hooked up with the obscene—with the flirty caller?"

"Shut up about that, Charly, why don'tcha? Put it outa your mind, don't bring it up again. Think of her as Margaret Winston de Boliver, F.F.L."

"What's F.F.L.?"

" 'Former Fat Lady.' " He giggles in his Feinblatz. "Charly, listen, we want you to stand up for us, okay?"

"At the wedding?" I says. "Or the divorce?" I don't know why I said it, it just come out. When I have a few ales I get silly sometimes.

"Ya need a best man at a divorce?" The poor simp looks thunderstruck.

What the hell, the laughs've been few and far between lately. I says, "Why, certainly! Chief Grant, he was best man at my divorce from Marilyn."

"No lie?"

233

Four rounds later Ax and I got the whole divorce ceremony laid out. It'll be a church affair, I'll stand up for him, Lulu'll be the maid of honor and Plummer'll give the husband away. We'll have the whole thing catered, and there'll be no sweat for Ax except it'll cost him a couple hundred.

"I'm wondering about the honeymoon," I says after we got all the other details laid out.

"What honeymoon?" Ax says, ordering up his fifth or sixth Feinblatz.

"You and Francine," I says. "After the divorce ceremony."

"Fuck off, why don'tcha?" Ax says, sputtering in his stein. "There ain't no honeymoon after a divorce, dummy."

"Oh, right," I says. "I wasn't thinking."

Sometimes a loot's got time on his hands, the district's quiet, the firebugs are off at their annual convention, the chiefs are kind of relaxing on their oar, but it's been five or six months since it was peaceful around Station 12. My head's spinning with details—housework, reports, inspections, departmental red tape, plus we got arson patrol twelve hours a shift and only six bodies to split it between, now that Les is out, plus there's also the undercurrent that Fire 5's gonna be split up and disbanded. Every five minutes the bush telegraph goes off and I get the latest communiqué:

"Charly, this is Billy Ruben at Eighteen's. Superchief just pulled out with Slater. Said something about transferring you and Bedrosian over here."

"Sprockett, this is Estes. Lieutenant at Six's? Yeh, right. They got you ticketed for Mountain Heights. Your firebroad —she'll go back to training school, help with the teaching. Chief Armstrong clued me this morning."

"Charly?" I recognize Al Grant's voice. "It looks like one more week at most . . . Right, pal . . . I'm doing everything I can . . . Yeh? I held 'em back this long, didn't I?"

*One more week.*

Fire 5 won't go up the spout, goddamnit, if I got to incinerate headquarters myself.

No, I wouldn't go that far. Just get rid of Slater. A small bomb under the front wheel of his . . . Jeez, I'm flipping out. Like him.

Speak of the devil, he pops up for roll call and pulls a gasket inspection. Every fireman's suppose to have an extra inch-and-a-half gasket and a two-and-a-half-inch gasket in his coat in case they're needed at a hydrant. It turns out half the platoon don't have them. "Well, Sprockett?" he says to me.

"I don't understand, Chief. I checked two days ago and everybody had 'em." The God's honest truth.

"Mine were in my pocket last night," Plummer calls out. "I'm a hundred percent positive."

"Take that man's name," Slater snaps to his driver standing there with a pencil.

"Pardon me, Chief," I says. "What for?"

"For talking in ranks."

Christ! He's gonna nit-pick us to death before he breaks us up.

"How about you, Sprockett?" he says, holding out his bare hands.

"What about me?"

"Your gaskets."

That's one problem I'll never have. I keep two sets: one in each pocket.

Empty.

"Chief," I says, "something's funny here. I know my men, I know myself—"

"Explain it at the hearing," he says, and marches off. I swear he's snickering. I think I know why. I bet he went into the locker room and pilfered them himself.

\*       \*       \*

236

*       *       *

One o'clock in the afternoon. Tyree's got chicken croquets frying in deep grease. He just don't understand, you never fry anything that's porous and soaks up grease. You end up bloated and overweight, like him.

An oh-shitter's burning in the Hopfner Building downtown, and I got to stand around the scullery smelling Tyree D'Arcy's croquets. None of the guys stray more than a few feet from their turn-out gear, we been waiting to get special-called ever since the second alarm about five minutes ago.

Plum's got the portable radio at the end of the table and his head's practically stuck inside the speaker. He jumps up and says, "Hey, they're sending more companies!"

"Turn it up!" somebody hollers, and we hear the voice loud and clear:

*"Engine Nine, Eighteen, Ladder Two, Battalion Three. Five and Main. The Hopfner Building. Engine Nine . . . "* Everybody but us.

"Fuck off, why don'tcha?" Ax yells at the radio.

"P-p-piss on 'em," Sonny says.

"I'm cooking y'all a nice lunch," Tyree says. "Now don't go getting your juices riled." Satchel Paige, 1957. I notice his boots and coat are right next to the stove, and he keeps looking sideways at the pole hole.

The messages crackle back and forth, and pretty soon we find out the fire's burning on the second, fifth and sixteenth floors, must of traveled up a ventilation opening or an elevator shaft. Either that or a conduit took off on a short circuit. It's odd they haven't called us yet. With three floors involved, you'd think they'd be having manpower problems.

*"Deputy Two to Portable Two, what's your position?"* The combat chief's trying to contact one of his crews.

*"Portable Two. We don't know. Sixteenth floor's all we know*

237

*for sure. Over.*" He talks like he swallowed a couple quarts of snot. Sounds like Eddie Cushman. I knew him at 17's. Damn good fireman.

"Those poor guys must a got off at the fire floor," Mustacci says. "Now they're trapped."

"Whattaya mean?" Fenstermacher says. He's been listening to the same calls as the rest of us, he ought to know what Mike means.

"Didn't they teach you anything at training school?" I says.

"Teach me what, Loo?" He's smiling at me. Hard to get sore at the kid, he's so good-nature.

"To never take an elevator direct to the fire floor?" I says. "Always get off one floor below, hook up to the standpipe, then hump the hose up the stairs."

"Why?"

"Because in the first place if there's an oh-shitter burning and you open the elevator door in the face of the fire, you're grilled, right? And in the second place, you know those electric eyes that open and shut the elevator doors?"

The kid nods.

"They can't tell a body of smoke from a body of human," Plummer puts in. Lulu's just walked into the scullery, I guess he wants to display his knowledge.

"I still don't get it," Fenstermacher says.

"The doors won't shut, kid," Plummer says patiently. "You open the door and the smoke rushes into the elevator and breaks the light beam and the door won't shut again and you're f— you're f— you're in plenty trouble. The standpipe's maybe down the hall, way the other side of the fire, and you're standing there with an armful of dry hose, and you can't move."

The radio blares again. *"Portable Two, I dunno how much longer"*—he stops to cough, and cough again—*"how much longer we can hold out Over."* It's Eddie Cushman for sure.

238

Nice wife, three kids, one's got the asthma.

*"Two three nine. You inside a room?"* 239's the assistant chief, second in command in the whole city, he's running the show now.

*"Affirmative. Help comin'?"* Cushman sounds like he's talking clear from his ankles, he's gagging so bad.

*"That's affirmative. Hang on."*

Sure, help's coming, hang on, what else can he say? How's anybody gonna help now? Apparently the whole sixteenth floor's involved, the elevator's jammed open, Eddie's crew's trapped. They don't even have a charged line with them to open up a fog and generate some oxygen. They're in deep, those poor bastards. You break the rules, you pay dear. Sad but true.

When everybody in the scullery realizes what's happening, they crowd around the radio, practically laying on top of each other, all except Lulu, she's standing a few feet back and her face looks flushed under the Orphan Annie red hairdo. A curl of smoke drifts over the stove, and somebody yelps, "Your croquets're burning."

"Fuck my croquets!" Tyree says, leaning closer to the portable unit. "Excuse me, Lulu."

She reaches over and slides the pan off the flame, the croquets won't be bad once they're scraped. Just as she gets back to the table, the bells ring and the radio says, *"Fire Five, Fire Five,"* and the joint explodes. We're into our turn-out gear in about two seconds flat and spinning down the pole like skydivers.

We're so excited, we barely even listen to the directions. Where else could they be specialing us in? A Dempsey Dumpster? A fat lady stuck in a bathtub?

*"Fire Five, Fire Five,"* the dispatcher says as we roll out of the station. *"Five and Main, the Hopfner Building . . . "*

I grab for the microphone, but Plummer almost knocks it out of my hand as he rams the gearshift into second.

*"Fire Five okay,"* I respond, my voice shaking. We want this one bad.

I turn around and count my firemen, I mean my firefighters.

Lulu's on the tailboard with Fenstermacher and Sonny. Her hat's too big, but otherwise she looks ready. No skin's showing, Plummer'll be disappointed.

Everybody else is crowded into the cab, zipping and tugging and snapping. "Ax," I says over my shoulder, "wipe your mouth!"

"What?" he says.

"It don't look good, slobbering before you get to the fire."

"Oh, yeh, Charly, right, right," he says. Poor guy, never knows when I'm serious.

We're a block from the Hopfner Building when a red hat flogs us down. "Stash it here," the lieutenant hollers. "Report to the manpower chief on foot." The old story, not enough firefighters. Well, we'll fill the gap. That's our job. You'll hear no complaints from Fire 5.

"Lulu," I says, "stay with the rig. They might need it moved."

"Oh, shoot!" she says. She's mad she can't come to the party.

"I'm sorry, honey," I says. "It's the probie's job."

"Rats," she says.

We run toward the fire ground, skipping over the spaghetti and trying to keep up with Tyree and Fenstermacher. I hear Lulu call from back at the rig, "And don't call me honey!"

"She's right, Loo," Plum says, panting alongside me. "It's honeyperson."

By this time the kid and Tyree are far ahead. I'm carrying a Halligan tool and Sonny has two plaster hooks and Ax has the thirty-inch chain saw, but we wouldn't of been able to keep up with those other two if we'd been wearing propellers.

"Fire Five reporting," I says when I reach a white hat in front of the building.

"Here's whatcha do, Loo," he says. "Take your crew and go up in the freight elevator. We got men trapped on the six-teenth floor, they're—"

"We know the situation, Chief."

"Good. Need ventilation bad, we can't save 'em otherwise. Take and go to the roof and break out every goddamn thing you can see. Skylights, any fucking thing. We got a couple other crews working their way up from the fifteenth floor, but it's slow."

"Right, Chief."

Another fireman hands me a portable radio unit and leads us through the smoky lobby to the back of the building. A freight elevator's standing open. The way it smells it must of carried a couple dozen firemen up to the fire and a couple

241

dozen down, most of them with the heaves and Krispy Kritter ears at the same time.

"Okay, you're relieved," I says to the guy that led us over. "Chief told me to run the elevator."

"Thanks, we'll take care of it," I says, ushering him out. Fire 5 works as a unit.

I see buttons marked 1 to 16 and a blank button just above the top. I push the blank and we start moving upward, pretty fast for a freight elevator. Then the doors slide open and we step into the middle of an Erector set, girders and steel ladders and catwalks all over the place.

I realize we're in the service area with the air-conditioning and heating and ventilation equipment. We ought to be able to get to the roof from here. Then it'll be up to Ax with his mighty chain saw. The smoke isn't too bad, but the heat's terrific—maybe 140 degrees—more like 240 under our heavy work clothes.

"Stay here," I says to Fenstermacher. "You're in charge a the elevator."

"Where'll you be, Loo?"

"High as we can climb." We're off, Sonny and Mike and Plummer and Ax, with Tyree and me bringing up the rear.

At the top of the first ladder, we come to a grill-steel landing and more catwalks branching out, and Mike spots another ladder, this one narrower gauge, and up we go till we're standing on a flat metal grid right under a ceiling.

"Stay clear!" Ax yells and cranks the chain saw.

The whole landing is maybe two by six feet. Ax slams the whining saw blade against the ceiling, and sparks fly. I recognize a basic health hazard, count your arms and legs, everybody.

"There ya go, you fucker!" Ax yells over the scream of the saw, and I look up and see the blade poking through to daylight. "Gimme that!" I says, and grab an ax from Sonny.

Whack, slash, bang, bam, we're shredding the roof, enlarging the hole, pretty soon it's four foot wide. With a whoosh and a whistle the hot air and the smoke from below start venting through the hole like the valve on a pressure cooker.

"Get down, get down!" I holler. The draft rushes through the vent so fast I halfway expect to see somebody get sucked out and go flying into space like Batman.

"Let's move!" I says, and start back down the ladder.

My idea is to break another vent, there's too much heat and smoke concentrated in this one spot, maybe we can spread it around a little and distribute the outflow. Our hole must be the first in the roof and it's drawing all the smoke off the fire floor, which is what we wanted to do, but it's filling this service area like Slotnik the baker filling an eclair.

At the bottom of the thin metal ladder, the visibility's almost zero. "Grab hands!" I says, and we creep across a catwalk trying to feel for another approach to the roof.

We've covered maybe twenty feet when a big cloud of foul smoke surges up from below. I turn around and I can't see who I'm holding on to.

"It's okay, it's okay," I holler, wishing we'd brought masks. "Let's keep trucking, we'll hit some clear air." It's too late to double back to the elevator, we'd never find the right ladder down. I wonder about Fenstermacher. He'll be okay. Freight elevators don't have electric eyes, he can always shut the door and ride it down.

Behind me some of the crew's starting to cough and spit, but we keep moving straight ahead on the catwalk. We're gabbing all the time to keep up communication, the way all firemen are taught, and then I come up to a closed door so quick I bang my helmet and half stun myself.

"Okay, Loo?" Sonny says.

243

"C'mon," I says, and I shove the door open.

The smoke's swirling inside, but not quite as thick as out on the open catwalk. "Hurry up," I says. "Get in and shut the door!"

Ax is the last man in. He barrels through the opening like a tight end and just as he gets inside Plummer screams, *"Freeze!"*

"Whatsa matter?" I says.

"There's a big hole," Plummer says, breathing hard. "This must be the elevator loft."

"Madonna," Mike Mustache says softly.

"Can you make out the shape?" I ask.

"I think it's about ten feet across," Plum says. "I'm feeling my way around the edge."

I try to get a look, figure out where he is, but the smoke's pouring in, all I can make out is a faint outline.

"Everybody stay down," I says. "On your knees. Follow the wall to the back side, away from the door. Less heat."

I bump into somebody and it's Tyree. "Here," I says, "gimme your hand." Pretty soon we got a regular daisy chain, and we all make it around to the far side of the hole.

"Now just sit tight," I says. "And for Chrissakes, stay back from the shaft!"

"That's a real fucking express," Plum says.

"Yeh," Mike says. "Non-stop service to the first floor, no waiting, folks."

I crawl on my belly to the lip of the hole and look down. No elevator as far as I can see, Fenstermacher must of got called away, or driven away. Can't blame him. The way the smoke was, he's lucky he saved his own ass, let alone ours. We'll be all right. Patience, that's all.

*"Portable Three to Two three nine,"* I says into the radio.

*"Two three nine, how's it going up there, Portable Three?"*

244

I don't know exactly what to tell the assistant chief. How can I explain that we come up here to ventilate for the guys trapped on the sixteenth, and now we're trapped ourselves? Fire 5's in enough trouble with the brass already. *"Okay, Two three nine,"* I says. *"We opened her up."*

*"We noticed. She's already clearing out on sixteen."*

*"Roger."* I don't usually bother with that radio-manual jargon, but what else can I say?

"What now?" Ax says.

"Sit!" I says, like I'm drilling Ladder 10's Pomeranian Chihuahua. "The fire's banking down on sixteen. Smoke can't last long."

Famous last words. Pretty soon it's coming right up the elevator shaft, it's seeping under the door cracks. We might as well be inside a can of mushroom soup.

"Hang tough," I says. Sound like Slater. No, he'd say, "Hang tough, double time!"

I crawl to the edge of the hole again to see if there's any sign of fresh air, and I catch a smell of wintergreen, it's like the Life Saver Corporation's burning below us. Maybe this is where they keep their reserve stocks.

Behind me, Mike lets out a laugh. "What's so funny?" I says into the darkness.

He laughs twice as loud.

"You got a weird sense of humor, man," I says, crawling back and propping myself against the wall. I seen kids like him in the neighborhood high on dope, giggling their head off at a cloud or a moth.

"Control yourself, Mustacci," I says, feeling a little silly myself. He lets out a long string of giggles.

Maybe he's getting hysterical. No, that don't make sense, he's been through far worse than this. This isn't the end of the trail, I mean we're stuck in an elevator loft because outside the loft it's a whole lot worse, but what the hell, we all smoke Camels, we can handle it. Just a question of sit tight, wait till the air clears, and then it's back to Station 12 for a game of pinochle.

"Hey, Loo!" Tyree calls. "Don'tcha wish I had my coronet?" He snorts at his own remark. "A li'l recital while we wait?"

"Yeh," I says, "too bad you left it, man."

"Fenstermacher can bring it up in the elevator," Tyree says, and breaks himself up.

I heard funnier lines at Loo's funeral, but I laugh. Then I take another whiff of wintergreen and I says, "Stop acting like an asshole, Tyree," and I burst out laughing louder than him. Don't know why.

*There's no sun up in the sky.*

*Stormy weather . . .*

Jeez, I'm getting goofy. Got to clear my head.

The wintergreen again. Hey, this is crazy! Ax grunts and says something, and Plummer says, "What? I can't hear ya, I got a Halligan tool in my ear."

We're drunk, we're stupid, I can't figure it out. We're all scrunched down on the floor, there's about a foot of air down there and the Sargasso Sea above us, and we're all giggling.

It's like the . . . the . . .

The fire in the Medical and Dental Building, that's it! The time a couple tanks of nitrous oxide burst, and we couldn't keep a straight face for three hours.

Happens to every fireman, one time or another. We call it Silly Gas. Chief Stieglitz use to say it comes from acoustic tile sometimes, or insulating foam, forget which. He oughta know. The night they were carrying out the body of the old night watchman and the aid man couldn't stop laughing and Stieglitz was gonna write him up, and then he gets a whiff of the gas himself and he says to the morgue chauffeur, "Here, take this party anyplace he wants, the fare's on me."

Seen all kinds, fires that make you laugh, fires that make you cry . . .

"Whoopee!" Ax yells, and slides his chain saw toward the elevator hole like a shuffleboard weight.

"Hey, hey!" I says, trying to keep a straight face, "whatsa matter with you? That's fire department property."

Guffaws all around, plus a fart from Tyree. I didn't know Silly Gas had that property.

Sonny pipes up, "It's such a nice day here at the beach. I think I'll take a d-d-d-dip."

"You are a d-d-d-dip," Plum says, and everybody guffaws. Including me.

*Especially* me.

Then I realize Sonny's voice came from the edge of the shaft.

"Hey, you jack-off!" I yell.

"Watch that first step," Mike says. "You working out a fancy dive for us, Sonny?"

"Right," Sonny says. I can picture him with a silly grin on his face, dangling his feet down the hole. "A sixteen-and-a-half with a f-full t-twist."

"Goddamn!" Mike says. "This's fun. Let's get trapped again tomorrow."

"Sonny," I call out, inhaling another toke of the heavy wintergreen smell, "quit playing games, man. Get away from that hole. Sit tight."

"Keep a tight ass," Tyree says. I wish he'd remember his own advice.

"Come on, you guys," I says, trying to get serious. "Reach out. Let's grab hands again. No more fooling around." But I'm giggling as the words come out.

247

"Hey, man, that Ax, he really got big balls, don't he?" Mike squeals.

"He sure do," Tyree says. "One's the size of a pea, and the other's a itty bitty thing."

Something's crackling in my ear. Rice Krispies. "Hey, quieten down!" I holler. I can hardly talk, I'm laughing so hard.

A voice comes in, sounds like the superchief. *"One one one to Portable Three."*

It *is* the superchief, speaking to me from my neck. That's his code: 111. Hey, *hey,* the big chief's hanging around my neck, talking to me!

Oh, yeh, it's my portable unit.

I punch at the button, miss it the first couple times, then hit it. *"Hey, Chief,"* I says, *"how's your hammer hanging?"*

*"One one one to Portable Three,"* the Superchief repeats.

*"Right on, your holiness,"* I says, but I don't know whether I remembered to punch the button or not.

*"What's your location, Portable Three?"*

*"Right now?"* I says. *"Around my neck, Chief."*

He don't answer right away, I imagine he's holding his portable unit out in front of him and shaking it. Then he says, *"One one one to Portable Three, hold your position. I'm sending Chief Slater up to find you. He's got the building plans."*

Now isn't that just like Slater? The fire's blacking down, the danger's over, so he'll put on his mask and be a hero.

"How'd we get up here?" Plummer says. "Anyway?"

"Followed the rule," Mike says. " 'Anything worth doing's worth fucking up.' "

Sonny makes a vomiting sound. "Listen," Mike says, "if you don't like my humor, just sit quiet."

"Yeh, don't insult the author, or he'll pull off your dick and use it for a punctuation mark."

"A comma?"

Wish I could tell who's talking. Sometimes I think it's me, sometimes it's them, sometimes it's all of us.

"Best damn p-p-party we had in months!"

"You can say that again."

"Best damn p-p-party we had in months!"

"Aw, fuck off, why don'tcha?"

Huh? I'm proud of this outfit. We have more runs than any other company in town. Especially when we eat at Joe's.

Thanks for the mammaries.

Did I say that or just think it? No, Irving Berlin said that. I-r-v-i-n . . . "Hey," I says, "how d'ya spell Irving?"

"Dunno," a voice says, it sounds like our author. "What's it mean 'to irv?' "

"To irv is human, to forgive . . ."

The life of a fireman. Sitting on the edge of an elevator shaft, cracking wise. Buncha schoolkids, hanging moons in the boys' room.

*"Battalion Four to Portable Three. Come in, Portable Three."* Sounds like Slater.

I push the button and do the Indian Love Call. *"When I'm calling yoo-oo-oo-oo oo-oo-oo."*

*"Get back down here!"* It's Slater for sure, he sounds like somebody stole his rubber duck.

*"Back down where?"* I says. I still can't see two feet in front of my face. I take another couple sniffs, and this time it don't smell like wintergreen, it smells like plain old conduit smoke, sharp and biting.

*"What's your location, Portable Three? Goddamnit—"* He cuts himself off, I guess he just remembered that every word goes on monitoring tape at the alarm office. Then he comes back on all formal and proper: *"Battalion Four to Portable Three, maintain your position. I'm coming in."*

We're saved, we're saved! Massa, we're saved . . .

249

Everybody quietens down. Where's the laughter, the fun, where's the dumb jokes, the old comraderie?

"Hey, Loo?" It's Tyree.

"Yeh?"

"I'm sick, man." I hear this awful sound, like he's spewing a sackful of elderly soul food.

"Me too," Mike says, and he throws up, and then somebody else a few feet away. This isn't the world's worst fire but it sure puts out a variety of smoke.

A clank.

Just outside the door.

Somebody's on the catwalk. I narrow my eyes to slits and lay my head on the concrete floor, where the smoke's the lightest, but I still can't see more than a foot or two.

"Anybody in here?" It's Slater's voice, I'd know it anywhere.

Behold unto ye, a savior is born, and his name is H. Walker Slater.

"You scumbags in there or not?"

The door creaks.

"Hey, what's going on?" He's inside now, and he sounds scared. I remember what Captain Nordquist told me about him. Chokes up in a fire room.

"C'mon, you bastards, answer me!" His voice sounds skittery.

A whisper cuts across the smoky room, not loud but distinct. *"Right over here, Chief."*

I hear a couple of footsteps.

"No, wait, Chief!" I start to yell, but nothing comes out.

There's a muffled cry and the sound of a body slamming against the side of the elevator shaft.

Then it's quiet again.

"Hear that?" I says.

"Jesus, Mary and Joseph," Mike says. It's not a curse.

250

"Sonny?" I says. I hope he's still dangling his feet. "See anything?"

"T-t-too smoky, Charly. B-b-b-but I ... heard."

I crawl on my belly and look down the shaft. Nothing in sight. The cables are moving up on one side and down on the other, the elevator must be in use. How the hell? Poor Slater, he must of landed on top.

Who said it?

*"Right over here, Chief."*

In a few minutes we hear glass breaking in the distance, then the door swings open and there's the whine of a portable fan and the smoke begins to clear. No danger now. Was there ever? Just a matter of time. A sniff of smelling salts, a good noseblow and a swallow of cold water, and we'll never know it happened.

What happened?

Back at the rig, I position Fenstermacher and Lulu Ann on the tailboard, the rest of us in the cab. "Drive slow," I order Plummer.

All the way down seventeen flights of steps, following the ladderman with his flashlight, nobody'd opened his yap. The rest of the guys still don't look like they want to talk. Fine.

"Now listen," I says as Plummer eases the rig onto Fifth Avenue and back toward the station. "Nobody heard a word up there, understand? Nobody heard—one—goddamn—word!"

Somebody starts to say something, but I cut them off quick. "Wait!" I says. "Nobody talk!"

Silence.

Plummer stops for a red light and glances sideways at me. "Pay attention," I says. "Now look, I heard it, we all heard it." The other guys lean forward on their jump seats. "Somebody said, 'Right over here, Chief.'"

251

"It wasn't—"

"*Shut up!*"

Ax shuts up. I'm beginning to get pissed. I got to make them see that the only protection for the guy that did it is for all of us to hang together, not talk about it, not share secrets or hints, nothing. Just act like it never happened. A chief fell down an elevator shaft. Tragic. But it's got nothing to do with us. Not if we dummy up.

"Right now," I says, "one guy in this cab knows who said it, and five guys don't. Whispers are whispers, they all sound the same, right?"

Nobody answers. I got their attention.

"One of us sent Slater down that shaft. Five of us didn't. Let's leave it at that."

"Huh?" Ax says, screwing up his face like he don't get it.

"Whichever one·did it," I says, "don't ever confide in anybody, take it to your grave."

"What's our story then?" Mike says.

"Simple. Slater walked in, asked if we were there, and that's the last we heard."

"Do we say where he went?" Ax says.

"Goddamn!" Plummer says, sounding aggravated. "He went bye-bye. How're we suppose to know where he went?"

Plummer always was quick. I turn around and study the other faces in the half-dark cab. They're all nodding except Ax. He still looks confused.

Tyree says, "Don'tcha see, man? Don'tcha see? We all jes' keep quiet—"

Ax interrupts. "But I didn't do any—"

"*Shut your fucking mouth!*" I says, spinning around on my seat and raising my hand like I'm gonna swat him. "*Don't say you didn't do anything!* Can't you see that narrows it down? Don't say a word! Not now. Not ever."

252

The long shift finally ends, we're sitting around the bullpen waiting to get the word. We can't really talk, guys from Ladder 10 are drifting in and out, plus guys from the next shift, ready to relieve us at eight o'clock. We sit like mummies, waiting to hear the death signal: twenty bells at slow cadence. Just like they did for Loo.

Ten minutes after shift, and still no bells. "Hey, whatsa matter with you pogues?" Lieutenant Steve Peterson says. "Ain'tcha got homes?"

"Right, Steve," I says, and nod toward the door. The men get up and follow me out. Down at the parking lot, somebody suggests a round at Joe's. I cast the deciding veto. "No boozing tonight, no sitting around jabbering. Everybody go home and stay by your phone."

"Makes sense," Tyree says.

"And watch what you say," I says. "A little birdie might be listening."

"A little birdie?" Ax says, scratching his crew-cut.

"Explain to him, Plummer," I says, and head for my apartment.

Three hours later I'm listening to my scanner. It's all routine business, still no death notice.

My phone keeps ringing. "Hey, Charly, you heard anything?"

"Nope."

A few minutes later: "Hey, Charly, *ar uh*—any word?"

"No word."

I flip on the TV, but they're showing a bunch of Japanese kabuki warriors whacking each other. I switch quick to Johnny Carson, but I can't hear his jokes because the announcer's laughing so loud, and I finally turn the thing off and open a book by Dan Jenkins that usually improves my spirits, but not even that crazy Puckett family can take my mind off what's eating me tonight.

Did I dream it? Can six guys share a nightmare?

The laughing gas. Maybe that had something to do with it. Acoustic tiles, I bet. Takes a lot of heat to get them started, but once they reach the flash-point you better have your mask ready. Should of brought masks with us. My fault. A horse on me.

The phone.

"Oh, hello, Ax."

"Charly—*om ah*—I was just wondering."

"I'm sure you were, Ax."

"*Ar uh*—what's new? I mean, what's the word?"

"The word is sleep, Ax," I says. "I guess they're holding the —*er*—the announcement till morning."

"What announcement?"

No doubt about it, he's our weak link. "About your mother's got the clap!" I says, practically screaming into the phone. "What other announcement we been waiting for?"

"Oh, yeh, right, Charly. Right, right. Thanks, Charly. G'night."

Goddamn idiot.

Next thing he'll be down at the morgue asking can he place

some begonias on the body, and the attendant'll ask him how he knows there's a body, there hasn't been any announcement yet, and Ax'll say . . .

He can't be that dumb.

Can he?

Six A.M. Haven't even undressed. I walk to the newsstand, grab the morning paper. Headline:

ALBUQUERQUE THREATENS DEFAULT
Prez Calls for Prayers

It's cold out there on the street, but by the time I get back to the apartment I've checked every page.

Not a word.

I can't help myself, I dial the housewatchman. "Who's this?" he wants to know.

"Lieutenant Sprockett."

"Holy Christ, Charly!" I recognize Tommy Frasch's voice, he's a Ladder 10 tillerman. "Whatchew waking me up for, man? It's an hour till roll call."

"Nothing special, Tom," I says, giving it the old nonchalant. He's a nice guy, won't hold a grudge for more than five or six months. "Couldn't sleep," I says. "Felt like talking. How'd it go last night?" I'm expecting him to break in and tell me that the bells went off early in the morning, twenty rounds at slow cadence, and then the announcement over the squawkbox, "The Fire Department mourns the loss of H. Walker Slater, Chief, Fourth Battalion, killed in action. Funeral services will be . . ."

*"How'd it go?"* Tommy's repeating. "It went great, till you woke me up. Didn't get turned out once. Whatsa matter with you, Charly? You miss the old place too much? I mean, you been off-shift nine or ten hours already."

255

I fake a laugh, but it comes out as a dry gurgle.

"Boozing all night, yes or no?" he says.

"Huh? Oh, yeh, right, Tom. Hoisted a few."

"Sleep it off, Charly," he says. "Sleep it off." The phone goes dead.

*Why are they holding up the announcement?*

They must know what happened, every detail, and they're trying to drive us off the wall, make us break down and confess. I heard of that technique.

If nobody else caves in, they can depend on good old Ax, he'll tell all. No, he's loyal.

Well, who's disloyal then? Let's see. Sonny? Plummer?

They're all loyal. One hundred and ten percent.

How'd headquarters find out? Maybe my radio was locked in the transmitting position. Happens sometimes. Maybe they got every word on the big monitoring tape at the alarm office.

*Right over here, Chief . . .*

I'm getting paranoid. Who wouldn't? There's a dead chief in the elevator shaft, which they should of found him—let's see —eleven hours ago. *Had* to of found him by now. Hit the roof of that elevator about ninety miles an hour, they couldn't miss hearing it.

My phone's ringing every fifteen minutes, Ma Bell's gonna declare an extra dividend. Plummer calls me, I call Ax, Ax calls Sonny, it's like a chain letter.

The phone rings again and this time it's Allan Grant.

"Whattaya say, Al?" I says, trying to sound normal.

"What's all the racket?"

Jeez, I forgot. My two radios are on and so's my TV. I'm trying to listen to every news program I can find, plus I got my scanner at top volume to override the others if the bells come in. Sounds like a rock festival.

"My neighbors," I says.

"The baker? At nine o'clock in the morning?"

"Yeh. Having a party."

Grant lowers his voice. "Listen, Charly, I thought you oughta be the first to know about Chief Slater, then you can tell your shift."

"I already heard," I says. Jesus Christ on a crutch, what made me blurt *that* out? I must of just graduated from stupid school. That's the trouble with having a completely up-front relationship with a guy, you can't even fake him out when your life depends on it.

"You already heard? Boy, news travels."

"Well, *ar uh*—"

"Really too bad, don'tcha think, Charly? I mean, the man wasn't easy to get along with, but he had ideas. We need ideas, Charly."

"Yeh, right, Al."

I call Plummer with the news and tell him to pass it on, and then I figure I'll drop in at the station, see the reaction when the bells go off. When the bells rang for Loo, there wasn't a sound in Station 12, some of the guys were actually bent over with grief. It'll be different this time.

When I walk in, it's business as usual. Probably they don't know yet. I'll straighten up my locker, look busy.

"Hey, Sprockett, what're you doing here?" It's Peterson, the Fire 5 lieutenant.

"Just can't keep away," I says, halfway turning around. "Miss you girls too much. Did ya hear about—"

I almost mention Slater, but something tells me to keep my mouth shut.

"Hear about what?"

"The fire last night?"

"Naw. I'm deaf in one ear and can't hear outa the other."

"We got the Silly Gas," I says, not knowing what to say.

257

"No kiddin'? Never had the pleasure, me."

After a while I wander down to the watch office, check the log. The latest entry is a false alarm at seven A.M., and the last one before that is Fire 5 back in service from the Hopfner Building last night. Not a single word about Slater.

I check the punch-tape that keeps a record of our bells, looking for twenty straight holes, but it's blank. Headquarters is sure acting weird. Could it be they can't locate the next-of-kin? Hard to believe.

I sit in the scullery and sip a cup of black coffee—I had at least three quarts since the fire, my mouth tastes like an elephant's jockstrap. Willie Guminski of Ladder 10 comes in and says, "You're gonna miss Slater, huh, Loo?"

"For sure," I says, trying to sound sincere. "Hey, when're they gonna ring the bells?"

"The bells?"

"Yeh. The twenty bells, slow cadence."

Willie laughs and then frowns. "Boy, Charly, you got a really grizzly sense a humor, man."

I can't take much more of this double-talk. I'm beginning to feel like Alice in Wanderland. Time to go home, feed the cat, crash for a couple hours.

Out of the corner of my ear I hear bells, and the squawkbox announces, *"Battalion chief in quarters."* I rinse my cup and head for the exit.

Down at the shadowy end of the hall, a familiar figure limps slowly in my direction. He's in civvies, a dark double-breasted suit, but I'd know him anywhere.

It's H. Walker Slater, or his ghost.

He gets to the top of the stairs, sees me and stops short, like he's slammed into a wall. Then he hurries down, falling all over himself, and he's out of sight before I can make a move.

I stagger home like a man in a three-legged race.

The cat must be hungry, haven't fed him since last night. "Tom," I says. "Here, Tom."

He crawls out behind the sofa, sees me and races through his exit-door, his tail between his legs.

What's everybody know that I don't know?

Just as I'm running down my front steps after the cat, a car pulls up and a voice says, "Hiya, Loo," and I jump three feet.

It's Fenstermacher. "Goddamn, Wallace," I says, "do ya have to sneak up like that?" Then I notice our probie, lifting her shapely legs out of Fenstermacher's old Corvette. "Excuse my French, honey," I says. "I had a long night. What're you two doing here?"

"Oh, I was talking to Plummer on the phone," Fenstermacher says, "and we got to chatting about the fire and he said you always enjoy post-mortems and stuff, so Lulu and me—we weren't doing nothing, we thought we'd drive over and rap."

"Sure," I says. "Terrific." It's great to have company after you've been sitting up all night waiting for a message that never come in and then top it off by seeing a zombie and your own cat won't speak to you.

"Also," Lulu Ann says as we're climbing the stairs, "Wallace's scared witless."

"Of what?" I says, stopping on the landing.

"I'd rather not talk in public, Loo," the kid says, nodding toward my door.

We go in and I notice they're holding hands. A matched pair: the first two red-headed firefighters I ever seen holding hands off-shift. Too bad. I thought Sonny had the inside track. "Whatsa problem, kid?" I says, puttering around with the coffeepot in the kitchen.

"Oh, nothing," he says.

"Nothing?" Lulu says, her big sapphire eyes opening like pie plates. "You keep me up till daylight talking about it, and then you say it's nothing?" She looks like she's ready to choke off the romance right now. "You just tell Loo the whole story. He'll understand."

Fenstermacher hesitates.

"C'mon, now!" she snaps. "Tell him! *This instant!*"

"Yeh, well, Loo, it's just—something freaky happened last night, Loo. I don't know how to explain it."

He stops again, and Lulu kicks him in the ankle. Lucky she's wearing red tennis shoes, about a size three, or we'd have another man on the wounded list.

"Loo," he says, gulping, "I don't know what came over me. You remember I brought Chief Slater up in the elevator to find you guys?"

No, I don't remember. I knew that somebody brought Slater up, but I didn't know it was Fenstermacher.

"So I was waiting for him in all the smoke on the top floor and I got on a laughing jag, I just couldn't stop. Embarrassing! I was leaning over, I was trying to get my breath, the whole thing just seemed so *funny* to me, Loo. Do you believe me?"

"Believe you?"

"Loo, I'm telling you, I was doubled over trying to control myself. Then the chief stepped through the ceiling."

"The ceiling?" My coffee cup breaks in the sink.

"Yeh, the roof of the elevator. You didn't hear? You know how those ceilings are, Loo, they're not built to bear weight. He just flops next to me, and I'm giggling so hard I can't quit. I said, 'Chief, you figured out a new way to get on an elevator.'

261

Laughed and laughed, had to cover my mouth with my hand."

"With your hand?" I says.

"Yeh," Lulu says. "He laughed and laughed. Right in the battalion chief's face."

"What'd Slater say?"

"He turned white, he was so mad. He points his finger down, like 'Get me outa here!' and I took us down express."

Jesus Llewellyn Christ.

The elevator was up.

Now Slater knows what we tried to do. He'll pick us off one by one, like a killer that walks by night. No wonder he ducked when he seen me at the station.

I'm so upset I pour more coffee on my visitors' laps than I pour into their cups, I guess they figure I got the d.t.'s. Lulu grabs the pot and takes over.

"Am I in bad trouble, Loo?" the kid says. He looks like he's about to bawl.

"In bad trouble?" I says, still dumbfounded. "You in trouble?"

"Thinks he'll be suspended," Lulu says, sitting on the edge of my divan and crossing her slim ankles.

"Tell me something, Wallace," I says, regaining consciousness, "how come you didn't mention this till now?"

"Well, Loo, when you guys came out of the building, you didn't talk, remember? You looked shook, and then you jumped in the cab. Lulu and me, we rode the tailboard. Besides, I was still feeling stupid. From my laughing jag."

I try to comfort the young lovers, assure them their future's not in jeopardy, battalion chiefs got better things to do than bear grudges against dizzy rooks. By the time they leave, an hour later, they're calmed down and holding hands again.

I flop on my bed and study the polka-dot design on the ceiling. My eyes feel like they been dusted with Drano, my heart's doing the funky pheasant from the coffee, my breath's coming in short spurts.

Something don't add up, but I'm too punchy to concentrate. The phone call!

That's it. The call from Grant. What was it he said? "I thought you oughta be the first to know about Chief Slater."

The first to know what?

"Really too bad, don'tcha think, Charly?"

What's "too bad" about stepping through a plastic ceiling?

My hands shake as I dial headquarters. What'll I say when he comes on the line? *Hi, Al, this is Charly. Listen, Fire Five tried to murder Slater last night but it misfired. Al, would you mind explaining* . . . Wouldn't that sound just lovely?

"Charly," he says, "what's happening? I'm kinda busy."

"Allan, what were you trying to tell me about Slater a while ago?"

"You said you already knew."

"I was just kidding. You know how I jack around." I throw in a laugh, but it sounds more like a death gurgle.

"You mean you don't know?"

"Nope."

"Slater put in for accelerated retirement."

*"What?"*

"He's on terminal leave right now. Said that's it. Finished. Kaput."

I'm gulping. *"Uh . . . uh . . . did he say why?"*

"Not really. Said it was a personal decision. Something about a business opportunity in another city."

"Holy balls.".

"Maybe he figured somebody was out to get him," Grant says into the phone.

"Jeez," I says, trying to sound cool, "I don't know where he'd get a crazy idea like that."

263

I call Plummer, and Plummer calls Ax, and pretty soon everybody knows what's happened and I take my phone off the hook. It's two o'clock in the afternoon before I drop off, and even then it's a kind of a half-sleep, thinking and dozing, dozing and thinking, all the way till dark.

I keep hearing Al say, "Maybe he figured somebody was out to get him."

I wonder how much they know at headquarters.

Poor Slater. He must of thought we were on his case. A nice man like him. All he done was put Cap and Les in the hospital and damn near wipe out Fire 5. Who'd be annoyed over little things like that?

Guess he figured we'll get him sooner or later. The elevator won't always be up.

How'd he last as long as he did, pushing so hard, leaning on people? It can happen, it can happen, especially in an outfit where everybody tries to be loyal. It's us against the world, and if a guy screws up, you try to pretend it was an accident, not his fault, he'll do it right the next time. Then you wake up one morning, like Cap said, and Charlie Manson's your commanding officer.

Well, Charlie Manson made one big mistake.

He tangled with Fire 5.

Isn't that why we were set up in the first place, to handle special problems?

It's been three weeks since H. Walker Slater rose again from the dead and sitteth at the right hand of his travel agent, and life's been so beautiful I'm thinking of re-enlisting for another twenty-year hitch. Headquarters moved Fiddler Gorman over from Battalion Six to replace Slater, and he's a good ole boy, raised in Pointe-a-la-Hache, Louisiana, but not one of your beady-eyed redneck types. Fiddler tries to laugh and have fun and be liked. Tyree D'Arcy says he'd rather have Gorman for a battalion chief than anybody else, including Dwight Bethea the black chief at Battalion Three. "That Bethea," Tyree says, "he always trying to out-white whitey. House nigger! Now Fiddler, he *know* he's white. Don't have to signify all the time."

The whole Fire 5 "B" shift's been practically living at the hospital. Les is in a cast up to his waist, going bananas in his private duplex room. We bring him old logbooks so he can run his finger down the list and see what fires would of made him the maddest.

Cap Nordquist said goodby to his wife and every man in Station 12 and let Ladder 10's Pomeranian Chihuahua lick him and then checked into the operating room for surgery. Two hours later he got wheeled out by a couple of smiling ward boys and a smiling brain surgeon and two or three smiling nurses.

They found brain damage, all right—a blood clout the size of a dime, left over from one of the six or eight times Cap got knocked out fighting fires. They scraped the clout off and now Cap's as frisky as any other elderly gentleman with heart trouble and emphysema. He makes noises about coming back to work, but headquarters says that's a little too much to expect, although Cap'll always be welcome in any scullery or bullpen in the district. The way they worked it out, he gets a full pension whether he comes back or not, that's the beauty part.

I'm sitting in the watch office thinking about Les and Cap and kind of smiling inside when Plummer hollers that somebody wants me on the phone.

"This is Cindy," the voice says.

Hot damn, I says to myself, maybe we got a new obscene caller. I mean, *flirty* caller.

"Hi there, Cindy," I says.

"Do you remember me?"

"Well, I—*ar uh*—"

"The chick on the light-pole?"

"Oh, yeh," I says with my usual charm and gift of gab which has kept the young ladies beating down my door for many a year.

"Cindy Lindgren?" she says. "The girl with . . . the arm?"

"Oh, *Cindy!*" I says, pretending I'm thrilled to death. What's she doing with a name like Cindy? Your hippie chicks, they usually got names like Sunflower, Moondust. She's pretty, though, I remember that. Damn near beautiful, with the long hair and all. Jeez, it must be six months since I climbed out and listened to the story of her life. Whole world's changed since then. Real slim figure, I remember that much.

"Listen, Mr. Sprockett—"

"Charly to my old friends."

She laughs like a schoolkid. "Charly," she says, "I've been going to a Bible group lately. Part of my therapy, ya know? But I quit because they're too far out—speaking in tongues and all, ya know?—and I'm not ready for that, not yet anyway."

Why's she telling me all this? What am I suppose to say?

"*Om eh*, how's your love life?" I says. Dumb question. She's got me tongue-tied, rising up from the past like this. We already discussed her love life a long time ago, hanging over the Freeway. Nice intimate atmosphere out there on the light standard.

"Great!" she says. "I met a heavy dude—a doctor."

A doctor! "Terrific," I says.

"Thanks—*er uh*—Charly."

There's another one of those pregnant pauses. I guess this isn't any easier for her than it is for me. So why'd she call? "Well, *uh*, what can I do for ya, Cindy?"

"Oh, I forgot why I called. I'm *so* silly. But I'm getting better. Not so depressed, ya know?"

"Good, good. Next time we meet, maybe we can pick a quieter place. People're starting to talk."

"Far out," she says, giggling. "Listen, here's why I called. It's probably nothing, but just in case, ya know?"

"Right. Just in case."

"This Bible group I've been meeting with, there's a guy that's really square, I mean like a cube, ya know? Thin ties and wing-tip shoes and all? Ya know what I mean?"

No, I don't. There's nothing I like more than a nice wing-tip oxford with a fleur-de-lis pattern on the toe, and I got a closetful of thin ties, mostly knits. Marilyn use to go for them. But luckily I don't have to comment, Cindy rattles right on. "He keeps raving about the saved and the damned, how the city's

267

being polluted by bums and heathens, and God's gonna reach down and strike 'em dead in the streets. Stuff like that, ya know?"

She's still got me baffled. I'm a fire lieutenant, not a psychologist.

"Anyway, I've been steering clear of him, he's spacier than I am, but then I bumped into him tonight and I thought I oughta tell somebody."

"Tell somebody what, hon?"

"Well, I was walking along Tyner? About the Six-hundred block?"

"Yeh?" The eastern edge of Skid Row.

"And he comes down the street with a drunken old man, I mean a real derelict, and he was kind of helping the man along, ya know? So I thought, Well, that's nice, I mean all I ever heard him do is scream about sending the winos to hell, ya know? Purify the city in fire, that kinda crap, but now he's helping his fellow-man, ya know?"

"Purify the city in fire?"

"That's what he said. So I followed along for a half a block or so, till the two of them stopped in a doorway. The wino sat on the stoop, and Mr. Fremont, he pulled something out of his coat pocket and handed it over. By that time I'd almost caught up to them, and Mr. Fremont, he turned and saw me and acted pissed off, ya know? Said something about the vengeance of the Lord and hurried on down the street alone."

*Purify the city in fire? Vengeance of the Lord?*

"Then I saw what he'd handed the wino. It was a bottle, in a paper bag. So I had to wonder—"

"—why he's trying to get a wino drunk," I finish the sentence for her. "My God, Cindy," I says, talking fast. "Holy Jesus where are you? Listen stay right there till I can make a call Cindy *where are you anyway?*"

268

"Hey, be cool, Mr. Sprockett—Charly. I'm not going anyplace. I'm at the corner of Senz and Geraghty. A phone booth."

I know the corner well. It's about four blocks away. Two dingy barrooms catty-corner from each other, and on the other two corners a boarded-up building and a plumbing-supply warehouse.

And no streetlight.

I look at my watch: 10:13 P.M.

"Stay right there!" I says.

"But—"

"Stay in the goddamn booth!"

No answer.

"You okay, Cindy?"

"It's him," she says. Her voice is so low I can hardly hear.

"Who?" I says.

"Mr. Fremont. He just came around the corner."

"Toward you?"

"Yeh." She's whispering now.

"Can he see you?"

"The booth's lighted."

"Crack the door till the light goes out."

No response.

"Crack the door!"

I hear a sharp intake of breath.

"Cindy! *Cindy!*" The dial tone comes on.

I reach up and hit the alerter button.

"Code Red," I says when Plummer slides the pole. "Senz and Geraghty."

As he climbs into the cab, the rest of the guys hit the rig and I jump up on the side by the chemical tank.

"Charly," Plum calls out, "aren't you riding up here?"

"We got the Torch!" I yell to the whole crew. "Put me right

269

next to the phone booth on the southeast corner!"

The old Kenworth coughs once and turns over. By the time we turn left out the door, Plummer's got its ears laid back. On a Code Red, we're allowed ten miles an hour over the posted limit, but I swear we're doing fifty by the end of the first block. The siren's wailing and Sonny Wicker's yanking the bell cord like he's flagging a colt at Santa Anita.

I'm on my knees in the midsection of the rig, holding on to a stanchion with one hand and trying to keep my balance while I pull the locking pin on the chemical ball.

*Got it!*

I cradle the nozzle in my hand and squirt out a little Purple-K, to make sure it's cleared. Nice flow of powder.

We burst through the Meredith Street intersection. Two blocks to go.

There's a car in front of us at Baker, and Plummer swings out and passes and forces him up on the sidewalk. He'll move over, the next siren he hears.

At Senz, we take the turn wide and just miss three Salvation Army workers.

Now I see the corner.

There's movement on the sidewalk, just behind the phone booth.

"The booth!" I scream at Plummer over the siren.

He sees what I see and jerks the rig into the incoming lane of traffic and slams on the brakes.

The guy's got her down, his knee's in the small of her back. The match flickers in his hand.

There's a flash and a puff and two silhouettes are outlined in bluish flame.

The Purple-K spurts through the air and smothers the fire as quick as it started. Cindy and the Bible nut are dusted with lavender powder from head to foot, looks like they went to a

270

Mardi Gras party. But they're squirming, they're alive.

The guy gets up and stumbles, but Ax knocks him back down. "Don't move, I'll break your fucking arm!"

Plummer radios the dispatcher, and I wipe the purple off Cindy's face with my handkerchief. Underneath, she's smiling. I look for burns, but she looks normal. "Feel anything?" I says.

"Just shook," she says, her voice shaking. "It's him, isn't it?"

"Who else?"

I wipe more chemical off her neck and hands. She reeks of gasoline, but her clothes aren't even charred. The powder snuffed the gas just at the flash-point, before it built up heat. You can do funny things with gasoline—soak your hand in it, light it, shake it out before it hurts you. Fire-eaters know the trick, too. Just don't inhale.

"Hey, look!" Mike says. He holds up a faded enameled pin flecked with gold.

"Where'd you get that?" I says, trying to read it in the dim light.

"He was wearing it. The Texaco Kid here."

I make out the inscription: *Perfect attendance 10 years. Grace Evan. Church.*

"Nice record," I says, leaning over the Torch. "You oughta be proud."

He grunts. He's short, soft-looking, heavy around the middle, with a receding forehead and plastic-rim glasses. The kind of guy when you're introduced, you forget his name in the middle of the handshake.

"You learn to kill people in Sunday School?" Ax says, still holding the man down.

"Unclean," the guy says. He's frothing at the mouth, but I can't tell whether it's Purple-K or his own mental problems.

"Euphonious fucker," Mike Mustache says. I guess he's thinking about Loo and the others. Who isn't?

271

The aid car finally pulls up, plus about six black-and-whites, and they rub the Torch clean and pat him down. No wonder he looks fat, there's three hot-water bottles strapped to his waist.

"I guess he don't smoke," Plummer says. "Woulda saved us a lotta trouble."

The cops also find a white-leather Bible in an overcoat pocket and a waterproof matchbox issued by the Boy Scouts of America, with eight or ten big kitchen matches inside. "Be prepared," that's their slogan.

All of a sudden I remember what the dying wino said to me and Ax, *"Ba ba,"* till I leaned over and realized he was saying, "Bible." I should of paid attention, passed the tip to the marshals. But then what? Arrest everybody that carries a Bible? We would of got our best citizens. Besides, marshals don't listen much to firemen.

"What's your name, ya fuck ya?" one of the cops says with their usual courtesy. He licks the point of his stubby pencil.

"I am The Fourth Angel," the Torch says slowly. His eyes move back and forth at us, like he's measuring for suits, but he don't seem scared. Probably figures God is on his side. Jeez, I hope he's wrong.

"The Fourth Angel, huh?" the cop says. "Nice to meetcha. I'm Judas Iscariot, me. Funny I didn't see ya at the dinner."

"It's Fremont," I says.

"Huh?"

"His name's Fremont. At least that's what he uses."

Somebody's tugging on my arm. I turn around. It's Cindy, her clothes splotched with Purple-K and her long hair dangling like she stepped out of a showerbath. "They're taking me to the hospital for observation," she says. "I just wanted to thank you."

272

"Thank *me?*" I says. "You cleared the case, sweetheart. The city oughta put your name up in lights."

"My mother always taught me, when somebody saves your life twice, the least you can do is thank them." She plants a big wet kiss on my cheek, and a couple of the guys start tittering behind me.

"Hey, Cindy," I says. "Tell me one thing. Why didn't you call the cops? What is it with you and cops anyway?"

"Oh, it's not that I don't like 'em," she says. A good thing, because Zacarelli the beat cop's standing right behind us, flipping his nightstick, taking it all in. "It's just that . . . you were so nice and all. Besides, I always follow the golden rule of city living."

"The golden rule of city living?" I wish I knew what she's talking about.

" 'When you need help quick, dial a fireman.' "

"Your mother teach you that, too?"

"No, Charly. You did."

An hour later the phone rings at the firehouse, and one of the marshals tell us they got a full make on "The Fourth Angel." He's a three-time inhabitant of the state loony bin, Drexel Hill. He went out on a twenty-four-hour pass and stretched it into a year of fun and excitement. Real name: Fremont Allardyce. Occupation: night desk clerk. Place of business: The Harbor Light Mission.

Al Grant drops in at my apartment. After the swarm of newspapermen and TV cameras and the guys from the mayor's office, I'm glad to see a plain old fireman, even if he is a deputy chief. "Charly," he says, "I can't say it flat out, but I'm authorized to give you a hint."

"A hint?" I says. "Jeez, Al, do I offend?"

"Charly, take a whack at the captain's test."

What a joke. I couldn't even pass the test for loot. I'm lucky I passed the test for recruit.

"Don't laugh," Grant says, helping himself to a cup of coffee. "Nordquist got his medical, there's gonna be an opening. Who we got better'n you?"

"Let's see, there's McKenzie at Seventeen's, Lieutenant Monahan at the fireboat, there's Moose Salter, there's Peterson, Simmons, Shrack, Cram, O'Boyle, Roginski, maybe another couple dozen I could name."

"Charly, you got veteran points and longevity points and merit points. All you'd have to do is squeak by with a passing grade and you're in."

"Sure," I says, "it sounds easy." I motion for him to sit, he's making me nervous pacing up and down, and he's bugging my cat. "Al, I don't want the job in the first place. I had enough of this brass-hat crap."

"You don't like being an officer?"

I get up and dump the dead film packs out of his ashtray. "Strictly a bummer," I says. "Nothing personal, but I don't know how you stand it, pal. The only good times're rolling on fires and jacking around with the guys, and you don't have to be an officer to do neither one. Besides," I says, thinking how stupid it's gonna sound, "I like to cook."

"Well, you could still cook!" he says, looking at me like I'm the one with the brain clout and not Nordquist.

"An officer that cooks?" I says. "C'mon, Al, when'd I have the time?"

"Look, Charly, take the test! There's captain's bars in it."

"The only bar I'm interested in is Joe's. You oughta know that better'n anybody."

For a minute he don't talk. He cocks his head to one side and then the other like an Irish setter that can't quite pick up the scent.

"You might have something there, Charly," he says finally. "All this upward mobility . . ." He blows out a deep breath. "Sometimes I'm sitting in my office late at night, making up rosters till my eyes cross. It's like a jigsaw puzzle that never gets solved. I ask myself, Is this why you came on the department? To shuffle papers?"

"That's it exactly."

"I says to myself, Wouldn't it be nice to wrestle a nozzle again?"

"Fun, man. You big shots should try it once in a while."

He kicks at me with his shiny Class A shoe. "Same old Charly," he says. "Incorrigible."

"I don't know what that is, Al, but if you do it, you gotta clean it up."

He puts on his hat, checks it in the mirror and heads for the door. "Charly, the trouble with you is you don't know enough to come in outa the flame."

"Yeh," I says, slapping him on the back, "just lucky, I guess."

That night the survivors are sitting in Joe's. Mike Mustacci reads his latest writing exercise from a laundry stiffener:

"The fire flickered around the uniform, lighting up the white of his helmet, revealing that the fireman was a chief, as only chiefs wear white hats. This was in a fire at 539 S. Aberdeen. The second I saw the hat I knew who it was, for there was only one chief who wore a jeweled emblem in front."

He stops. "How d'ya like it so far?"

"Terrific," Plummer says, blinking slow like Rip Van Winkle.

"Holds your interest," Tyree says, rolling his eyes.

"M-m-moves right along," Sonny says through his fingers.

"It was Chief Slattery, the man that taught me all I know about fire suppression. I crawled valiantly across the floor to save him, but then the second tank of gas exploded in my ear and the chief was gone. A helmet whistled past my ear, and to my dissension, it was white."

He stops again. "Like that touch?"

"What touch?" I says, looking up from the wet circles on the table.

"The hat whistling past my ear."

"Very interesting," Plummer says. "Is that about the end?"

"Not quite."

"He was a brave and indubitable man. They had to retire his uniform, as it was splattered around the room. And so the sad afternoon ground to a weary halt at 539 S. Aberdeen."

276

"That's my ender," Mike says. His voice cracks, his writing touches him deeply.

"Hey, how about another pitcher?" Ax says, and snaps his thick fingers at Joe. "Mike'll buy. Cheer him up a little."

After Joe sets the brimming pail of Feinblatz in the center of the table and slips back behind the bar, Ax says halfway to himself, "I wake up in the middle of the night and I wonder who coulda said it."

"Said what?" I says.

" 'Right over here, Chief.' "

"I got a flash for ya," Plummer says. "I wonder, too."

"Beats the shit outa me," Mike says.

"We never gonna know," Tyree says.

"It's the S-s-s-secret of Fire Five," Sonny says.

There's one of them pregnant pauses, and then every head turns in my direction. "How 'bout you, Charly?" Ax says. "Don't it keep you awake at night, wondering?"

I stare back at the innocent faces. "Most everything does," I says.

JACK OLSEN is the author of *Alphabet Jackson, Massy's Game, The Bridge at Chappaquiddick, Night of the Grizzlies, The Man with the Candy, The Girls in the Office,* and *Silence on Monte Sole.* Mr. Olsen lives in Bermuda with his wife and his daughter, Sara.